U0077408

…文化

…群◎著

職場菜鳥's 英文升職筆記

那一些老鳥不會說的秘密！

與其凡事碰壁、還不如自己救自己

職場上班族必看!!!

64個短篇**情境對話**
- 完整呈現工作中必定會遇見的各式情境及流程

16個職場**補給站**及**16**個前輩**巧巧說**
- 偷偷地揭露職場中不欲人知的成功小撇步

看完本書，會讓
笨鳥會飛　菜鳥快飛
中鳥突飛　老鳥猛飛

雖然說『**菜**久了，就是你的』，
但是到底還要**菜**多久？
就從本書開始，由自己來決定！

特約編者序

我很推薦上班族，尤其是社會新鮮人，購買此書成為學習商業英語的基礎。此書將職場常見對話分成十六主題單元由淺入深導入各部門之情境對話；其中“職場補給站”單元不僅教導職場禮儀常識，也教導與同事客戶之間的溝通應對技巧。“你應該要知道的小小事！”單元更是讓準備踏入社會的職場菜鳥獲益良多。“Word Bank”列出基本關鍵字並以例句幫助讀者有效率地學習運用單字。此外，“In Other Words”單元，用換句話說的方式讓讀者可以活用英文文法來學習對話句子，讓讀者不僅熟悉口說會話，也可學習到以正確文法撰寫電子郵件或書面信函，達到不重複死板的英語學習。這是一本公司各部門人員，尤其行銷業務、行政、客服人員，都需要的語言學習參考書。我期待也深信這本書將幫助讀者更有自信地面對外國客戶和應用英語在職場和生活上。

王富美

編者序

這是一本針對職場新鮮人及進入職場已有一段時間，但卻一直覺得還是抓不住「眉角」的上班族而編寫的書。以業務、總機、助理、總務、人資、採購還有秘書這幾種常見的職位，來為您透析職場中必需要知道的一些小撇步。

以生動活潑的職場情境英文對話，為您介紹每種職位的重點工作，讓您更加熟悉工作中的流程。再加上職場補給站及老鳥巧巧說的單元，為您偷偷補給職場上許多前輩不太願意告訴您的密技。重點單字加例句，讓您的職場英文字彙多更多，應用句型加分！各式短句的換句話說，讓您成為英文會話達人，不管怎麼說都流利！

本書不只教您英文，還為您補充許多專業知識及一些職場上大家都不願分享的秘密，以雙管齊下的方式為您增加職場經驗值。我們誠摯地希望每位讀者在讀過這本書後都能職場經驗值滿級，成為無往不利的職場大紅人。

倍斯特編輯部

12:30 PM

PART 1

Sales 業務

*Unit 01　新手業務來報到

*Unit 02　新手業務上戰場

*Unit 03　產品說明

*Unit 04　客戶生氣了！

1-1 新手業務來報到

The First Day at Work
第一天報到

Brian arrived for his first day at work, and he is about to deliver a brief self-introduction to his colleagues in the meeting.

新手業務Brian正式進入公司報到，在會議中向其他同仁做一番簡短的自我介紹。

Brian – the new employee 新手業務
Dennis – colleague 業務同仁
Rita – sales executive 業務主管
Sophie – colleague 業務同仁

Dialogue

Rita	Good afternoon, everyone. I am very happy to introduce you to our newest staff member, Brian Chen, who will join us as a **sales coordinator**. Let's give him a warm welcome.	大家午安。很開心為大家介紹我們的新成員Brian，他將加入我們的業務專員行列，讓我們熱烈地歡迎他。
Brian	Thank you very much. My name is Brian Chen and I am 24 years old. I am a middle child of two **siblings**. My father is a store manager at a restaurant and my mother is a housewife. I graduated from Taipei University about two years ago. I am a people person. I am **outgoing, cheerful**, and have lots of friends. I am very happy to be here and be part of the team.	謝謝大家。大家好，我叫Brian，今年24歲。我在家中排行老二，父親是一間餐廳的店長，母親則是一位家庭主婦。我約兩年前畢業於台北大學。我是一個很好相處的人。我的個性外向開朗，且擁有許多朋友。我很高興能來到這裡成為團隊的一份子。

	I am a good thinker and quick learner. I will work hard and **give my best** to the company. So nice to meet you, thank you!	我是一個善於思考的人，也能很快地學習新事物。我會努力工作，一定為公司全力以赴。很高興認識大家，謝謝。
Rita	Is there anything else you would like to know about Brian? Any questions?	有人想多了解Brian一些嗎？有任何問題想問嗎？
Dennis	Hi, I am Dennis. It's very nice to meet you. What was your major in school?	嗨，我是Dennis，很開心見到你。你的主修是什麼？
Brian	My major was Business Administration. As you can see, my major is **relevant** to this job.	我的主修是企管。所以，這份工作和我的主修相關。
Sophie	Hello. My name is Sophie. It's great to have a young guy in the office. Have you just finished your military service?	嗨，我是Sophie。公司裡有年輕人真是太好了。你服完兵役了嗎？
Brian	Yes, but I worked a number of part-time jobs while I was studying at the University. I was a pizza delivery boy, waiter, and store clerk. These experiences helped me learn the right **attitude** to deal with customers.	是的。但我讀大學時曾經做過許多兼職的工作，我曾當過送比薩的小弟、服務生，以及店員。這些工作經驗讓我學習到如何用正確的態度來面對顧客。

sales coordinator　業務專員

Mark is interested in the position of sales coordinator and has applied for it.
Mark 對業務專員職位很有興趣，也提出應徵。

sibling　n.　兄弟姊妹

I am happy to have siblings as the company in my life.
我很高興在我一生中有兄弟姊妹與我為伴。

outgoing　adj.　外向的

One of the job requirements for a sales coordinator is to be outgoing.
業務專員職務的條件之一就是需要個性外向。

give one's best　全力以赴

I always give my best to help people.
我一直都是全力以赴去幫助別人。

relevant　adj.　有關聯的

The detective is seeking for relevant clues about the case.
這偵探正在尋找此案件的相關線索。

clerk　n.　店員

The clerk asked me to sign on the receipt.
店員請我在收據上簽名。

attitude　n.　態度

His positive attitude leads to his success in many aspects.
他的正面態度讓他在多方面都很成功。

In Other Words

I am a people person. I am outgoing, cheerful, and have lots of friends.
我是一個很好相處的人。我的個性外向開朗，且擁有許多朋友。

- I am very popular, easy-going, friendly and like to meet and talk to new people.
  我非常受歡迎，容易相處，友善，喜歡與新人認識交談。
- My personality is considered as outgoing, cheerful, bright, and popular. I am not afraid of meeting strangers and enjoy making friends.
  別人認為我的個性是外向，喜樂，陽光，也是很紅的人。 我不害怕面對陌生人也喜愛交朋友。

I will work hard and give my best to the company.
我會努力工作，一定為公司全力以赴。

- I will work diligently and do my best to make a contribution to the company.
  我會勤勞工作盡全力貢獻給公司。
- I will devote all my time and myself to benefit the company.
  我會投入所有時間和自己來造福公司。

These experiences helped me learn the right attitude to deal with customers.
這些工作經驗讓我學習到如何用正確的態度來面對顧客。

- I learn from these experiences how to face customers by the right manner.
  我從這些經驗學到如何以正確態度來面對客戶。
- Through my past working experiences, I learned to handle customers with the positive attitude.
  經由我以前的工作經驗，我學到以正面態度來處理客戶問題。

1-2 新手業務來報到

Get to Know the Work Place
認識工作環境

Rita gives Brian a quick office tour and provides him with an introduction of the company's profile, as well as the Sales Department.

Rita帶Brian認識公司環境，並說明公司及業務部門架構。

Brian - the new employee 新手業務
Rita - Sales executive 業務主管

Dialogue

Rita	This is your desk. You are sitting next to Joe, who has been working here for two years. You may **consult** him if you have any questions at any time.	這是你的座位，你的旁邊是Joe，他在這裡工作已經兩年了。若你有任何問題，可以隨時諮詢他。
Brian	That is great to know.	好的。
Rita	Restrooms are outside of the reception area and the **break room** is on the other side. Follow me, I will show you around your workplace. This is the work area. Over here we've got a copier, fax machine, printer, and **paper shredder**.	洗手間在接待區的外面，茶水間在另一邊。請跟我來，我帶你參觀一下你的工作環境。這裡是工作區，有影印機、傳真機、印表機，以及碎紙機。
Brian	I see. What is the room across the hall?	瞭解。走廊另一邊的房間是什麼？

Rita	That is the file room where we **store** important business records and documents. Come this way and I will show you the meeting rooms; they are the second, third, and fourth rooms behind the file room.	那是文件室，專門存放重要的商業紀錄和文件。走這邊，我帶你去看看會議室，文件室後面的第二間、第三間以及第四間都是會議室。
Brian	Why are there so many meeting rooms?	為什麼會有那麼多間會議室？
Rita	Room A is a **conference room**. It is **equipped** with audio-visual, computer, and presentation **facilities.** It can hold up to 60 people. Room B and Room C are general meeting rooms where we have our regular department meetings or any meetings with customers. Now let's have a seat in Room B, so I can take my time to tell you the information about our company on a need-to-know basis.	會議室A是大型會議室，設有影音、電腦和簡報用的設備，可容納60人。會議室B和C是一般會議室，用來進行部門定期會議和招待顧客。現在我們先在會議室B坐一下，讓我大致跟你說明一下公司須知。

★你應該要知道的小小事！

稍具規模的公司，在新人報到第一天，就會提供公司章程和員工守則給新進員工看，內容包括公司的組織架構、人事規定（請假相關規定、遲到扣薪）、考績評等…等內容，因為與自己本身的權益有很大的關係，都應仔細閱讀清楚。

Word Bank

consult v. 諮詢

My mother always consults her doctor when she doesn't feel well.
我媽在生病時總是去諮詢她的醫生。

break room 茶水間

We have a birthday party at the break room for our coworkers.
我們在茶水間幫我們的同事舉辦生日派對。

paper shredder 碎紙機

Please take the confidential documents to the paper shredder for shredding.
請把這些機密文件拿到碎紙機碎掉。

store v. 儲存

The USB disk is able to store a large quantity of data.
這USB隨身碟可以儲存大量資料。

conference room 會議室

All the executives are having a meeting at the conference room.
所有主管都在會議室開會。

equip v. 有……設備

The training program will keep you equipped with competitive skills.
這些訓練課程會讓你備有具競爭力的技能。

facility n. 設備

The office is equipped with a variety of technology facilities.
這辦公室裝設了各式各樣的科技設備。

In Other Words

You may consult him if you have any questions at any time.
若你有任何問題，可以隨時諮詢他。

- If you have any questions, feel free to ask him at any time.
  如果有任何問題，都隨時可問他。
- Do not hesitate to let him know, if you have any questions.
  如有任何問題，儘管問他。

Room B and Room C are general meeting rooms where we have our regular department meetings or any meetings with customers.
會議室B和C是一般會議室，用來進行部門定期會議和招待顧客。

- We hold general meetings, including routine department meetings and common meetings with customers at Room B and Room C.
  我們在會議室B和C召開一般會議，包含定期部門會議和招待客戶。
- Room B and Room C are common conference rooms for regular department meetings and for meeting with customers.
  會議室B和C是召開定期部門會議和招待客戶的一般會議室。

I can take my time to tell you the information about our company on a need-to-know basis.
讓我大致跟你說明一下公司須知。

- Let me spend some time to present our employee handbook in which you must be informed of some relevant information.
  讓我花些時間來跟你說一下我們的員工手冊，裡面有些相關須知。
- Let's take some time to check out our company handbook, which you are requested to know.
  我們花點時間來看一下公司規章，這是你需要知道的.

1-3 新手業務來報到

Know Your Job Duties
瞭解工作職責

Rita explains the company framework and background to Brian, as well as his job duties.

Rita為Brian介紹公司的架構和背景，並且說明他的工作職責。

Brian - the new salesperson 新手業務
Rita - sales executive 業務主管

Dialogue

Rita	Green Day is a medium-sized enterprise with 110 employees. It was founded in Taichung in 1980 by Mr. Kao, the president of the company. The company owns and operates two product lines, hair and skin care. It also has a large number of customers throughout Taiwan. Are you familiar with our products?	Green Day是一間中型企業，旗下有110名員工，由高先生，即我們的董事長，於1980年於台中成立。公司擁有且經營兩種品牌，分別是頭髮和護膚產品，在台灣擁有為數眾多的顧客。你對我們的產品熟悉嗎？
Brian	I think so. My mother and my younger sister are fans of the company's shampoo and skin lotion.	我想是的。我母親和妹妹都是公司洗髮精和乳液的愛用者。

Rita	That's wonderful to hear. Health insurance, labor insurance, and festival bonuses are available for all the employees, including probationers. For other regulations, the company will follow the Labor Standards Act. Do you have any questions so far?	這真是太棒了。所有員工皆享有健保和勞保，以及三節獎金，包括仍在試用期內的員工。至於其他的規定，公司一切依照勞基法。到目前為止，你有任何問題嗎？
Brian	No, please continue.	沒有，請繼續。
Rita	As a **probationary** sales coordinator, you are responsible to **source** client information, develop sales **promotional** materials, prepare sales reports, **follow up** on sales activities, and **participate** in sales events.	身為一名業務專員，在試用期內，你的職責是整理客戶資料、開發業務宣傳工具、準備業務報告、追蹤業務活動的後續發展，以及參與業務活動。
Brian	Don't I need to develop sales **proposals** as well?	我不需要開發業務提案嗎？
Rita	No, not until you pass the probation. In general, the probation period lasts three months, but if you do well, that may be reduced.	不需要，直到你通過試用期為止。一般而言，試用期為期三個月。但如果你工作表現良好，則可提早通過試用期。
Brian	I will spare effort to prove to you that I can do the job.	我將竭盡全力向你證明我能夠勝任此工作。

Word Bank

probationary adj 試用的

David got a job offer last week and has started his probationary period.
David 上週得到一份工作，已開始他的試用期。

source v. 分類整理

The secretary is requested to source the business cards by alphabetical order.
秘書被要求要依照字母次序分類整理名片。

promotional adj 促銷的

The department store is crowded with people due to the promotional activities.
這百貨公司因為促銷活動，到處都是人。

follow up 追蹤後續

The salesperson follows up every potential customer who he has contacted.
這業務人員持續追蹤每位他所聯絡過的潛在客户。

participate v. 參與

My brother is very active to participate in every activity of the community.
我哥哥積極參與每個社區活動。

proposal n. 提議

The sales executive has approved proposals for products advertisement.
這業務主管批准了產品廣告企劃案。

In Other Words

Health insurance, labor insurance, and festival bonuses are available for all the employees, including probationers.
所有員工皆享有健保和勞保，以及三節獎金，包括仍在試用期內的員工。

- All employees, including probationers, are eligible for health insurance, labor insurance, and festival bonuses.
  所有員工包含試用期內的員工皆享有健保、勞保和三節獎金。
- All employees and probationers enjoy health insurance, labor insurance, and festival bonuses.
  所有員工和試用期內的員工皆享有健保、勞保及三節獎金。

As a probationary sales coordinator, you are responsible to source client information, develop sales promotional materials, prepare sales reports, follow up on sales activities, and participate in sales events.
身為一名業務專員，在試用期內，你的職責是整理客戶資料、開發業務宣傳工具、準備業務報告、追蹤業務活動的後續發展，以及參與業務活動。

- During the probationary period of being a sales coordinator, your duties are client information collection, promotional material development, sales reports preparation, sales activities follow-up, and sales events attending.
  在業務專員的試用期間，你的工作是收集客戶資料、開發業務宣傳工具、準備業務報告、追蹤業務活動的後續發展，以及參與業務活動。
- Being a probationary sales representative, you are in charge of classifying client information, expanding sales promotional materials, preparing sales reports, tracking sales activities, and attending sales evens.
  身為試用期間的業務專員，你的工作是分類客戶資料、開發業務宣傳工具、準備業務報告、追蹤業務活動的後續發展，以及參與業務活動。

1-4 新手業務來報到

Job Review
工作回顧

Brian has been in the company for about a week, and Rita wishes to have a meeting with him to discuss his working conditions and how well he has adapted to the new environment.

Brian已進公司一週，Rita希望和他開會，討論他這一週以來的工作情況，以及對新環境的適應。

Brian - the new salesperson 新手業務
Rita - sales executive 業務主管

Dialogue

Rita	Good morning, Brian. So, you have been here for almost a week. Is there anything you would like to share or ask?	早安，Brian。你已經進公司將近一個星期了，你有什麼想問或分享的嗎？
Brian	I've been learning something new and useful every day. I knew it was not easy to be a salesperson, but now I **realize** the job is more than just selling things. <u>There is so much to pick up.</u>	我每天都學習到新的和有用的事物。我以前就知道當一名業務員並非易事，但我現在才意識到這份工作不僅僅是賣東西而已。有太多東西需要學習了。
Rita	Do you **get along with** your co-workers?	你和同事之間相處得融洽嗎？

Brian	They are very good to me, especially Joe. He takes time to explain things to me **step by step** even though he is busy with his own work.	大家都對我很好，尤其是Joe。即使他自己的工作很忙，他仍然花時間一步步地跟我解釋許多事情。
Rita	So far what is the hardest part of the job?	到目前為止，你覺得最難的部分是什麼？
Brian	I have been here for only one week, so I cannot really say at this moment. Everything is new and fresh to me, and I know there are more **challenges** ahead.	我才來一個星期，在這時刻我真的無法回答。每一件對我而言都是新奇的，而我也知道未來會有更多的挑戰。
Rita	You are **absolutely** right about that. Are you worried or afraid?	你說的對極了。你會擔心或害怕嗎？
Brian	No, I am excited and nervous, in a good way.	不會，我感到興奮且緊張，正面的那種。
Rita	I am glad to hear what you have just said. That is the **spirit** we need and you should be proud of yourself. You are doing very well. Keep up the good work.	我很開心聽到你這麼說，這正是我們所需要的精神，你該以自己為傲。你做得很好。再接再厲。

★你應該要知道的小小事！

新人在報到後的一段時間（依各單位情況不同，面談時間也會調整），主管會找新人聊聊適應的狀況，看是不是有什麼地方需要出面協助或是指點，或是針對新人的表現給予讚賞或提出一些建議與想法。

Word Bank

realize v. 意識

The older I get, the more I realize it is not easy to be a good teacher.
隨著年紀的增長，我更加了解到要當個好老師不容易。

get along with 相處融洽

Amy is easygoing and gets along with everyone in this company.
Amy 很隨和，跟公司內的每個人都相處融洽。

step by step 逐步地

The teacher is patient to teach the students to solve the questions step by step.
這老師有耐心地教導學生逐步地解決問題。

challenge n. 挑戰

The teenagers are taught to face the challenges bravely.
這些青少年被教導要勇敢面對挑戰。

absolutely adv. 絕對地；一點也不錯

I believe you are absolutely qualified for the position.
我相信你絕對可勝任此職務。

spirit n. 精神

Keep the positive spirit and you will be successful at all aspects.
持續保持正面的精神，你在各方面都會成功。

In Other Words

There is so much to pick up.
有太多東西需要學習了。

- I have so many things to learn.
  我有太多東西需要學習。
- It is necessary for me to learn much more.
  對我來說有太多東西需要學習。

He takes time to explain things to me step by step even though he is busy with his own work.
即使他自己的工作很忙，他仍然花時間一步步地跟我解釋許多事情。

- He spends time to instruct me things stage by stage, although he is busy with his tasks.
  雖然他自己的工作很忙，他仍然花時間階段性的教我。
- He is still willing to spend time in guiding me, though he is not always available.
  雖然他沒空，他仍然願意花時間指導我。

That is the spirit we need and you should be proud of yourself.
這正是我們所需要的精神，你該以自己為傲。

- That is one of the requirements we are looking for, and you certainly deserve the pride.
  這是我們需要的條件之一，你要替自己感到自豪。
- You have the spirit which we desperately need and you should be proud of yourself.
  你擁有我們極為需要的精神，你應以自己為榮。

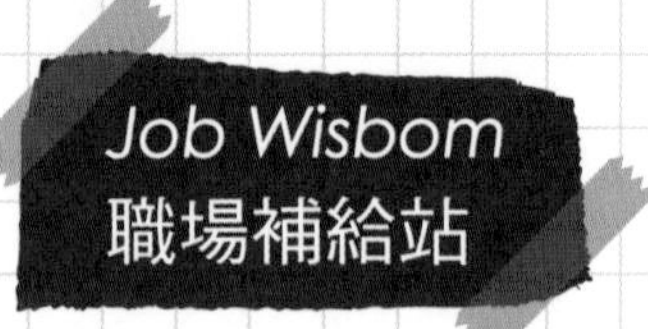

成為人見人愛的新進員工小撇步！

★記住名字

尤其是任職於業務領域的人，這點絕對是第一法則！許多客戶的注意力和感受往往就集中在一些看似微乎其微的地方上，對新手而言，別以為進了公司之後只要花心思在職務內容上就篤定過關，其實從你一進門至下班打卡回家，主管和同事都在觀察你。

★笑口常開

俗話說伸手不打笑臉人，第一天的印象非常重要，所以第一天上班一定要讓人看見你充滿朝氣和笑臉迎人的一面。

★發問和尋求協助

遇到不熟悉、不清楚或是不懂的事情，別害怕開口問人。會發問表示你對事情的關心，想找答案代表你有想解決或弄清楚問題，這些都是會讓自己加分的要點，問問題不會有壞處，這不僅加深他人對你的印象、看好你的態度之外，自己也從中學習到不少東西。但要想清楚問題再問，不合宜的問題千萬別說出口。

★勤作筆記

將主管或同事所交代或建議的事項抄下來吧。做筆記也可增強自己的思考能力和有效理清思緒。

★保持低調且合群

新人一進入公司，保持低調和學習合群是很重要的。無論你過去的學經歷有多麼輝煌，在新的環境裡，你就是新人。你要學習新的企業文化，適應新的環境和同事。在職務和細節上，保持合群，當然這並非要你像個小媳婦一般地一聲不吭，但也千萬不要成為一個意見王，少數服從多數，儘量跟著大家意見一致就是了。

★別愛比較

比較難免會有得失心和抱怨，這些無形的負面情緒都會直接影響你的工作效率、態度和人際關係。

用字篇

! 業務專員 – sales coordinator

在台灣，許多公司行號會將專員這職稱翻譯成specialist，其實specialist顧名思義是指某個領域的專家，在一般公司行號中，專員是指負責指定職務的一般職員，所以應該使用的職稱應該是coordinator，負責處理和協調事物的人員。

! meeting room和conference room的差別

meeting room和conference room雖都解釋成會議室，但其規模和使用性卻有所不同。兩者皆為召開會議所用，裡面設置有科技設備，例如投影機，影音設備等。差異之處在於，conference room基本上都較大，可容納10人以上（規模以不同機構或組織而異），一定附有影音設備。meeting room可大可小，可以大如像conference room的規模，但也可小於一般僅有桌椅的會客室。

業務前輩看哪裡？

自信心：對自己要有信心，才能有機會把你的產品給推銷出去。

誠心：必須要有一顆真誠的心，誠懇地對待客戶和同事。

執行力：一定要說到並且做到，才能贏得主管和客戶的心。

韌性：要能屈能伸，遇到挫折時不要輕易被打敗，回去好好檢討，時時檢視自己，是不是有什麼不足？調整心態再出發。

學習力：將在職場上所接觸到的所有資訊，內化成為自己的力量。不斷的學習，不懂的就問。

團隊合作：Team work永遠會比一個人的力量來得大上許多，互相支援以獲得最大的效益。

2-1 新手業務上戰場

On the Way to Visit a Customer
拜訪顧客的途中

Brian accompanies Sophie on a visit to a regular customer.
Brian跟著Sophie拜訪公司的老客戶。

Brian - the new salesperson 新手業務
Sophie - the salesperson, Brian's colleague 業務，Brian的同事

Dialogue

Brian	May we go over the customer information again?	我們可以再複習一次顧客的資料嗎？
Sophie	Sure. We are on the way to pay a visit to Ms. Wu, the **procurement** manager of Spa Village, a regular customer of ours. Spa Village is a four-star hotel in Beitou, with a good **reputation** and popularity.	當然。我們要去拜訪的是Spa Village的採購經理吳小姐，他們是我們公司的老主顧。Spa Village是一間位於北投的四星級飯店，享有聲望且備受歡迎。
Brian	How is this Ms. Wu? What is she like?	那這位吳小姐是什麼樣的人呢？
Sophie	She is very friendly and smart, the type of person you want to **hang out** with. But when it comes to business, she's very **shrewd**.	她很友善且聰明，是那種你會想繼續跟她往來的人，但一旦論及公事，她則是非常精打細算。
Brian	How old is she?	她幾歲呢？

Sophie	I am not sure about her **exact** age, but I think she is in her forties.	我不確定她的實際年齡，但我想她應該是四十幾歲左右。
Brian	I hope I will make a good **impression** on her. I am a bit nervous. What if she doesn't like me? What if I say something wrong?	希望我可以給她留下一個好印象。我有點緊張，如果她不喜歡我怎麼辦？如果我說錯話呢？
Sophie	Relax. You will do fine. Here we are, the **headquarters** of Spa Village.	放輕鬆。你沒問題的。我們到了，Spa Village的總部。

★你應該要知道的小小事！

新手業務在外出拜訪前，一定要先做好事前的功課，要先熟悉自己公司的產品，這樣不管客戶提出什麼樣的問題，你都能從容應對不緊張，還有記得先從前輩那裡打聽客戶的喜好和地雷，避免說錯話，這樣才能在客戶心中建立不錯的第一印象哦！

★你應該要知道的小小事！

新手業務外出拜訪客戶時，因為對公司產品的熟悉度還不足，所以遇到客戶詢問一些關於產品比較深入的問題時，很容易會因為不知道如何回應而冷場；或是有的客戶可能會問到與其他公司同性質產品的比較，這個對於新手業務來說，也是比較棘手的問題。所以在了解公司產品之後，可以針對市場上一些較受歡迎的競爭產品列出比較分析，藉以累積自身的經驗，這樣在外出拜訪客戶時就不用怕了！

Word Bank

procurement n. 採購

Jeff is in charge of the procurement of raw materials from abroad.
Jeff 負責自國外採購原料。

reputation n. 信譽、名譽

The hotel has a good reputation for its service.
此飯店以服務佳而得享信譽。

hang out 來往

John always hangs out with his coworkers after work.
John 下班後總是和他同事們出去。

shrewd adj. 精打細算的；強悍的

Mark is a shrewd businessman.
Mark 是個精明的生意人。

impression n. 印象

The sales representative always makes good impressions on the customers.
這業務員總是給客户好印象。

headquarters n. 總部

Most of the corporations' headquarters in Taiwan are located in Taipei.
大部分的台灣企業總部都設在台北。

In Other Words

Brian accompanies Sophie on a visit to a regular customer.
Brian跟著Sophie拜訪公司的老客戶。

- Sophie leads Brain to pay a visit to an old customer.
  Sophie帶領Brain去拜訪一家老客戶。
- Brain visits a regular customer with Sophie.
  Sophie陪伴Brain去拜訪一家老客戶。

Spa Village is a four-star hotel in Beitou, with a good reputation and popularity.
Spa Village是一間位於北投的四星級飯店，享有聲望且備受歡迎。

- Spa Village, a four-star hotel, is located in Beitou with a good reputation and popularity.
  Spa Village是一間四星級飯店，位於北投並享有聲望和受人歡迎。
- Spa Village, which is a four-star hotel in Beitou, is respectable and well-liked.
  Spa Village是一間位於北投的四星級飯店，享有聲望且備受歡迎。

She is very friendly and smart, the type of person you want to hang out with.
她很友善且聰明，是那種你會想繼續跟她往來的人。

- She is so nice and clever that you definitely feel like to make friends with her.
  她非常善良聰明，你一定會想要跟她交朋友。
- She is very kind and intelligent and you absolutely would like to be her friend.
  她非常仁慈且聰明，你一定會想要當她的朋友。

2-2 新手業務上戰場

Visiting a Customer 拜訪客戶

Sophie and Brian are paying a visit to Ms. Wu.

Sophie和Brian拜訪吳小姐。

Brian - the new salesperson 新手業務

Sophie - the salesperson, Brian's colleague 業務，Brian 的同事

Ms. Wu - customer 客戶

Dialogue

Ms. Wu	Hello, Sophie, how long has it been?	哈囉，Sophie，我們有多久沒見了？
Sophie	Hello, Ms. Wu. <u>It has been at least three months since the last time we met.</u>	哈囉，吳經理。距離我們上次見面，至少有三個月了。
Ms. Wu	Only three months? I thought it had been longer than that.	才三個月？我還以為更久呢。
Sophie	That is probably because you miss me so much. May I introduce my new colleague to you? This is Brian. He just joined us this month.	那是因為妳很想我吧。我可以向妳介紹一位新同事嗎？這位是Brian，他這個月才剛加入我們。
Brian	How do you do?	您好。
Ms. Wu	How do you do?	你好。

Brian	Thank you for giving me the chance to meet with you. Sophie has been telling me how **sincere** you are. Such an important customer like Spa Village must be hard to come by.	感謝您願意抽空見我。Sophie不斷地告訴我您待人有多真誠。以及貴公司Spa Village是何等重要且不可多得的客戶。
Ms. Wu	Don't mention it. You are very polite.	不必客氣。你很有禮貌。
Sophie	**Politeness** is one of his **virtues**. Brian has a **degree** in Business Administration, and over the past month, we have found him to be very **hardworking** and **conscientious**.	有禮貌是他的優點之一。Brian擁有企管學位，在這個月以來，我們發現他既努力且認真。
Ms. Wu	What a **valuable** new player. Alright, now what can I do for you?	好一個生力軍。好了，現在我能為你做些什麼呢？
Brian	Allow me to introduce you our newest **toiletry** package. Not only does it suit your needs but save a lot of money, too.	容我為您介紹最新的化妝品方案，不僅符合您的需求且更省錢。
Ms. Wu	It sounds interesting. Please continue.	聽起來很有趣，請繼續。

sincere n. 真誠的

Peter is a sincere and down-to-earth person.
Peter 是個真誠實在的人。

politeness n. 禮貌

A person with politeness must be very popular.
一個有禮貌的人一定很受歡迎。

virtue n. 長處、優點

I am proud of my brother, who is a man of great virtue.
我以我哥哥為榮，他是品德高尚的人。

degree n. 學位

He finally gained a degree in Economics after studying hard for a few years.
他在幾年努力念書後，終於拿到經濟學位。

hardworking adj. 努力工作的

Alice is a hardworking teacher.
Alice 是個認真的老師。

conscientious adj. 認真的

She is conscientious about everything.
她對每件事都很認真負責。

valuable adj. 有價值的

The husband bought a valuable ring for his wife.
這先生買了一個貴重的戒指給她的太太。

toiletry n. 化妝品

The woman carried a lot of toiletries with her.
這女人隨身攜帶很多化妝品。

In Other Words

It has been at least three months since the last time we met.
距離我們上次見面，至少有三個月了。

- It is more than three months since we met last time.
  自從我們上次見面後，已經超過三個月了。
- We have not seen each other for over three months.
  我們有三個月多沒見面了。

Politeness is one of his virtues.
有禮貌是他的優點之一。

- One of his merits is being courteous.
  他的優點之一是有禮貌的。
- He behaves with decorum, and that's one of his best characteristics.
  他總是舉止得宜，而這就是他的優點之一。

Allow me to introduce you our newest toiletry package.
容我為您介紹最新的化妝品方案。

- Let me take the liberty to present you our newest cosmetics package.
  恕我冒昧來為您介紹我們最新的化妝品方案。
- It is my pleasure to display our newest cosmetics package to you.
  我很榮幸能替您介紹我們最新的化妝品方案。

2-3 新手業務上戰場

After a Deal Was Closed
生意談成之後

Sophie reviews the deal Brian has just closed, reminds him of things he needs to pay attention to, and offers him some advice.

Sophie檢視Brian剛談成的一筆生意，叮嚀他一些該注意的事項以及提供一些建議給他。

Brian – the new salesperson 新手業務
Sophie – the salesperson, Brian's colleague 業務，Brian 的同事

Dialogue

Sophie	Congratulations on your first **deal**!	恭喜你達成第一筆交易！
Brian	Many thanks to you, too. I couldn't have pulled it off without your help.	很感謝你，如果不是你的幫忙我也無法完成。
Sophie	I did not do much. You did a great job. Keep up the good work.	我沒做什麼。你做得很好，再接再厲。
Brian	Should I inform the **warehouse** first as soon as I get back?	回去後我應該先通知倉庫嗎？
Sophie	No. The first thing to do is to report to Rita, our executive, and ask her for **advice** or suggestions. After that, you should file all **documents**, prepare forms, and inform **related** operation units and departments of the goods and services ordered.	不。回去後的第一件事，應該是將此筆交易向我們的主管Rita報告，尋求她的指點和建議。接著，你應該將所有文件歸檔、製作表單，並通知相關的營運單位及部門訂購的商品及服務。

Brian	Don't I need to check with the warehouse to make sure we have enough **inventories**?	我不需先跟倉庫確認是否有足夠的庫存嗎？
Sophie	You need to complete an **order form** and pass it to the warehouse. And then they will follow their own step by step procedure.	你需要先完成訂單並交給倉庫。接著他們會依照程序逐步完成。
Brian	I see. Thank you very much.	我了解了。非常感謝你。

★你應該要知道的小小事！

業務通常在談case的流程是這樣：

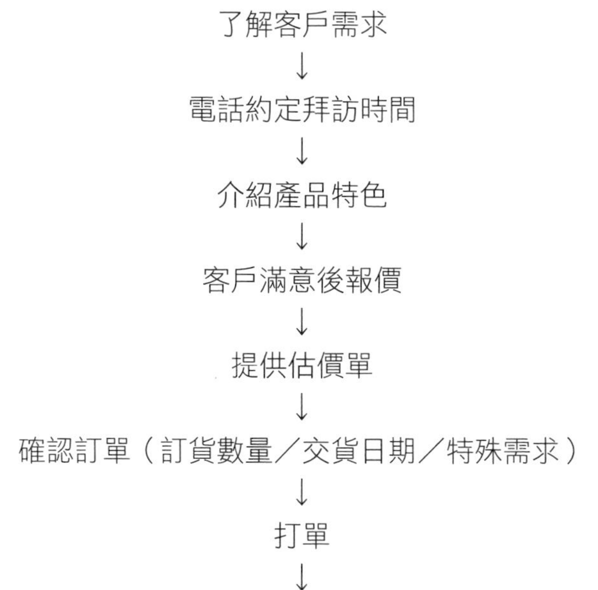

Word Bank

deal　n.　交易

The new sales representative was lucky to make his first deal during the probationary period.
這業務代表很幸運的在試用期間完成他的第一筆交易。

warehouse　n.　倉庫

The receiving clerk is checking and unloading the shipments at the warehouse.
收貨員正在檢查及卸貨到倉庫裡。

advice　n.　指點、建議

The doctor always gives advice of doing exercise regularly to his patients.
這醫生總是建議他的病患要規律運動。

document　n.　文件

To file the documents is the first task for every new clerk.
對每位新進人員的首件工作就是整理文件。

related　adj.　相關的

The student is looking for a part-time job to have related experience with his major.
這學生正在找一份與他主修有相關經驗的兼職工作。

inventory　n.　存貨

The department store made an inventory of everything before the holiday season.
這百貨公司在假期前夕已儲備每樣商品的存貨。

order form 訂單

It is required to fill in an order form before placing an order.
在下單前需要填寫訂單表。

In Other Words

I couldn't have pulled it off without your help.
如果不是你的幫忙我也無法完成。

- Without your assistance, I couldn't have it accomplished.
  如果沒有你的協助，我無法完成。
- Thanks to your help, I perform it successfully.
  託你的福，我成功地完成了。

You did a great job. Keep up the good work.
你做得很好，再接再厲。

- You did an excellent job. Keep doing on it.
  你做的很棒，再接再厲。
- Well done. You are always doing a good job. Do keep doing that!
  做得好。你總是做得這麼好。繼續保持啊！

And then they will follow their own step by step procedure.
接著他們會依照程序逐步完成。

- And then they will follow their SOP (standard operating procedure).
  接著他們會依照標準作業程序進行。
- And then all procedures will be followed step by step by them.
  接著他們會逐步進行所有作業程序。

2-4 新手業務上戰場

Final Check-up
最後檢查

Brian calls to make sure the order is processing smoothly and goods will be ready and delivered to the customer on time.

Brian 打電話確認訂單處理狀況一切順利，商品已備妥並準時送達客戶處。

Brian - the new employee 新手業務
Daisy - the warehouse staff 倉庫人員

Dialogue

Brian	Hi, Daisy. This is Brian. I am calling to **ensure** everything is in hand and we will be able to deliver the goods on time.	嗨，Daisy，我是Brian。我想確認一切已就緒且我們能夠準時將貨物送達。
Daisy	Everything is fine ... just one thing... we do not have enough soap in stock.	一切都順利……只有一件事……那就是我們肥皂的存貨不夠。
Brian	Oh, no! How come you did not tell me this earlier? What are we going to do about it? Is there enough time to manufacture the soap?	喔，不！妳怎麼沒早點告訴我？那妳打算怎麼做？還有足夠的時間製造肥皂嗎？

Daisy	Sorry. It was our fault. We went through the inventory **rapidly** and miscounted some items. I have already checked with the factory, and it will take two weeks to **make up** the **insufficient** stock.	很抱歉，這是我們的疏失。我們清點得太快以致漏掉了幾樣項目。我已經聯絡了工廠，將存貨補齊需要兩個星期的時間。
Brian	Two weeks! That will only leave us about one week to pack and **load**. How can we make it on time?	兩個星期！如此一來，我們大概只剩一個星期的時間來包裝和裝貨了。這樣來得及嗎？
Daisy	I will add night **shifts** to speed up the work as soon as we receive the goods. You can count on me for this.	我們一收到貨品之後，我會增加晚班人手以加快工作進度。這一點你可以相信我。
Brian	Are you sure? This is my first deal and Spa Village is a regular customer, so I cannot afford to **disappoint** them.	你確定嗎？這是我的第一份交易，而且Spa Village是老主顧了，所以我不能得罪他們。
Daisy	No worries. I give you my word.	別擔心。一言為定。

★你應該要知道的小小事！

業務處理客戶訂單時，一定要小心謹慎，因為每一位客戶都是公司的貴人；當遇到那種很重要的大客戶的訂單或是比較複雜難應付的客戶，就得再更加地仔細，可以特別叮嚀負責出貨的部門要留意這幾張單。如果有什麼突發狀況，千萬不要就裝傻，或是先放在那邊等客戶打來再處理，這樣很有可能讓你陷入更大的危機當中。當一了解狀況，應馬上做緊急處理，雖然得在第一時間就面對客戶的不悅與怒氣，但這比較有可能讓對方覺得你有擔當，不會遇到事情就跑去躲起來，才有可能未來還有合作的機會。

Word Bank

ensure v. 保證

The mechanic double checks the engine to ensure that it is in excellent condition.
技師再次檢查引擎以確定運作正常。

rapidly adv. 迅速地

It is incredible that the R&D department rapidly solved the problem.
不可思議的是研發部門如此迅速地解決此問題。

make up 補足

The buyer called the seller for a shortage of delivered goods and asked them to make it up.
買方致電賣方數量短缺並要求補足。

insufficient adj. 不足的

The student is aware of having insufficient knowledge and would like to learn more.
這學生知道自己知識不足，想要再多學習。

load v. 裝載

The ship is loaded with a great deal of goods.
這艘船可以裝載大量商品。

shift n. 輪班

The nurse is working at the night shift.
這護士正在上夜班工作。

disappoint v. 使失望

The student's behavior disappointed his teacher.
這學生的行為讓他的老師很失望。

In Other Words

I am calling to ensure everything is in hand and we will be able to deliver the goods on time.
我想確認一切已就緒且我們能夠準時將貨物送達。

- I want to make sure that everything is ready to have the goods been delivered on time.
  我想確認一切已就緒可讓貨物準時送達。
- I am calling to confirm that our products can be delivered to our customer punctually.
  我打來是想確認我們的貨物能準時送到客戶那裡。

You can count on me for this.
這一點你可以相信我。

- You can rely on me for this.
  這一點你可以信賴我。
- Trust me, I won't disappoint you.
  相信我，我不會讓你失望的。

I give you my word.
一言為定。

- You have my assurance.
  我向你保證。
- I'll do as I promised.
  我會照我承諾的做。

如何給顧客好印象！

★穿著得宜

許多交易的成敗取決於第一印象。相反的，若打扮得過於花枝招展或是標新立異，同樣也會產生負面的印象。重點是整潔、合乎專業和身分。避免擦味道過濃的香水或古龍水。

★用溫和的口吻交談

耐心且仔細聽取客戶的觀點。還有，保持微笑和互動。例如：當客戶侃侃而談時，不時要點點頭或揚揚下巴，切記不要擺出一張撲克牌臉，即便臉上並無顯露出惡意或不耐，也不能擺出一付無動於衷的模樣。

★不要打斷客戶的發言

打斷別人説話或是干擾是很不禮貌的，而且會讓客戶覺得沒誠意。要記得關掉手機或是轉成震動模式。

★千古不變的道理－顧客永遠是對的

要記住，你是提供服務的一方，若沒有客戶，你就不會有工作。即便知道客戶是錯的，也最好順從客戶的想法。不二法則就是，寧可咬著牙撐過去，也好過失去一筆生意。

★不要一開始就裝熟

很多人都以為和顧客之間應該營造一股「打成一片」的氛圍，才有利於生意的成交。其實這並非正確的觀點，初次見面時，還是要保持一點距離，但要不失禮貌和專業的態度。初次見面就擺出一付哥兒們或好姊妹的態度，會讓人覺得過於輕挑，還會讓對方小看你的能力和責任感。

★盡心盡力替客戶排除萬難

試著從客戶的觀點看事情，探索為何會有那樣的想法或感觸，將心比心。

★要保持樂觀進取的態度

盡全力但別強求，因為本來就不可能滿足所有客戶，若有幾個人給你釘子碰，不要懷疑自己，再接再厲。

用字篇

! Goods以及Products的差別

兩者皆可解釋為商品/產品，以致許多人以為這兩個單字是通用的，其實兩者之間是有差異的。

goods: 相較於products，goods則較為廣泛使用，泛指一般公司行號所生產的物品，包括電器用品、醫療用品、美容用品、飲食用品等，但必須是實體產品，例如保險商品或金融商品，則不可使用goods。

products: 用法同於goods，但products可用於實體以及非實體物品。

老鳥巧巧說

業務拜訪一定要留意的「眉角」

在做業務拜訪時，除了盡力介紹自家的產品之外，在拜訪過程中也要時時注意客戶的表情和反應，有些話跟問題，客戶可能不會說也不會問。但如果你夠機靈、觀察夠仔細，你就可以藉由他們的facial expression和body language來看出他們對產品是不是滿意或是有什麼其他的問題，你就可以立即做出說明，得到他們的信任，也讓他們知道你不僅僅是介紹產品，希望他們購買，同時你也在乎他們的感受。有些業務剛入行，熱血沸騰，好不容易約到拜訪某位客戶，就想著：我今天來一定要把所有想要講的都講完，目的不達成，我絕不離開，只要發揮我強大的說服力，這筆訂單我一定會拿到。但如果真的遇到客戶在忙，或是剛好有急事要處理，業務一定要會看臉色，不要一直硬講，可以先快速做個ending，並約定下次拜訪的時間，讓客戶能趕緊處理要事，這樣客戶也會覺得你很貼心，也不會拒絕你的下次再訪。

3-1 產品說明

We Are Interested in Buying Your Product
我們想購買貴公司的產品

Melissa Tsai, an overseas customer, calls for some product information.
來自海外的顧客－Melissa蔡來電詢問一些產品資訊。

Steve - the senior sales representative 資深業務
Melissa Tsai - a potential customer 潛在的客戶

Dialogue

Steve	Good afternoon. Green Day. Steve speaking. How may I help you?	哈囉，我是Steve，有什麼可以為您服務的嗎？
Melissa	Hi, my name is Melissa Tsai. I am calling **on behalf of** Nick's Hair. We are a chain of hair salons, located in Hong Kong, and own a total of six shops.	嗨，我是Melissa蔡，我代表Nick's Hair來電，我們是香港一間連鎖髮型沙龍，旗下共擁有六間分店。
Steve	Hello, Ms. Tsai. This is Steve, a **senior** sales representative. Thank you for calling us. May I ask, how did you know about our company?	您好，我是Steve，是資深業務代表。感謝您的來電。我可以請問您是如何知道我們公司的呢？
Melissa	Your products are not available in the market here. We made a purchase on your website. We are interested in buying your products. The **herbal** shampoo and conditioner series.	在香港市面上買不到你們公司的產品，我們之前是透過你們公司的網站訂購的。我們想購買你們公司的產品。草本洗髮乳和潤髮乳系列。

Steve	Our natural herbal series is one of the top-selling hair care products on the market. They are made of natural **ingredients**, and completely safe for all hair types.	我們的天然草本系列是市場上最熱賣的頭髮護理商品之一，全部是天然原料製造，適用於各類髮質。
Melissa	That is why we are interested in it.	這就是我們對它有興趣的原因。
Steve	May I have your phone number, e-mail, and mailing address? I will send you some free samples and our latest **catalog**.	可以給我您的電話、e-mail以及通訊地址嗎？我會寄給您一些免費樣品以及我們最新的型錄。
Melissa	That would be great. My number is 2338-5650, my e-mail is melissa@nickshair.com, and the address is 10th Fl., No.28, Willington Street, Central, Hong Kong.	那太好了。我的電話是2338-5650，e-mail是melissa@nickshair.com，地址是香港中環威靈頓街28號10樓。
Steve	The samples and catalog will be sent tomorrow and you should receive them in less than a week. Thank you for calling and giving us the opportunity to send you the samples. Please feel free to **contact** us at any time.	明天我就會將樣品和型錄寄出，而您應該在一星期內會收到。感謝您的來電，讓我們有機會將試用品寄給您。如有任何需要，請隨時來電。

Word Bank

on behalf of　代表

I am writing on behalf of my company to express our appreciation.
僅代表我的公司致函表達謝意。

senior　adj.　資深的

She has worked in this company for 30 years and is a senior employee.
她在此公司已工作30年，是個資深員工。

sales representative　業務代表

The big company hires 10 sales representatives to promote the new product.
這大公司聘僱10位業務代表來推廣新產品。

herbal　adj.　草本的

The organic and herbal hair care products are very popular and sold out.
這有機草本護髮產品因太受歡迎而銷售一空了。

ingredient　n.　原料、材料

What are the ingredients of the pizza?
比薩的原料是什麼？

catalog　n.　型錄

The latest catalog displays the newest products line.
最新的目錄標示了最新產品類別。

contact v. 聯絡

Remember to contact me when you arrive in the US.
到了美國要記得跟我聯絡。

In Other Words

I am calling on behalf of Nick's Hair.
我代表 Nick's Hair 來電。

- I represent Nick's Hair to call you.
  我代表Nick's Hair來電。
- I'm calling from Nick's Hair.
  我這裡是Nick's Hair。

They are made of natural ingredients, and completely safe for all hair types.
商品全部是天然原料製造，適用於各類髮質。

- All are produced by natural ingredients and suitable to all hair types.
  商品全部是天然原料製造，適用於各類髮質。
- Our products are all manufactured with natural ingredients and fit all types of hair.
  商品全部是天然原料製造，適用於各類髮質。

Thank you for calling and giving us the opportunity to send you the samples.
感謝您的來電，讓我們有機會將試用品寄給您。

- We appreciate your calling and chance to offer you samples.
  我們感謝您的來電及能提供試用品給您的機會。
- I'm appreciated for the opportunity to provide you our product samples.
  我很感謝能有這機會提供試用品給您。

3-2 產品說明

Making an Appointment 安排會面

Melissa wishes to visit the company. She is making an appointment with Steve by phone.

Melissa想來拜訪公司，她和Steve在電話中安排會面時間。

Steve – the senior sales representative 資深業務
Melissa Tsai – a potential customer 潛在客戶

Dialogue

Steve	Good afternoon, Ms. Tsai. How did you like the samples?	蔡小姐午安，請問您對我們的樣品還滿意嗎？
Melissa	We liked them very much. We would like to make an **appointment** to visit you and know more about the natural herbal hair care **series**.	我們很喜歡。想跟您約個時間拜訪貴公司，並多了解有關天然草本護髮系列的產品。
Steve	That is wonderful. You are most welcome. When do you plan to arrive?	那太好了，我們誠摯歡迎您，您計畫何時抵達呢？
Melissa	If it is not too much trouble, we would like to visit you at your office on October 12th.	如果不會給你們造成麻煩的話，我們希望可以在10月12日到貴公司拜訪。

Steve	No trouble at all. I shall make an **arrangement** to **pick** you **up**. What time will you arrive and how many will be in your **party**?	一點也不麻煩。我應該安排接機。您們什麼時間會抵達以及來訪人數呢？
Melissa	That is very **generous** of you. I am not sure about the exact **arrival** time yet, but I will let you know as soon as I find out. There will be two of us.	您真是太客氣了。我尚不確定確切的抵達時間，一旦我確定後我會儘快讓您知道。我們屆時一共會有兩個人。
Steve	May I know the name of the other party?	我可以知道另外一位來訪者的大名嗎？
Melissa	Of course. His name is Robert Chow, the head stylist.	當然。他是我們的首席造型師Robert周。
Steve	Can you tell me what products you are interested in?	可以告訴我您們對哪些產品有興趣呢？
Melissa	The natural herbal shampoo and conditioner, and fragrance oils.	天然草本洗髮乳和潤髮乳，以及香精油。
Steve	Thank you. I look forward to meeting you.	謝謝。我期待能見到您們。
Melissa	Me too. Thank you very much. See you soon.	我也是。非常感謝你，到時候見。

Word Bank

appointment n. 會面

I have an appointment with the client at 10:00am.
我和客户十點有約。

series n. 系列

The whitening series of skin care products are on sale.
保養美白系列產品正在打折中。

arrangement n. 安排

The secretary is making arrangements for the conference.
秘書正安排準備會議。

pick sb. up / pick up sb. 接某人

Melissa is leaving for picking up her child.
Melissa 正出發去接她的小孩。

party n. 一行人

The two parties try to make terms and sign the contract.
雙方試著達成協議並簽署合約。

generous adj. 大方的；慷慨的

Jeff is always generous in giving help.
Jeff 總是樂於助人。

arrival n. 到達

Everyone is waiting for the arrival of the newborn baby.
每個人正等候新生兒的到來。

In Other Words

She is making an appointment with Steve by phone.
她和Steve在電話中安排會面時間。

- She is making a phone call to set up a time to meet with Steve.
  她打電話和Steve約定會面的時間。
- She is calling Steve for making an appointment.
  她打電話給Steve約會面時間。

What time will you arrive and how many will be in your party?
您們什麼時間會抵達以及一共有幾位呢？

- When will you supposedly arrive and how many visitors does your party have?
  您們預計何時會到達，一行共有幾位呢？
- What is the approximate arrival time and how many people will come?
  您們大約何時會到達，有幾位會到訪？

I am not sure about the exact arrival time yet, but I will let you know as soon as I find out.
我尚不確定確切的抵達時間，一旦我確定後我會儘快讓您知道。

- I am not certain about the exact arrival time yet, but I will keep you informed upon finding out.
  我尚未確定確切的抵達時間，一旦確定後我會儘快通知您。
- I am not sure yet about what the exact time we will arrive is. However, I will advise you once I get it.
  我還不確定我們將抵達的確切時間，但確定行程之後我會儘快通知您。

3-3 產品說明

Preparing for a Product Presentation 準備產品說明會

Steve reports to Rita and Tony about the arrangement with Melissa. The three of them are planning a product presentation together.

Steve 向 Rita 及 Tony 報告 Melissa 即將來訪一事。他們共同策劃一個產品說明會。

Steve – the senior sales representative 資深業務
Rita – the sales supervisor 業務主管
Tony – the sales director 業務協理

Dialogue

Steve	A **client** plans to visit us on October 12th, along with their head stylist.	我的客戶連同他們的首席造型師想在10月12日來拜訪我們。
Tony	Tell us more about this client.	跟我們說說你的客戶。
Steve	Her name is Melissa Tsai, the vice general manager of Nick's Hair. <u>Nick's Hair is a chain of hair salon in Hong Kong with six shops.</u> They have used our products before.	她叫Melissa蔡，是香港連鎖髮廊Nick's Hair的副總經理。Nick's Hair是香港一家有六間分店的連鎖髮型沙龍。他們之前就曾使用過我們的產品。
Rita	When will they arrive at the airport?	他們幾點抵達機場？
Steve	At 2 p.m. and I will pick them up **in person**.	下午兩點，我會親自去接機。

Tony	October 12th! That leaves us with less than a month. What products are they interested in?	10月12日！那麼我們只剩下一個月不到的時間，他們對哪些產品有興趣呢？
Steve	The natural herbal hair care series and fragrance oils.	天然草本護髮系列和香精油。
Rita	We need to start building a product presentation as soon as possible.	我們需要儘快著手籌備一個產品說明會。
Tony	Correct. Before you start, I want you to **gather** as much information about the target client as you can. And then ask the Art Department to help prepare the **visual aids**. Steve, you will be **in charge of** the presentation, and Rita, you will supervise him.	沒錯。在你開始進行之前，我希望你們能夠儘量收集越多關於目標客戶的資料越好，接著再請美術部門協助製作視覺輔助道具。Steve，說明會由你全權負責，然後Rita妳在一旁給予指導。
Rita	Yes.	好的。
Steve	Understood. **I will get right on it.**	了解。我馬上就著手進行。

★你應該要知道的小小事！

在第一次準備產品說明會時，難免會緊張；其實可以透過一些事先演練，像是準備好介紹的內容後，對著鏡子中的自己從頭到尾講一次，看看自己的表情是不是很僵硬、聲音是不是太平，然後再慢慢調整。

Word Bank

client n. 客戶

Remember the clients' demands are always our first priority.
記得客户需求永遠是我們的第一優先考量。

along with 連同

Please have everything ready along with the samples for the presentation.
請準備好各樣資料連同樣品來做簡報介绍。

in person 親自

The man is excited about meeting his cyber acquaintance in person next week.
這男人很興奮下週要與網友會面。

gather v. 收集

The new clerk is assigned to gather potential customers information.
這新員工被派去收集潛在客户資料。

visual adj. 視覺的

The audiences have visual satisfaction with this movie.
觀眾從此電影得到視覺上滿足。

aid n. 有輔助作用的事物

A good dictionary is an aid of learning foreign languages.
好的字典是學習外語的助手。

in charge of 負責

Steve has been transferred to the Marketing Department and in charge of advertisement division.
Steve 被轉調到行銷部負責廣告部門。

In Other Words

Nick's Hair is a chain of hair salon in Hong Kong with six shops.
Nick's Hair是香港一家有六間分店的連鎖髮型沙龍。

- Nick's Hair is a hair salon group with six chain shops in Hong Kong.
  Nick's Hair是香港一家有六間連鎖店的髮型沙龍集團。
- Nick's Hair is a Hong Kong based hair salon chain with six shops.
  Nick's Hair是香港一家有六間分店的連鎖髮型沙龍。

That leaves us with less than a month.
我們只剩下一個月不到的時間。

- We have no longer than a month.
  我們只剩下一個月不到的時間。
- It remains less than a month for us.
  我們只剩下一個月不到的時間。

Steve, you will be in charge of the presentation, and Rita, you will supervise him.
Steve，說明會由你全權負責，然後Rita妳在一旁給予指導。

- Steve, you will be responsible for the presentation, and Rita, you will be his supervisor.
  Steve，你全權負責說明會，然後Rita妳當他的指導員。
- Steve, you are assigned to arrange the presentation, and Rita, you are authorized to instruct him.
  Steve，你負責安排說明會，然後Rita妳負責指導他。

3-4 產品說明

Making an Inquiry
詢價

After the product presentation, clients from Hong Kong wish to make an inquiry.
產品說明會結束之後，來自香港的客戶希望能夠詢價。

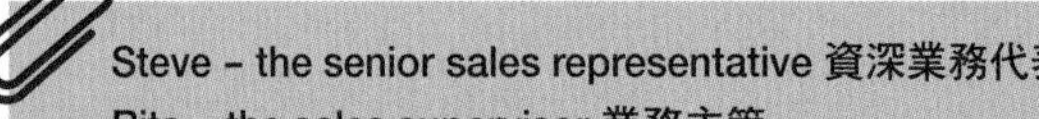

Steve - the senior sales representative 資深業務代表
Rita - the sales supervisor 業務主管
Melissa Tsai - the client 客戶　　Robert Chow - the client 客戶

Dialogue

Robert	That was an **impressive** presentation.	這真是一場令人印象深刻的說明會。
Melissa	And we would like to know the price, **excluding** tax, of the natural herbal shampoo and conditioner, and water lily fragrance oil.	我們想知道天然草本洗髮乳、潤髮乳以及睡蓮香精油不含稅的價格。
Steve	Tell us the **quantity** you **require** so that we can work out the **offers**.	請告訴我們您們所需要的數量以便我們報價。
Robert	3,000 dozens of herbal shampoo and conditioner, 1,500 each, and 1,200 dozens of water lily fragrance oil.	草本洗髮乳和潤髮乳各1,500打，共3000打，以及1,200打睡蓮香精油。
Melissa	We are planning to go back to Hong Kong the day after tomorrow.	我們計畫後天回香港。
Robert	So, we would **appreciate** it if you could give us the **quotations** before we leave.	所以如果您能夠在我們回去之前就提供報價的話，我們會非常感激。

Steve	Here is the thing. First of all, we need to check with the warehouse to see if we have enough inventories, and then we need to consult with the director.	是這樣的。首先我們必須先向倉庫確認有足夠的存貨，然後還必須請示協理。
Melissa	If you can speed things up, we should be able to place an order before we leave.	如果您們動作能加快的話，或許我們在回去之前就能下訂單了。
Rita	How about this? We'll give it a try and call you tomorrow.	這樣如何？我們會儘量試試看，然後明天會給你們電話。

★你應該要知道的小小事！

通常業務在製作估價單時，公司內部都會有一個正常的處理時間，如果遇到緊急的狀況的話，新人其實可以請教前輩是否有什麼樣的應變方法可以加速這個case的處理。將估價單交給客戶之前，一定要再三確認折扣、金額、數量，避免造成公司損失及後續可能會產生的麻煩。

Word Bank

impressive adj. 令人印象深刻的

The President made an impressive speech to the people.
總統對他的人民發表了一個令人印象深刻的演說。

exclude v. 將……排除在外；不包括……

All people, excluding children under 12 years old, are allowed to attend the exhibition.
所有人，除了十二歲以下兒童，都可以進來參觀展覽會。

quantity n. 數量

The unit price will be reduced if the order is placed in large quantity.
如果下單量很大，單價就會降低。

require v. 需求

Some personal information is required for the member registration.
要加入會員需要準備一些個人資料。

offer n. 報價

Our client accepted my offer and placed an order.
我們的客户接受我的報價並下單。

appreciate v. 感激

I always appreciate what God has given every day.
我總是感激上帝每天給我的恩賜。

quotation n. 估價單

The sales representative is responding the inquiries with quotations.
此業務代表正在以估價單回覆詢價。

In Other Words

That was an impressive presentation.
這真是一場令人印象深刻的說明會。

- I was very impressed by this presentation.
  我對此說明會印象非常深刻。
- The presentation really impressed me.
  此說明會令我印象非常深刻。

If you can speed things up, we should be able to place an order before we leave.
如果您們動作能加快的話，或許我們在回去之前就能下訂單了。

- We should probably be able to place an order before we leave if you can accelerate the process.
  我們在回去之前就能下訂單了，如果您們動作加快的話。
- If you can expedite things up, we should be able to place an order before we leave.
  如果您們動作能加快的話，或許我們在回去之前就能下訂單了。

We'll give it a try and call you tomorrow.
我們會儘量試試看，然後明天會給你們電話。

- We'll try our best and call you tomorrow.
  我們會儘量試試看，然後明天會給你們電話。
- We'll make our every effort and ring you up tomorrow.
  我們會儘量試試看，然後明天會給你們電話。

成交的撇步！

★不簽署書面文件絕不死心

口頭上的承諾永遠不夠且不可靠。人的想法可以在一秒鐘之內而有所轉變，不要因為客戶在口頭上給予了承諾而鬆懈或放慢腳步，記住一定要簽署書面協議才算大功告成。

★營造一股緊迫感

客戶往往會三心二意、舉棋不定，這時你必須讓客戶了解，若不儘快做出決定，可能佔不到便宜或利基，所以你必須適度且適時地給予一些「利多」，例如價格的折扣、免費或低價的包裝，或是較為優惠的保固等等。

★以競爭力做為誘餌

要讓客戶明白，倘若不和你簽約，那麼你會找其他人，如此一來其他人的競爭優勢將強過於他/她。在談生意時，或多或少需要施展一點「說話天花亂墜」的技倆。

★抱著「最新潮流」不放

任何人，尤其是生意人，最能讓他們心動的一項要素就是「最新潮流」，所以必須讓客戶明白，與你合作絕對符合潮流，而且是目前市場上最新或是正在流行的機制。

★獨一無二的優越感

要讓客戶明白，不是每家公司行號或是每個人都適用於你所推銷的產品或服務，若非有點「本事」或「實力」，還不見得適用。

★理念至上

在提倡面面俱到的這個時代，單單只有產品和服務的特性已無法滿足千變萬化和多元的市場環境。每種產品和服務都需具備一種理念、信念。例如，若你推銷的是電子產品，那麼你必須以「科技代表進步」或是「擁有電子科技才是活在當下」等琳瑯滿目的口號，作為產品的信念。

★提出實證

讓客戶知道其他人用過此產品或服務的經驗以及良效，最好是具有知名度或信譽的公司行號或是個人。

★做好「不會成交」的心理準備

必須做好可能一切努力到頭來都是白費的心理準備，但千萬不要因此變得消極，雖然生意做不成，但仍然可以經營人際關係，說不定能透過該客戶讓周遭的人獲得其他機會，又或是與客戶保持互動，有朝一日他/她會被你感動也說不定。注意！「保持互動」，如同字面上的解釋，僅須保持，而非糾纏。

完美說明會的秘訣大公開

了解及熟悉產品的特色：

這是最重要的一點，一定要完全掌握特色，如果可以，也要了解其他家廠商同性質產品的特色，到底公司有沒有什麼勝出的地方，如果有就一定要大大的提；相反的，如果介紹的產品有比較弱一點點的地方，就輕輕帶過，千萬不要做出誇大不實的介紹，避免讓自己陷入尷尬的狀況。

簡單明瞭的重點說明：

掌握時間，15分鐘的產品說明會和30分鐘的產品說明會，介紹的方式一定不一樣，一定要會變通，才能在有效時間之內先做完重點說明。

說話的條理性：

在有限的時間內要讓客戶很快掌握你的說明重點，條理一定要分明，不要東講一個西講一個，這樣客戶會很難follow，說明會的成效就會打折。

4-1 客戶生氣了

The Deal Is Off
交易取消

A major client, Mr. Li is not pleased with the quotations; therefore, the deal is off.
大客戶李先生不滿意報價；因此，交易取消。

Sophie - the salesperson 業務
Mr. Li - the major client 大客戶

Dialogue

Mr. Li	The price you're offering is **beyond** what is acceptable for us.	你們的報價高出我方所能接受的範圍太多了。
Sophie	Allow me to explain. Our offer is in line with the **prevailing market price**. The market hit bottom and soon will pick up.	容我解釋一下。我們提供的報價與市場價格一致，市場已經盪到最低點，不久後一定會回升。
Mr. Li	That is **nonsense**. Your offer is **ridiculous**. The quotations are not only higher than other sources, but are even higher than the market price. We have been a loyal customer of your company for a **decade**.	胡說八道。你們提供的報價太荒謬了。你們的報價不僅比其他公司的報價來的高，甚至還高於市價。過去十年來，我們一直是貴公司忠誠的顧客。
Sophie	Mr. Li, please calm down. There must be some mistake.	李先生，請冷靜下來。這其中一定有什麼誤會。
Mr. Li	Let me ask you again. Is this the best you can do?	讓我再問你一次，這是妳能給的最好價格了嗎？

Sophie	I am afraid it is the lowest price we can offer now.	恐怕這已經是我們目前可以提供的最低價了。
Mr. Li	How **disappointing**!	真令人失望！
Sophie	Let me check again with my supervisor.	讓我再和我的主管確認一下。
Mr. Li	There is no need to do that. The deal is off. I am not going to place an order. <u>And we will never do business with you again.</u>	不需要了。交易取消。我不會下訂單的，而且我們再也不會和你們做生意了。

★你應該要知道的小小事！

業務在跟客戶談到折扣的時候，一定要特別小心，如果客戶所提出的要求已經超過你的職權範圍，也不用馬上很強硬的跟對方説不可能這幾個字，避免讓客戶有不好的感覺，可以先婉轉告知你可代為請教上級主管，會盡快回覆消息給客戶。

如果真的遇到很難應付的客戶，一直跟你“盧”價格或是折扣，也不要跟對方動氣，因為凡事以和為貴，不要因為無法控制一時的情緒，而必須花兩倍甚至是三倍的時間來善後，這樣很划不來。當下若真的無法處理，可以先想辦法有禮貌的結束對話，待稍冷靜之後，再仔細思考或是請教前輩如何處理這樣的狀況比較OK，儘量用比較圓融的方式來與客戶周旋，千萬不要硬碰硬！

Word Bank

beyond adv. 超越、超過

I am blessed to have everything beyond my expectation.
我很蒙福擁有超過我所求的一切。

prevailing adj. 主要的

English is the prevailing language in the world.
英文是世界上主要語言。

market price 市價

He was lucky to buy this house by lower than the market price.
他很幸運以低於市價買到這棟房子。

nonsense n. 胡說

Don't be fooled by his nonsense.
不要被他的胡說八道給騙了。

ridiculous adj. 可笑的、荒謬的

It is ridiculous that you have made this mistake again and again.
你一再犯此錯誤真是荒謬。

decade n. 十年

It has been two decades ago since I met him last time.
我上次見到他是二十年前。

disappointing adj. 失望的

The singer's performance is disappointing to her fans.
這歌手的表現令他的歌迷失望。

In Other Words

A major client, Mr. Li is not pleased with the quotations; therefore, the deal is off.
大客户李先生不滿意報價；因此，交易取消。

- One of our key accounts, Mr. Li, is unsatisfied with the offer; therefore, the business is closed.
  我們的大客戶之一–李先生，不滿意報價；因此此次生意宣告結束。
- The offer is not satisfactory to Mr. Li, who's one of the important clients, and results in the business being terminated.
  重要客戶之一的李先生，不滿意報價；導致此次的交易終止。

Our offer is in line with the prevailing market price.
我們提供的報價與市場一致。

- Our quotation is consistent with the major market price.
  我們提供的報價與市場一致。
- Our offer is the same as the market average price.
  我們的報價跟與市場的平均價格是一樣的。

And we will never do business with you again.
而且我們再也不會和你們做生意了。

- And we will terminate the business relationship between us forever.
  而且我們會永遠停止我們之間的生意關係。
- From now on, we won't purchase anything from you ever again.
  而且從現在開始，我們會停止買賣關係。

4-2 客戶生氣了

Making an Offer
進行報價

Dennis, a salesperson, provides a very good offer to the client, Mrs. Ku. Mrs. Ku is very attracted by the low price and places a large order.

業務員丹尼斯向客戶古太太提供很理想的報價，古太太被低價吸引，並且下了一筆很大的訂單。

Dennis – the salesperson 業務
Mrs. Ku – the client 客戶

Dialogue

Mrs. Ku	I am afraid your price is above my limit.	你的價格恐怕超出了我的底限。
Dennis	I wish I could please you, but your **suggested** price is **rather** on the low side.	我很希望能夠讓您滿意，但您建議的價格實在偏低。
Mrs. Ku	Dennis, I have been doing business with you for a long time. Is this the lowest price you can offer?	Dennis，我跟你們做生意已經有一段時間了。這是你所能開出的最低價嗎？
Dennis	You have always been a great customer, but I do not think we could cut the price to that **extent** as required.	您一直是很優質的顧客，但我想我們無法將價格降到您所提出的限度。
Mrs. Ku	Your prices are always higher than other sources.	你們的價格總是比其他公司的還要高。

Dennis	Our products may cost more, but I can **assure** you, that they are worth every penny.	我們的產品或許是貴了點，但我可以跟您保證，一分錢一分貨。
Mrs. Ku	Is it possible to **reduce** the price a little?	有沒有可能把價格再降低一點呢？
Dennis	Alright. I may offer you a special discount of 15%, and this is my **bottom line**.	好吧。我可以提供您八五折的特別折扣，這已經是我的底線了。
Mrs. Ku	Well, then. I will make an order for twenty dozens of olive skin lotion.	好吧，那麼我就下訂單了，我要20打的橄欖油護膚乳液。
Dennis	Thank you! Let me get the contract ready.	感謝您。讓我將合約備妥。

★你應該要知道的小小事！

業務在查詢產品價格的時候，千萬要特別留意！因為公司的產品很多是系列商品，所以在同一個系列下可能會有許多的品項，在查價時，品項名稱一定要看清楚，才不會誤看價格，報錯價，這樣對客戶也很不好交代。有的客戶，可能會在聽過解釋之後，覺得沒關係，人都難免出錯，所以會原諒業務的這個小失誤。但有的客戶則會覺得是業務報錯價，所以業務必須負起全責。這時，如果是遇到那種價差大或是訂購量較多的狀況，就會相當的棘手。

Word Bank

suggested adj. 建議的

You should read the suggested instructions of the manual before you activate the device.
在啟動機器前，你應該要閱讀手冊的建議事項。

rather adv. 頗；相當地

The new clerk works rather hard and efficiently.
這新員工相當認真和有效率地工作。

extent n. 限度、程度、範圍

To a certain extent, both the parents and teachers are responsible for the education of children.
在某種程度上，父母親和老師都應該對小孩的教育負責任。

assure v. 保證

The salesperson assured me of the quality of the merchandise.
業務員向我保證此商品的品質。

reduce v. 降低

The department store reduced the price of many items on the annual sale.
這百貨公司在週年慶時將很多項目降價。

bottom line n. 底線

The customers are trying to find the bottom line before making bids.
客户在下標前想找出底價。

In Other Words

You have always been a great customer, but I do not think we could cut the price to that extent as required.
您一直是很優質的顧客，但我想我們無法將價格降到您所提出的限度。

- You have always been one of our superior customers. However, we are unable to reduce the price to meet your satisfaction.
  您一直是我們優質顧客之一，但我們仍無法將價格降到您滿意的程度。
- Even though you are always an excellent customer, we still can't cut the price per your request.
  即使您一直是我們優質顧客，但我們仍無法依您要求將降價。

Our products may cost more, but I can assure you, that they are worth every penny.
我們的產品或許是貴了點，但我可以跟您保證，一分錢一分貨。

- I can guarantee you the quality of our products, though they have higher price.
  我可以保證我們的產品雖然價格較高，但一分錢一分貨。
- The value of our products is assured for every penny, though they cost more.
  我可以保證我們的產品雖然價格較高，但一分錢一分貨。

I may offer you a special discount of 15%, and this is my bottom line.
我可以提供您八五折的特別折扣，這已經是我的底線了。

- I can give you a special discount of 15%, which is my best offer.
  我可以提供您八五折的特別折扣，這已經是我的最低報價了。
- Fifteen percent off the price, which is the best discount that I can offer you.
  八五折，這是我所能提供您最好的折扣了。

4-3 客戶生氣了

A Major Mistake
重大失誤

Rita finds a major mistake in the contract which Dennis has just signed with Mrs. Ku. Dennis offered an unacceptable discount. The bottom line should be 10% instead of 15%.

Rita在Dennis和其客戶古太太所簽署的合約中發現重大失誤。Dennis居然給出一個公司無法接受的折扣。底線本應是九折，而非八五折。

Dennis - the salesperson 業務
Rita - the sales supervisor 業務主管

Dialogue

Dennis	Rita, do you want to see me?	Rita，妳想見我？
Rita	Come in. Have a seat.	請進，坐吧。
Dennis	Are you reading the **contract** I signed yesterday? Is there anything wrong?	妳正在看我昨天才簽署的合約嗎？有什麼不對的地方嗎？
Rita	Did you offer a 15% discount to Mrs. Ku? How could you do that?	你向古太太提供了八五折的折扣嗎？你怎麼能這麼做呢？
Dennis	… I did check the reserve price of the olive skin lotion with you… a discount of 15% was within the extent we could offer…	……我的確和你確認過橄欖油護膚乳液的底價……八五折仍在我們可以提供的範圍之內……。

Rita	Oh, no! You have mistaken the olive skin lotion for the olive **sunscreen** series!	喔，不！你誤將橄欖護膚乳液聽成橄欖防曬乳液系列了！
Dennis	What! No way!	什麼！不可能！
Rita	The discount limit for olive skin lotion cannot **exceed** 10%. How many cases did your client order?	橄欖護膚乳液的折扣限制不能超出九折。你的客戶訂購了多少數量？
Steve	…20 dozens.	20打。
Rita	It could cause a great **loss** for the company. These skin lotions are not only our latest product, but made with expensive and **exclusive** ingredients.	這會替公司帶來重大損失。這些護膚乳液不僅是我們最新的產品，還是以非常昂貴且特有的原料所製成的。
Dennis	How can I fix it? Can I make a change…?	該如何補救？我可以更改……？
Rita	No, you cannot! The contract is **signed and sealed**. It is too late to make any changes.	不，不可以！因為合約已經經過雙方同意且簽字蓋章了！要做任何修改都已經太晚了。
Dennis	I am so sorry…	我很抱歉……。
Rita	Go back to your desk first. I will report the **situation** to Tony.	先回座位吧。我會將此情況向Tony報告。

Word Bank

contract n. 合約

It is important to read the contract carefully before you sign it.
在簽名前仔細閱讀合約是很重要的。

sunscreen n. 防曬乳液

I always wear sunscreen before going out.
我在外出時都會塗抹防曬乳液。

exceed v. 超出

The sales exceeded our expectation.
銷售超過了我們的預料。

loss n. 損失

You have to be responsible for this huge loss to the company.
你必須要對造成公司巨大的損失負責。

exclusive adj. 專有的、獨家的

The reporter got a piece of exclusive news.
這記者拿到一則獨家新聞。

signed and sealed adj. 經由正式的同意；正式生效

They won't get paid until the contract is signed and sealed.
這合約在正式生效之前，他們是拿不到錢的。

situation n. 狀況

His financial situation has been improved after getting a job.
在找到工作後，他的財務狀況有改善了。

In Other Words

You have mistaken the olive skin lotion for the olive sunscreen series!
你誤將橄欖護膚乳液聽成橄欖防曬乳液系列了！

- You have wrongly thought the olive skin lotion as the olive sunscreen series.
  你把橄欖護膚乳液弄錯成橄欖防曬乳液系列了！
- I'm afraid you are mistaken, 15% off is for the olive sunscreen series only, not the olive skin lotion.
  恐怕你是搞混了，85 折是針對橄欖防曬乳液系列，而不是橄欖護膚乳液。

It could cause a great loss for the company.
這會替公司帶來重大損失。

- It could bring on a huge loss for the company.
  這會替公司帶來重大損失。
- It could result in a huge loss for the company.
  這可能會造成公司的重大損失。

These skin lotions are not only our latest product, but made with expensive and exclusive ingredients.
這些護膚乳液不僅是我們最新的產品，還是以非常昂貴且特有的原料所製成的。

- The skin lotions, which are our latest product, are made with costly and unique materials.
  這些護膚乳液，我們的最新產品，是以非常昂貴且特有的原料所製成的。
- We use expensive and very special components to produce the skin lotions, which is the latest products of our company..
  我們使用價格昂貴和非常特殊的原料來製造我們公司最新的護膚乳液產品。

4-4 客戶生氣了

Reflection and Review
反省和檢討

Rita finds a major mistake in the contract which Dennis has just signed with Mrs. Ku. Dennis offered an unacceptable discount. Instead of 15%, the bottom line should be 10%.

Rita在Dennis和其客戶古太太簽署的合約中發現重大失誤，Dennis居然給出一個公司無法接受的折扣。底線本應是九折，而非八五折。

Dennis - salesperson 業務
Rita - sales supervisor 業務主管
Tony - sales director 業務協理

Dialogue

Tony	Dennis, how could you be so careless? Do you **realize** what you have done?	Dennis，你怎麼能如此粗心大意？你了解到自己犯了什麼錯誤嗎？
Dennis	I … I am **terribly** sorry…	我……我感到非常抱歉……
Tony	How long have you been working here?	東尼：你在這裡工作多久了？
Dennis	…about a year and half…	……大約一年半……
Tony	That means you are no longer a rookie. So tell me, why did you make such a mistake? Tell me again, what should you do before signing a contract?	那代表著你已經不是一個菜鳥了。告訴我，為什麼你會犯這樣的錯誤呢？再告訴我一次，你在跟客戶簽合約之前應該要做什麼？

Dennis	…I should read it carefully…, check the **terms**...	……我應該要詳細閱讀合約……檢查條款……
Tony	Such as?	例如？
Dennis	Such as prices, **mode of payment**, **term of delivery**, and discount.	例如價錢、付款方式、交貨日期，以及折扣。
Rita	As a supervisor, I am responsible for this, too. I should have double-checked the quotation before Dennis made an offer.	身為主管，我也有責任。我應該在Dennis提出報價單前再重複審核一次。
Tony	Indeed. I am very disappointed. Dennis, I am giving you a second chance. I hope both of you can learn from this **incident**.	的確。我感到很失望。Dennis，我再給你一次機會，希望你們二人從這一次的事件中好好學習。

★你應該要知道的小小事！

一般公司都會準備制式合約，職員在跟客戶簽約時，其實只會針對一些條文（合作內容、時間、金額……）做些修改，在完成修改之後，應再全部瀏覽一次，以防出錯。如果是新手，其實可以請主管或是前輩協助確認一下合約內容，完成的合約蓋上公司大小章和騎縫章之後，再請客戶簽名用印，一份給客戶，一份帶回公司收存。

Word Bank

realize v. 領悟；了解到

My mother realizes health is everything when she is getting older and older.
我母親年紀越來越大之後，就了解到健康勝過一切。

terribly adv. 非常地

I felt terribly sorry to hear that she misunderstood what I said.
我對她誤解我的意思感到非常抱歉。

term n. 條款

We have to read the terms of guarantee carefully after purchasing electric devices.
我們在購買電器用品後須仔細研讀保證書條款。

mode of payment 付款方式

The mode of payment is absolutely required to be stated on the quotation.
報價單需列出付款方式。

terms of delivery 交貨日期

The terms of delivery for regular orders are about three months.
一般訂單的交貨日期約三個月。

incident n. 事件

The teacher realized that it was an incident and did not want to talk about it.
老師認為這是單一事件而不想談論。

In Other Words

Do you realize what you have done?
你了解到自己犯了什麼錯誤嗎？

- Are you aware of the mistake you have made?
  你知道你所犯下的錯誤了嗎？
- Do you understand what you have done?
  你了解到自己犯了什麼錯誤嗎？

I should have double-checked the quotation before Dennis made an offer.
我應該在Dennis提出報價單前再重複審核一次。

- I should review the quotation before him mailed it to Mrs. Ku.
  我應該在Dennis在將報價單寄給古太太之前再重複審核報價單。
- It is my responsibility to check the quotation again before Dennis made an offer.
  我應該在Dennis報價前再重複審核報價單。

I hope both of you can learn from this incident.
希望你們二人從這一次的事件中好好學習。

- I expect both of you have learned from your mistake.
  希望你們二人已經從這一次的錯誤當中學到教訓。
- My expectation is that both of you could get a lesson from this incident.
  我的期望是你們二人都能從這一次的事件中學到教訓。

簽合約前應注意的事項！

★確認締約雙方

這是雙方合同，甲方和乙方往往即買方和賣方，常見的疏失就是搞不清楚到底應該填寫所有人的名字還是公司的名稱。若是代表公司簽約，那就一定要寫公司名稱、負責人（董事長）和公司的地址。

★確認合約中清楚載明雙方的責任和權利

合約內容當中，需要詳細地載明雙方的全立即責任，內容規定的愈詳細，日後發生爭議的機率也愈小。所以公司在擬合約時都會多方思考；業務人員也應該要了解合約內容，以便向客戶解釋。

★清楚載明糾紛的解決方法

在合約當中會清楚地寫出如有訴訟糾紛時的合意管轄法院，但建議在這之前可透過調解來解決爭端。

★有新增條文，務必請法律顧問確認

因為每個客戶的狀況可能都不太一樣，若有比較特殊的狀況或是case，可以在簽約之前提出，看是否可在既有的制式合約中，加入新的條文，遇到這樣的狀況，切記一定要先跟主管報告，看怎樣加入該條文內容，之後再請公司的法律顧問協助檢視文字是否有需要修改的地方。

★載明合約截止日期及終止方式

通常合約中會提出此約起始日期與終止日期，要特別留意有的合約在到期前沒有提出終止，代表自動再續約的狀況。

★蓋公司的大小章與騎縫章

因為都是代表公司簽約，所以合約的最後要記得蓋代表公司的大小章，另外合約書雖然都會釘起來，但蓋上騎縫章，表示這份合約是在雙方同意之下簽訂，而且簽訂之後無法片面修改合約。

★合約中有手寫的內容若經塗改，記得要在上方蓋章

制式化的合約，有一些需要手寫的內容，如果在寫的過程中不小心寫錯了，用立可白塗掉，並記得要在修改處再補蓋一個章。

★對於合約條文有不清楚的內容一定要提問

合約條文很多，用字也不像一般說話比較口語，如果對內容有點不太了解的話，要記得提問確認，不然當你在跟客戶簽約時，客戶問你，你卻說不清楚，這樣就會讓人有不太專業的感覺。

如何應付怒火中燒的顧客！

- 務必確認顧客究竟為何事而不悅
- 永遠不要說「公司規定就是如此」
- 顧客抱怨時，不要回嘴
- 多聽少說話
- 表現同理心

面對客戶發火三步驟

以往新人在處理客戶發火的狀況時都會很慌、很害怕，因為客戶再大怒的時候，其實說出來都會很傷人，因為他們的情緒已經跑在理智的前面，所以這時你應該要不斷地告訴自己：「我的理智一定要在我的情緒之前」，這樣才能有效地處理好事情，而不是兩個失去理智的人吵成一團，愈來愈亂。

基本上只要把握三個步驟，就可以將危機化為轉機，那就是「誠懇的道歉」、「仔細的聆聽」和「快速的處理」，盡量不要去理會客戶尖銳的言語，讓他們先宣洩心中的不滿，畢竟理虧的是我們，再來就是用最誠懇的態度努力道歉，可以學習日本人，以90度的鞠躬和最客氣有禮的話語來表達最深的歉意，最後就是要想盡方法最快找到因應之道，讓客戶滿意。

12:30 PM

PART 2

Receptionist / Assistant
總機／助理

1-1 總機接待

A Walk-in Visitor
訪客來訪

A visitor walks into the office and wants to learn about the company's products. Sarah, the receptionist, greets her and tries to find someone to assist her.

訪客臨時來訪並想了解公司產品，總機接待Sarah接待訪客並找同仁前來協助。

Sarah – the receptionist 總機接待
Maggie – the visitor 訪客

Dialogue

Maggie	Excuse me.	不好意思。
Sarah	Yes, what can I do for you?	有什麼可以為您服務的嗎？
Maggie	I am interested in your products. I have just **come by** and wish to get a catalogue.	我對你們的產品很有興趣，我正好路過，希望索取一份目錄。
Sara	Okay. Have a seat, please. May I have your name, please?	沒問題，請坐。請問您貴姓大名？
Maggie	Maggie Li. Just call me Maggie.	Maggie李，叫我Maggie就好。
Sarah	**Certainly**. So, Maggie, have you tried our products before?	沒問題。那麼，Maggie，您之前使用過我們的產品嗎？

Maggie	No, but I have heard many **positive** things about them from my friends, colleagues, and some **acquaintances**.	沒有，但我從我朋友、同事和熟人那聽過不少關於你們產品的好評。
Sara	May I get someone to help you, if you don't mind?	若您不介意的話，我可以請人來協助您嗎？
Maggie	I cannot stay for too long. I have to get back to my office.	我不能停留太久，我必須趕回辦公室。
Sarah	It won't take a long time. I'll get someone from the Sales Department to assist you.	不會花您很久時間的。我會請業務部的同仁過來協助您。
Maggie	All right. Please do.	好的。麻煩妳了。
Sarah	One moment please. Erm… Maggie, Sophie will be here in a minute. She is a sales coordinator. In the meantime, would you like some coffee or tea?	請稍候。嗯……Sophie會馬上出來協助您。她是業務專員。在此同時，您要來點咖啡或茶嗎？
Maggie	Coffee, please. Thank you.	請給我咖啡。謝謝。
Sarah	Not at all.	不必客氣。

Word Bank

receptionist n. 總機、接待

Jenny got a job offer of being a receptionist at a high-tech company.
Jenny 得到一個在高科技公司當總機的工作機會。

assist v. 協助

There are more helpers required to assist during hot seasons.
在旺季時需要更多助手來協助。

come by 路過

You are welcome to visit me whenever you come by.
任何時候你路過都歡迎你來找我。

certainly adv. 沒問題

You will certainly be rewarded by your hard-working attitude.
你認真工作的態度絕對會得到獎賞。

positive adj. 正面的

We should keep positive thinking towards life.
我們對生活應保持正面思考。

acquaintance n. 熟人

I have many acquaintances in the USA.
我在美國有很多熟人。

In Other Words

Sarah, the receptionist, greets her and tries to find someone to assist her.
總機接待Sarah接待訪客並找同仁前來協助。

- Sarah, who is the receptionist, greets her and looks for someone to help her.
  總機Sarah接待她並找同仁前來協助。
- The receptionist, Sarah, welcomes her and asks someone to assist the visitor.
  總機Sarah接待她並找同仁前來協助這一位訪客。

No, but I have heard many positive things about them from my friends, colleagues, and some acquaintances.
沒有，但我從我朋友、同事和熟人那聽過不少關於你們產品的好評。

- No, but I learned good comments about them from my friends, coworkers, and some acquaintances.
  沒有，但我從我朋友、同事和熟人那聽過不少關於你們產品的好評。
- Not yet, but I would like to have a try, since many of my friends and colleagues love your products so much.
  還沒，但我想試試看，因為我很多的朋友還有同事都超愛你們的產品。

May I get someone to help you, if you don't mind?
若您不介意的話，我可以請人來協助您嗎？

- Do you mind if I get someone to help you?
  你介意我請人來協助您嗎？
- Would you like me to ask someone to give you a simple introduction?
  您要不要我請人來為您做個簡單的介紹呢？

1-2 總機接待

He Is on His Way Back
他正在回來的路上

A visitor comes to the office and wants to see Steve, the senior sales representative, but Steve is not in the office right now. So, the receptionist helps the visitor to make an arrangement.

訪客來公司拜訪資深業務代表Steve，但他目前並不在辦公室。所以接待員幫訪客安排見面的時間。

Sarah - receptionist 接待員
Brandon - visitor 訪客

Dialogue

Brandon	Excuse me.	不好意思。
Sarah	Yes, how may I help you?	是的，有什麼可以為您服務的嗎？
Brandon	I'm here to see Steve, the senior sales representative.	我想見資深業務代表Steve。
Sarah	Let me check. One moment, please.	讓我查一下。請稍候。
Brandon	Sure.	好的。
Sarah	I'm sorry. He is not **available** now. Do you have an appointment?	不好意思，他現在無法見您。請問您有預約嗎？
Brandon	No, but we spoke on the phone yesterday, and he told me I could visit him **at any time**.	沒有，但我們昨天通過電話，他告訴我任何時候都可以來找他。

Sarah	He is not in the office right now. Would you like me to **give him a call**?	他現在不在辦公室。需要我幫您打電話給他嗎？
Brandon	Please do. It is very important for me to see him today, as I am **going back to** Taichung tomorrow.	麻煩您。我今天一定得跟他見面，因為我明天就要回台中了。
Sarah	Could you wait for a moment? And may I have your name, please?	您可以稍等一下嗎？請問您貴姓大名？
Brandon	Brandon Fan, the purchasing manager from Kitty Beauty.	我叫Brandon范，Kitty Beauty的採購經理。
Sarah	Thank you. (Talking on the phone)… Mr. Fan, I got **in touch with** Steve, and he is on his way back now. He is **sincerely** sorry. This way, please. I'll show you to the meeting room first.	謝謝您。（電話中）……范先生，我已經與Steve聯絡上了，他正在回來的路上。他為此深感抱歉。這邊請，我先帶您去會議室。
Brandon	When will he be here? I haven't got all day.	他什麼時間會回來？我的時間有點趕。
Sarah	In about fifteen minutes. Would you like some **refreshments**?	大約十五分鐘後。您想要來點飲料嗎？

available adj. 有空的

Are you available to have dinner with me tonight?
你今晚有空與我吃晚餐嗎？

at any time 任何時間

Please feel free to call me at any time
任何時間都歡迎打電話給我。

give sb. a call 打電話給某人

Don't forget to give your family a call when you arrive.
當你到達時，別忘記打電話給你的家人。

go back to 回到

The movie recalled me to go back to my childhood.
這電影讓我憶起我的幼年時期。

in touch with 和……聯繫

I hope we can always keep in touch with each other.
我希望我們可以一直保持聯繫。

sincerely adv. 真誠地、誠摯地

He sincerely made an apology and therefore was forgiven.
他很真誠地道歉，所以就被原諒了。

refreshment n. 飲料、茶點

There are refreshments available during the conference.
此會議有提供飲料。

In Other Words

No, but we spoke on the phone yesterday, and he told me I could visit him at any time.
沒有，但我們昨天通過電話，他告訴我任何時候都可以來找他。

- Although I didn't make an appointment with him, he told me at phone yesterday that I could visit him at any time today.
  雖然我跟他沒有約好，但他昨天在電話中告訴我今天任何時候都可以來找他。
- No, but I was informed to visit him at any time during our phone conversation yesterday.
  沒有，但我們昨天通過電話，他告訴我任何時候都可以來找他。

Would you like me to give him a call?
需要我幫您打電話給他嗎？

- Should I call him for you?
  需要我幫您打電話給他嗎？
- Would you like me to ring him up for you?
  需要我幫您打電話給他嗎？

I haven't got all day.
我的時間有點趕。

- I am in a hurry.
  我的時間有點趕。
- I have another appointment later this afternoon.
  我今天下午稍晚還另外約了人。

1-3 總機接待

Putting You Through
轉接中

A client calls to look for a sales coordinator, Sophie, but Sophie is not in the office right now. Sara, the receptionist, switches her to Sophie's colleague, Rita.

有位客戶來電想找業務專員Sophie，但Sophie目前不在辦公室。總機接待Sarah將電話轉接給Sophie的同事Rita。

Sarah – the receptionist 總機接待員
Bob – the client 客戶

Dialogue

Bob	Hello.	您好。
Sarah	Good afternoon. This is Sara. How can I help you?	午安，我是Sarah，有什麼可以為您服務的嗎？
Bob	Could I speak to Sophie from the Sales Department, please?	我可以和業務部的Sophie說話嗎？
Sarah	And may I ask who is calling, please?	請問貴姓大名？
Bob	This is Bob, from Happy Drug Store.	我是Happy Drug Store的Bob。
Sarah	OK. I'll try to put you through to her extension. I'm sorry; she is not in the office right now. Would you like to leave a **message**?	好的，幫您轉接她的分機。不好意思，她現在不在辦公室。您想要留言給她嗎？

Bob	Oh, no! I need to speak with him on an **urgent matter**. Can't you **reach** her?	喔，不！我有緊急的事情要跟她說。你無法連絡她嗎？
Sarah	I'll try again. One moment, please. Well… I'm really sorry. She did not answer the phone. May I **transfer** you to the sales executive? Her name is Rita.	讓我再試試，請稍候。嗯……不好意思，她沒有接電話。我可以幫您轉接給業務主管嗎？她叫做Rita。
Bob	That would be great. Thank you.	太好了，謝謝您。
Sarah	You're welcome. One moment please, I'm putting you through…	不客氣。請稍候，我將為您轉接。

★你應該要知道的小小事！

如果說業務是公司外部的門面，那總機接待就是公司內部的門面。總機接待通常會坐在公司大門一進門的地方，接待客人、收取快遞、接聽電話、轉接電話等等，不管是來公司拜訪的客人，或是打電話來公司的人，多數都會先由總機來接待，所以總機的儀態和禮貌就很重要。接聽電話時語調要輕柔有活力，轉接電話時如果遇到同事不在位置上，一直沒有將電話接起，就要立即主動跟來電者說明原因，留下對方的大名及連絡電話，並轉交給該同事，請同事儘快回電。

Word Bank

switch v. 為……轉接電話

One of the receptionist's tasks is switching every exterior line.
總機的工作之一是轉接電話。

extension n. 分機

Here is my office phone number and the extension number is 12.
這是我的公司電話號碼，分機是 12。

message n. 訊息

There was an error message popping out when I checked my emails.
當我檢查我的電子郵件時，有錯誤訊息跑出來。

urgent adj. 緊急的

It is urgent that the patient needs an operation.
這病人需要緊急開刀動手術。

matter n. 事情

It is a personal matter and should be concealed.
這是個人事情，不應公開。

reach v. 找到；連絡上

I can be reached during office hours on weekdays.
你可以在週間上班時間找到我。

transfer v. 轉接

He takes the MRT and then transfers to a bus to work.
他搭捷運轉接公車去上班。

In Other Words

I'll try to put you through to her extension.
我幫您轉接她的分機。

- I'll try to transfer your call to her.
  我將幫您的來電轉接給她。
- Please hold the line while I see if she's in.
  請稍候，我幫您看一下她在不在。

Would you like to leave a message?
您想要留言給她嗎？

- May I take a message for you?
  我可以幫您留言嗎？
- Would you like to leave her a message or talk to someone else in her department?
  您要留言給她或是跟她同部門的同事說話呢？

Can't you reach her?
你無法連絡她嗎？

- Are you unable to contact with her?
  你無法連絡她嗎？
- Is it possible for you to reach her?
  你有可能連絡上她嗎？

1-4 總機接待

The Line Is Busy
忙線中

A client calls, looking for the senior sales representative, but he isn't available at the moment. The receptionist, Sarah, asks the client's name and takes a message.

有位客戶來電想找資深業務代表，但該代表目前不方便接電話。總機接待 Sarah 詢問對方名字並記下留言。

Sarah - the receptionist 總機接待
Alice - the client 客戶

Dialogue

Alice	Hello.	您好。
Sarah	Good day, this is Sara. How can I help you?	您好，我是Sarah，有什麼可以為您服務的嗎？
Alice	Could I speak to Steve, please?	我可以和Steve說話嗎？
Sarah	<u>And may I ask who is calling, please?</u>	請問貴姓大名？
Alice	This is Alice Lin.	我是Alice林。
Sarah	<u>Sorry, I did not **catch** your name. Could you **repeat** that, please?</u>	不好意思，我剛剛沒聽清楚您的名字。可以請您再重複一次嗎？
Alice	Alice Lin. That is A-L-I-C-E, L-I-N.	Alice林，A-L-I-C-E, L-I-N.。
Sarah	Thank you. And where are you calling from?	謝謝您。請問您的公司行號是？

Alice	Daily Free Drugstore.	Daily Free Drugstore.
Sarah	OK, one moment, please. Hmmm… I am sorry but the line is **busy**. Would you like to **hold**?	好的，請稍等一下。嗯……不好意思，他目前電話忙線中。請問您想等待嗎？
Alice	Could I leave a message?	我可以留言嗎？
Sarah	Sure.	請說。
Alice	Please tell Steve that the **shipment** of 500 cases we **ordered** is late. It should have arrived by last Friday. Could you ask him to call me back **ASAP**?	請告訴Steve，我們公司訂的500份貨品的運送延遲了，在上週五以前就應該送達才對。可否請他儘快回電給我？
Sarah	I see. I will tell him. Thanks for calling.	我了解。我會告訴他。謝謝您的來電。

★你應該要知道的小小事！

總機如果遇到同事忙線中，無法接聽電話，除代為留言，也可請部門同事幫忙先接電話，因為部門同事可能對他的業務比較熟悉，如果來電者有比較緊急的事，部門同事也比較知道如何協助處理。機動性和彈性很重要，總機可能會面臨到的突發狀況比較多，要機靈一點、懂得隨機應變，才能夠更有效率地處理事情。除此之外，總機也必須對公司內部的組織有充份的了解，才能夠將電話快速地轉接給正確的部門、相關的人員，假設說公司內部很多位林先生，或是不只一位Gary，這時若來電者沒有主動告知是業務部的林先生、還是資訊部的Gary，就要主動詢問來電者是哪一個部份的業務內容需要協助，才能夠迅速地為來電者轉接給他想要找的人。

catch v. 聽清楚；理解

He is so smart that he can always catch the points of each conversation.
他非常聰明，所以總能抓住每次談話的重點。

repeat v. 重複

The teacher asked the students to repeat with her.
這老師請學生們跟她一起念。

busy adj. （尤指電話線）正被佔用的；忙線中

The line is busy and the call cannot be transferred.
線路忙線中，所以無法轉接電話。

hold v. 保留；持續、保持

Please hold on and wait for a moment.
請勿掛斷，等候一下。

shipment n. 運送

The goods are ready for shipment.
東西已準備好可以運送了。

order v. 訂購

The buyer ordered a large quantity of jeans last month.
這買家上個月訂購非常多的牛仔褲。

ASAP 儘快

I will reply to you ASAP.
我會儘快回覆你。

In Other Words

And may I ask who is calling, please?
請問貴姓大名？

- And may I know who is speaking, please?
  請問貴姓大名？
- And may I have your name, please?
  請問貴姓大名？

Sorry, I did not catch your name. Could you repeat that, please?
不好意思，我剛剛沒聽清楚您的名字。可以請您再重複一次嗎？

- Sorry, I did not hear your name clearly. Would you mind saying that again, please?
  不好意思，我剛剛沒聽清楚您的名字。可以請您再重複一次嗎？
- Sorry, I did not get it. Could you say again about your name?
  不好意思，我剛剛沒聽清楚。可以請您把您的名字再說一次嗎？

Could you ask him to call me back ASAP?
可否請他儘快回電給我？

- Could you tell him to ring me up right after he finished his phone call?
  可否請他講完電話之後立刻回電給我嗎？
- Please tell him to call me back as soon as he can.
  請他儘快回電給我。

接待人員不可不知的電話禮儀！

- 不要讓電話響太久
  一般公司規定電話響三聲內需接起
- 面帶微笑，即便是講電話，微笑可以使聲音聽起來柔和
- 親切的問候並先説自己的名字
  現在許多公司會規定接起電話時要説：「〇〇（公司名），您好，我是〇〇〇（自己的名字）。」
- 詢問對方貴姓大名
- 需請對方等候時，一定要先告知
- 不要打斷對方説話，先聆聽再給予回覆
- 若轉接不成功，記得要向對方道歉
- 溫和的口吻與有禮貌的態度
- 結束通話前記得要謝謝對方的來電
- 記錄來電者的名字和欲轉接的分機
  因為可能同時有很多通電話在線上，為避免講錯名字或轉錯分機的尷尬，做筆記是很重要的。
- 主動詢問，幫忙留言
  若知道某主管或某部門有會議在進行或目前不在位置上，應主動幫忙留言，避免讓客戶在電話那端等待太久。

如何應付難纏的訪客／顧客？

像是易怒、暴躁、不耐煩的客戶皆屬此類，都應更小心地接待，避免發生不愉快。

★仔細聆聽為上策

訪客氣呼呼的，心情很不好，這時候接待員除了聆聽之外，沒有其他更好的方式，若是開口詢問可能會更觸怒對方，所以當這類型的訪客上門，接待人員在打完招呼後，就準備洗耳恭聽吧，先讓訪客抒發一下心中不滿的情緒。

★顯露同情和同理心。

在聆聽對方抱怨的過程中，千萬不要一臉不耐或是滿臉憂愁，要展現同理心，發揮同情心，適時點頭並表現出你也很抱歉的樣子。

★讓對方知道你會儘可能地協助他/她。

聽完對方一連串的抱怨之後，在你開始要進行慣例性的詢問之前（姓名、電話、所代表的公司行號等等），先問對方有什麼是你可以幫上忙的。

★控制情緒

絕不能對訪客或顧客發怒，如果真的招架不住，可以用和氣的口吻請對方稍候，然後再請相關同仁出面協助處理，避免事情愈變愈複雜。

簡單工作不簡單

接待客人，接聽電話感覺很簡單，但其實有很多小地方都需要注意，才能夠將這份工作做得好，以下幾點要留意喔！

1. 有訪客要起身歡迎，如果手邊有是在忙，也要先用眼神跟訪客打個招呼，不要讓他們覺得站在那，怎麼都沒人理他們。
2. 不要以貌取人，千萬不要看訪客的穿著而有不同的接待態度，如果遇到有些來頭不小的人剛好穿著比較低調，這樣很容易不小心會得罪他們或是造成同事的困擾。
3. 遇到有訪客來找公司內的同事，不要讓訪客直接就殺到辦公區，這樣有可能會讓正在忙的同事措手不及。
4. 接聽電話留言時，一定要留下詳盡的資料，方便同事回覆，千萬不要僅僅告知同事有人找他，但卻沒有留下任何的相關資訊。

2-1 客訴處理

The Order Is Delayed
貨物延遲

A customer calls to ask why the order did not arrive on time, and the receptionist helps solve the situation.

顧客來電詢問為何訂購的商品沒有準時送達，總機接待協助解決問題。

Peggy – the receptionist 總機接待
Peter – the customer 顧客

Dialogue

Peggy	Good morning, this is Peggy. What can I do for you?	早安，我是Peggy，有什麼可以幫上忙的嗎？
Peter	Hi, this is Peter from Fashion Gate. I am calling to find out why our order did not arrive on time.	您好，我是Fashion Gate的Peter。我想詢問為何我們訂的貨物沒有準時送達。
Peggy	Oh, that is not good. When was the order **supposed to** arrive?	喔，真是糟糕。貨物原本應於何時送達呢？
Peter	Yesterday afternoon. I tried to contact the salesperson, but the line was busy. I left a message, but he did not **return** my call. He seemed to disappear into thin air.	昨天下午。我試著與業務員連絡，但電話忙線中，我有留言，但他並沒有回覆我。他好像從人間蒸發了。
Peggy	Understood. Could you give me your order number, please?	了解。可以請給我您的訂單編號嗎？

Peter	#B5510989.	#B5510989.
Peggy	Let me check with the delivery department and see what happened. One moment please.	讓我向貨運單位查明清楚，看看出了什麼狀況。請稍等。
Peter	Please do that.	麻煩您了。
Peggy	Hello, thank you for waiting. I just checked with the delivery department. There has been an **error** in the **process**. However, your order has already been **shipped**. It was sent out this morning.	您好，謝謝您的耐心等候。我剛才向貨運單位查詢過了，在處理過程中出了點差錯，不過您的訂單已於今早已送出了。
Peter	When will it arrive?	何時會送達呢？
Peggy	It should be there no later than three o'clock this afternoon. I **apologize** for any inconvenience this has **caused**.	今天下午三點之前應該會送達。對於造成您的任何不便，我們深感抱歉。
Peter	All right. Thank you.	好吧。謝謝您。
Peggy	You are welcome. Have a nice day! Good-bye.	不客氣。祝您有美好的一天！再見。

Word Bank

supposed to　應該

He is supposed to arrive in the US today.
他應該會在今天抵達美國。

return　v.　返回、回轉

Do you think that he'll return of his own free will as he had promised?
你覺得他會如同他所答應的自願回來嗎？

error　n.　錯誤

There are some errors made in the report.
這份報告裡有一些錯誤。

process　n.　過程

Your order has been in the production process.
你的訂單已在生產中了。

ship　v.　裝運

The goods will be shipped via a courier.
這些商品會經由快遞寄出。

apologize　v.　道歉

The manager sincerely apologized for the poor service.
這經理為了服務不佳很誠心地道歉。

cause　v.　導致

The accident was caused by his careless driving.
這場車禍是因他不小心開車而導致的。

In Other Words

Let me check with the delivery department and see what happened.
讓我向貨運部門查明清楚，看看出了什麼狀況。

- I will call the delivery department to find out what happened.
  我會打電話給貨運部門，看看出了什麼狀況。
- Let me check with the delivery department to figure out where the problem is.
  讓我向貨運部門查明清楚，看看問題在哪裡。

There has been an error in the process.
在處理過程中出了點差錯。

- An error occurred during the delivery.
  在運送過程中出了點差錯。
- Some mistakes happened in the process.
  在處理過程中出了點差錯。

I apologize for any inconvenience this has caused.
對於造成您的任何不便，我們深感抱歉。

- I am very sorry for any inconvenience occurred by this.
  對於造成您的任何不便，我們深感抱歉。
- Please accept my apology for any inconvenience caused by this.
  對於造成您的任何不便，請接受我們深摯的歉意。

2-2 客訴處理

Quantity Received Does Not Match Quantity Ordered
收到的商品數量與訂單不符

A customer calls to complain that the quantity of goods they received does not match the quantity on the order.

顧客來電投訴，收到的商品其數量和訂單不符。

Peggy – the receptionist 總機接待
Customer – 顧客

Dialogue

Customer	Good afternoon. I have a problem **regarding** the order we received.	午安，我有關於收到貨品的問題。
Peggy	Good afternoon, sir. May I ask where you are calling from?	先生午安。可否請教您的公司行號？
Customer	I am calling from Union Market.	我是代表Union Market。
Peggy	What seems to be the problem?	是什麼樣的問題呢？
Customer	We ordered 300 units of facial masks, but we received only 250.	我們訂了300組面膜，但只收到250組。
Peggy	I am so sorry. Could you please give me your order number and let me check with the warehousing department?	真的很抱歉。可否請您給我您的訂單編號？我會先向倉儲單位詢問看看。
Customer	#D00876521.	#D00876521。

Peggy	Please hold. … Sir, I would like to apologize for the error we have made. The warehouse is now **aware of** that, and the 50 units will be delivered as soon as possible.	請稍候……先生，容我為我們的疏失道歉。倉儲部門已了解此問題，剩餘的50組會儘快為您送達。
Customer	Can I get a **refund** on the 50 units?	剩餘的50組可以退費嗎？
Peggy	I am afraid not. The item was on sale, so refunds and returns are not **permitted**.	恐怕不行。貨品當初是有打折的，所以無法退費和退貨。
Customer	All right, just deliver those 50 units. The faster we receive them, the better.	好吧，就把那50組送來吧。越快越好。
Peggy	Certainly. We assure you that this will not happen again.	沒問題。我們跟您保證，這樣的事以後不會再發生了。

★你應該要知道的小小事！

出貨前基本上會再次確認出貨數量與訂單是否相符，但難免會有疏失，如果接到這樣的電話，應立即上電腦系統查詢出貨記錄，如果真的有疏失，應立即致歉，並告訴顧客處理需耗費多久的時間，掛上電話前也要再次表達歉意。

Word Bank

quantity　n.　數量

The unit price is negotiable by the quantity of orders.
單價可依訂單的數量來議價。

match　v.　符合

The quantity of the stock matches with that of the sale figures.
庫存數量與銷售數字符合。

regarding　prep.　關於

He will make a speech regarding the marketing strategies.
他將演講有關行銷策略的主題。

be aware of　知道的

I am aware of my weakness and trying to improve it.
我知道自己的弱點，正試著去改善。

refund　n.　退費

The store is reputable and offers a full refund to all customers for unsatisfactory goods.
商店聲譽佳並提供客户對不滿意商品之全額退款。

permit　v.　允許，許可

No smoking is permitted in the building.
此棟大樓禁止抽菸。

In Other Words

A customer calls to complain that the quantity of goods they received does not match the quantity on the order.
顧客來電投訴，收到的商品其數量和訂單不符。

- I got a customer complaint about the shortage of his receiving goods, which is inconsistent with the quantity that he ordered.
  我接到客戶投訴收到的商品數量短缺，與他所訂購的數量不符。
- A customer calls to complain about the quantities of goods received and ordered are unequal.
  客戶來電投訴收到的商品數量與訂單數量不符。

What seems to be the problem?
是什麼樣的問題呢？

- May I know what happened?
  我可以知道發生了什麼事嗎？
- Would you please specify the problem?
  您是否能詳細說明您的問題呢？

The item was on sale, so refunds and returns are not permitted.
貨品當初是有打折的，所以無法退費和退貨。

- No refunds and returns are permitted for the sale items.
  有打折的貨品無法退費和退貨。
- Refunds and returns are not applicable to the sale items.
  有打折的貨品無法退費和退貨。

2-3 客訴處理

Damaged Goods
損壞的貨品

A customer calls to complain that the order was delivered damaged, and the receptionist tries to solve the complaint.

顧客來電抱怨收到損壞的商品，接待員協助解決問題。

Sarah - receptionist 總機接待
Tina - customer 顧客

Dialogue

Sarah	Good morning, this is Sarah. What can I do for you?	早安，我是Sarah，有什麼可以為您服務的嗎？
Tina	I **purchased** three bottles of body lotion through your **website**. Upon delivery, I found one bottle **cracked**, and the lotion was **spilled** all over inside the box. Your service is poor.	我從你們的網站上訂購了三瓶乳液，貨品送達後，我發現其中一瓶已經破裂了，乳液灑得整個箱子都是。你們的服務真是太差了。
Sarah	Oh, I am very sorry. Could you give me the order number and let me check it out.	真的非常抱歉。可以給我您的訂單編號以便查詢嗎？
Tina	I don't have the order form with me now, but can I just give you my name and purchase date?	我手邊沒有訂單，但我可以給你我的姓名和購買日期嗎？
Sarah	Yes, that would do, too.	好的，那也可以。

Tina	Tina Wen, and the purchase date is August 10.	Tina溫，購買日期是8月10日。
Sarah	Please wait one moment, and let me see if we have the item in stock right now... Ms. Wen, we do have the same item you ordered in stock now. I can have someone send it out this afternoon. Would that be okay?	請稍等，讓我看看目前庫存是否有貨。……溫小姐，目前庫存是有貨的，我可以今天下午就幫您寄出，這樣可以嗎？
Tina	How long will it take? Do I need to send you back the damaged goods?	那需要多久的時間？我需要把損壞的商品寄回去給你們嗎？
Sarah	The delivery **normally** takes three to five **working days**. There is no need to send back the damaged goods to us. I am very sorry for what happened.	貨物送達通常需要三至五個工作天，您無須將損壞的商品寄回給我們。對於我們的疏失，我們深感抱歉。
Tina	All right. Bye.	好的，再見。
Sarah	Thank you for calling!	謝謝您的來電。

★你應該要知道的小小事！

顧客反應收到貨品有損壞，應立刻上系統確認顧客反應的品項是否與訂單上是相符的，然後跟顧客致歉，先做註記，如果無法立即跟顧客確認處理的方式的話，可先試著跟顧客爭取一些時間，做後續狀況處理，並於當天或隔天就做回覆，這樣才不會讓顧客覺得公司的服務不好。

Word Bank

damaged adj. 損壞的

Please return all the damaged goods to our company.
請將所有損壞的商品退回給我們公司。

purchase v. 購買

I prefer purchasing goods from the website.
我較喜歡在網站購物。

website n. 網站

The website offers free software for downloading.
這網站提供免費軟體供下載。

cracked adj. 破裂的

Watch out! The cracked glass is on the floor.
小心！地面上有破裂的玻璃杯。

spill v. 溢出

The water spills from the cup.
水從杯子溢出。

normally adv. 通常地

The manager normally gets to the office by 9:00am.
經理通常九點前會到達辦公室。

working day 工作天

There are five working days per week in our company.
我們公司每週有五個工作天。

In Other Words

I found one bottle cracked, and the lotion was spilled all over inside the box.
我發現其中一瓶已經破裂了，乳液灑得整個箱子都是。

- The lotion was spilled from one cracked bottle and spread all over inside the box.
  乳液從其中一瓶破裂瓶子灑出，弄得整個箱子都是。
- The box was full of the spilled lotion from one cracked bottle.
  整個箱子都是從其中一瓶破裂瓶子灑出的乳液。

Do I need to send you back the damaged goods?
我需要把損壞的商品寄回去給你們嗎？

- Do I have to return the damaged goods?
  我需要把損壞的商品退回嗎？
- Should I send the broken goods back to you?
  我應該把破掉的商品寄回給你們嗎？

The delivery normally takes three to five working days.
貨物送達通常需要三至五個工作天。

- In general, the delivery takes three to five working days.
  大致上，貨物送達需要三至五個工作天。
- It usually takes three to five working days for the delivery.
  貨物送達通常需要三至五個工作天。

2-4 客訴處理

Wanting to Make a Return
想辦理退貨

The receptionist, Sarah, responds to a customer who wishes to make a return of goods.

總機接待Sarah回應一名想要辦理退貨的顧客。

Sarah - the receptionist 總機接待
Mr. Johnson - customer 顧客

Dialogue

Sarah	Hello, this is Sarah, what can I do for you?	您好，我是Sarah，有什麼可以為您服務的嗎？
Mr. Johnson	I purchased five packs of facial masks through your website. I tried the mask, but the quality was not as good as I **expected**. I would like to return them for a **full refund**.	我從你們的網站上購買了五包面膜，用過之後發現品質不如我所預期。我想退貨並要求全額退款。
Sarah	I see. Could you tell me when you purchased the product? Or do you have the order number?	了解，可以告訴我您何時購買此商品的呢？或是您有訂單編號？
Mr. Johnson	I don't remember the exact date, but I can give you the order number. It's #C01998726.	我不記得確切的日期，但我可以給你訂單編號，#C01998726。
Sarah	One moment please… Here we go. Is this Mr. Johnson?	請稍等……好了，請問是Johnson先生嗎？

Mr. Johnson	Yes, it is.	是的。
Sarah	I am afraid we can't **offer** you a return. You purchased the product on June 7, and today is June 22. The **deadline** for returning the goods has **expired**.	恐怕我們無法提供退貨的服務。您是於六月七日購買此商品的，而今天是六月二十二日，已經過了退貨的最後期限。
Mr. Johnson	What?! This is **ridiculous**. It has only been about two weeks.	什麼？！這真是太可笑了。不過才過了大約兩個星期而已。
Sarah	I'm very sorry, but it says on our website that you must return goods within 10 days of purchase.	真的很抱歉，但我們的網站上有註明，您必須在購買後的十天內辦理退貨。
Mr. Johnson	I can't believe this. I will never buy anything from your company again.	真是令人難以相信。我再也不會購買你們公司的商品了。

★你應該要知道的小小事！

一般公司對於退換貨都會有一些相關的規定，新人在處理這類情況前，最好先問清楚，面對顧客詢問時，提供正確的資訊，避免先讓顧客以為可退貨、換貨或是退款，到後來竟然不行，這會讓顧客更生氣。退款的部份會與客戶當初的付款方式及公司內部作業程序有很大的關係，在確認可退款之後，公司會以什麼樣的方式進行退款，也應該跟顧客報告說明，避免造成對方誤解，而產生更多的麻煩。

Word Bank

expect v. 期待

The sales manager expects a significant sale during the coming Christmas holidays.
銷售經理期待在將來的聖誕節日有銷售佳績。

full refund 全額退款

You can get a full refund if you are not satisfied with the purchased goods.
如你不滿意所購買商品，你可得到全額退款。

offer v. 提供

The company offers a competitive benefit package to the employees.
這公司提供相當有競爭性的福利給員工。

deadline n. 最後期限

You have to submit the application before the deadline.
你必須在最後期限前遞出申請表。

expire v. 期滿；過期

My credit card will expire next month.
我的信用卡下個月過期。

ridiculous adj. 可笑的

It is ridiculous if you make this mistake again.
如果你再犯此錯就很可笑。

In Other Words

I tried the mask, but the quality was not as good as I expected.
我用過這些面膜之後發現品質不如我所預期。

- I tried the mask, but the quality was poor and didn't meet my expectation.
  我用過這些面膜之後發現品質很差，不符合我所預期。
- I am very disappointed at the poor quality of the mask which I tried.
  我對這些用過面膜的極差品質很失望。

The deadline for returning the goods has expired.
已經過了退貨的最後期限。

- Returning the goods is not applicable due to the expired deadline.
  已經過了最後期限無法退貨。
- It is not acceptable to return the goods because the deadline has expired.
  已經過了最後期限無法退貨。

But it says on our website that you must return goods within 10 days of purchase.
但我們的網站上有註明，您必須在購買後的十天內辦理退貨。

- But our website states the policy of returning goods within 10 days of purchase.
  但我們的網站上有註明必須在購買後的十天內辦理退貨。
- However, according to our return policy which has been stated on our website, it says that all goods have to be returned within 10 days of purchase.
  但根據我們網站上的退貨條款所載明，必須在購買後的十天內辦理退貨。

如何回覆客訴！

★認真看待客訴事件

不要以隨便的態度回應，要認真看待客訴事件。

★將客訴當作一個學習的機會。

客訴或許會使你感到疲憊甚至委屈，但不妨從另一個角度去看，將它當成一個學習的機會。站在服務和學習的角度看待客訴，可以避免自己的情緒受影響，亦可學習了解顧客心態以及其問題。

★保持冷靜

千萬不要動怒或是顯露不耐煩的語氣，也不要緊張，一緊張起來你便無法客觀地判斷或是專心地聆聽，而說話時可能也會顯得唯唯諾諾，保持冷靜和專業很重要。

★不要找藉口

認錯、正視、解釋。以上三個步驟是基本的，所謂的解釋並非找藉口搪塞，而是解釋為何會出現這樣的問題，若答案超出你所知道的範圍，也要據實以報，另一方面需要請求前輩、主管或是相關人員的協助。

★將心比心

從顧客的角度出發，若換作是你，你會希望得到怎樣的答覆或是回應，這樣能使你更貼切地了解顧客的心情和解決問題。

★記錄客訴事件

將所有客訴事件記錄下來，無論是呈報給相關單位或主管，或是留著給自己看，從經驗中學習、成長。

★徵詢顧客的建議和應該改進之處

聽完顧客的抱怨之後，可以問問對方有何建議或是公司該改進的地方，這樣一來，一方面能適當地平息顧客的怨氣和怒火，積極的態度也有助於避免公司成為對方的拒絕往來戶。

★承諾和保證必須實際

你可能會給予怒氣沖天的客戶一些保證或承諾，例如「我馬上為您處理」、「我會提醒XXX」、「我會儘快將貨品寄給您」等等。切記，既然給予承諾就要做到，所以不可以不切實際地保證一些你能力內無法達成的事情，免得讓客戶的印象更不好。

★感謝顧客來電

顧客願意來電，表示還有一線生機。所以仍然要感謝顧客，願意抽空撥電話告訴你事情的經過。

最常見的客訴和回應方式！

★客訴：「我等了老半天！」

回應：「不好意思，感謝您耐心等候。我剛已為您查詢，關於您的問題……」

★客訴：「我被你們轉接來轉接去的……」

回應：「對不起，讓您久等了，現在由我為您服務。……」

★客訴：「你一點都不在乎的樣子。」

回應：「我們非常在乎您的感受。請您給我個機會，我會盡力為您解決您的問題。」

★客訴：「遲遲等不到你們的消息！」

回應：「對不起，讓您等這麼久，真的很不好意思。可否請您先提供您的大名和電話，我立刻為您查詢。」

話術很重要

在處理客訴的案件，話術很重要，如果覺得自己在這方面的應對不太ok，最直接、快速的方式，就是多聽前輩說話，從中學習應對技巧，會是比較有效率的方式。遇到同事所面臨的狀況，也可以想想：如果今天換成是你，你會怎麼回應？這類型的實際演練是最有效的方式！

3-1 協助交辦事務

Customer Information
顧客資訊

The senior sales representative, Steve, asks the assistant, Cathy, to help update the customer information and send quotations to customers.

資深業務代表Steve交代助理Cathy協助更新顧客資訊，並將估價單寄給客戶。

Cathy – the sales assistant 業務助理
Steve – the senior sales representative 資深業務代表

Dialogue

Steve	Cathy, I need your help to **update** and **extract** customer information in Excel. <u>Are you **familiar with** Excel?</u>	Cathy，我需要妳幫忙用Excel更新顧客資訊。你熟悉Excel的操作嗎？
Cathy	Yes, I am. Where should I start?	是的。我該從哪開始呢？
Steve	First of all, you need to get lists of last month's customers from Sophie, Dennis, and Brian. Remember, only those who have done business with us. After you gather all the lists, you can begin to work.	首先妳需要向Sophie、Dennis，以及Brian拿上個月的客戶名單。記住，只需要拿那些和我們有交易的客戶名單。名單收集完之後，妳就可以開始進行了。
Cathy	When do you need it?	你何時要？
Steve	<u>Try to **complete** it by the end of the month.</u>	試著在月底以前完成。
Cathy	Yes, I will do that.	好的，我會的。

Steve	**By the way**, when you ask for lists of customers, ask them to give you the quotations made for the customers, too. **As soon as** you finish the customer information, go ahead and send out the quotations.	對了，當妳跟他們要顧客名單時，順便向他們要估價單，一旦完成顧客資訊之後，就直接將估價單寄出。
Cathy	No problem. Is there anything else?	沒問題。還有其他的事嗎？
Steve	That is all for now. Thank you.	目前就這樣，謝謝。
Cathy	You're welcome.	不客氣。

★你應該要知道的小小事！

助理通常協助處理一些比較單調、複雜度沒那麼高的工作，但這並不是表示助理的工作就很簡單、助理就不重要哦！假設一個部門裡如果有4-5個人的話，一個助理是要1個人對4-5個人，甚至有些公司在成本的考量之下，會幾個部門只配有2位助理，如果是這樣，那助理要處理的事務種類就更廣了，假設每一個人都交辦一件小事給助理，當十幾件小事加起來時，工作量也是相當驚人的呢！優秀的助理通常認真、負責、不推拖、動作迅速、細心仔細、能舉一反三，能適時提供各種協助，助理在一個部門裡就像是一個很重要的螺絲釘，有了優秀的助理協助，整個部門的效率也會跟著提高，所以要好好對待他們哦！

Word Bank

assistant n. 助理

Maggie works as an entry-level assistant.
Maggie 擔任基層助理的職位。

update v. 更新

The website is updated every week.
這網站每週都會更新。

extract v. 動詞 抽出

The reporter tried to extract some news about the singer.
這記者試著要找出有關這歌手的新聞。

familiar with 對……熟悉

I am very familiar with the downtown where I have lived for ten years .
我對市區非常熟悉，我在那裡住了十年。

complete v. 完成

I have to complete the report by this week.
我必須在這週前完成報告。

by the way 對了；順便一提

By the way, could you please pick me up this evening?
對了！你可以今天晚上來接我嗎？

as soon as 一……就……

We headed for the hotel as soon as we arrived in L.A.
我們一到洛杉磯時就去飯店了。

In Other Words

Are you familiar with Excel?
你熟悉Excel的操作嗎？

- Are you good at Excel?
  你擅長Excel的操作嗎？
- Are you excellent at Excel?
  你對於使用Excel拿手嗎？

Try to complete it by the end of the month.
試著在月底以前完成。

- Do your best to have it done by the end of the month.
  試著在月底以前完成。
- You had better finish it by the end of the month.
  最好在月底以前完成。

As soon as you finish the customer information, go ahead and send out the quotations.
一旦完成顧客資訊之後，就直接將估價單寄出。

- Go ahead and send out the quotations upon finishing the customer information.
  一旦完成顧客資訊之後，就直接將估價單寄出。
- After you have finished updating the customer information, go ahead and send out the quotations.
  一旦完成顧客資訊之後，就直接將估價單寄出。

3-2 協助交辦事務

New Staff Training Is Coming Up
新進員工訓練即將登場

The new staff training is coming up. Lynn, the personnel manager, asks Rita, the sales executive, whether she may get some help from one of Rita's assistants to make copies of handouts, etc.

新進員工訓練即將登場。人事經理Lynn詢問業務主管Rita，她是否可以請Rita的助理協助影印等事務。

Lynn - the personnel manager 人事經理
Rita - the sales executive 業務主管
Jay - the sales assistant 業務助理

Dialogue

Lynn	There you are, Rita. I've been looking all over for you.	Rita，原來你在這。我正到處找你呢。
Rita	What's the matter?	什麼事情？
Lynn	As you know, the new staff training is coming up soon.	妳知道的，新進員工訓練就快到了。
Rita	The Personnel **Department** is **organizing** it, that must really be keeping you hopping.	這是由人事部主辦的，你們一定忙的不可開交。
Lynn	That's right. I hardly have time to **breathe**. The thing is, our department is **short-handed**, so I was wondering if we could get some help from one of your assistants.	沒錯，我忙到沒有喘息的機會。問題是我們部門人手不足，所以我在想，是否可以請你們部門的一位助理幫忙。

Rita	No problem at all. What can our assistant help you with?	沒問題。我們的助理能夠幫上什麼忙？
Lynn	They can help us to make copies of handouts and set up the training area.	他們可以幫忙我們影印講義和佈置訓練場地。
Jay	Hello, Rita, Lynn.	妳們好，Rita，Lynn。
Rita	Speak of the devil! Jay, what a perfect timing!	說曹操，曹操就到！ Jay，你來的正是時候！
Jay	Yes?!	什麼？！
Rita	Lynn needs a hand with the preparations for new staff training. Why don't you give her a hand?	Lynn需要人手幫忙籌備新進員工訓練事宜。你何不幫她一下？
Jay	Why not! I'd love to.	何樂不為！我很樂意。
Lynn	Thank you so much.	謝謝你們。

Word Bank

come up　開始，發生

When does this question come up?
這問題是何時發生的？

personnel　n.　人事

All employees' information has been saved at the Personnel Department.
所有員工資料都存放在人事部門。

handout　n.　講義

Please have the handouts ready before the conference starts.
請在會議開始前把講義準備好。

organize　v.　主辦

The city hall is successful in organizing an annual marathon race.
市政府在每年的馬拉松比賽都辦得很成功。

breathe　v.　呼吸

I love to breathe deeply in the nature.
我喜歡在大自然裡深呼吸。

short-handed　adj.　人手不足的

The Personnel Department intends to hire more people to improve short-handed situation.
人事部打算招聘更多人來改善人手不足的狀況。

In Other Words

The Personnel Department is organizing it, that must really be keeping you hopping.
這是由人事部主辦的，你們一定忙的不可開交。

It is organized by the Personnel Department, which must be having you occupied. 這是由人事部主辦的，你們一定忙的不可開交。

The Personnel Department is in charge of organizing and that must really be making you quite busy.
這是人事部主辦的，一定讓你們非常的忙碌吧。

The thing is, our department is short-handed, so I was wondering if we could get some help from one of your assistants.
問題是我們部門人手不足，所以我在想，是否可以請你們部門的一位助理幫忙。

The problem is, we are so unmanned, so I was wondering if we can ask one of your assistants for help.
問題是我們部門人手不足，所以我在想，是否可以請你們部門的一位助理幫忙。

I was wondering if we can ask one of your assistants for help, 'cause we're actually a bit short-handed at this moment. .
我在想，是否可以請你們部門的一位助理幫忙，因為我們目前人手不足。

What can our assistant help you with?
我們的助理能夠幫上什麼忙？

What can our assistant be of any assistance?
我們的助理能夠幫上什麼忙？

What can our assistant do for you?
我們的助理能夠幫上什麼忙？

3-3 協助交辦事務

Market Research Report
市場調查報告

Hank, the enterprise planning coordinator, asks the assistant, Jenny, to write a market research report.

企劃專員Hank請助理Jenny幫忙寫一份市場調查報告。

Hank - enterprise planning coordinator/ 企劃專員
Jenny - enterprise planning assistant / 企劃助理

Dialogue

Hank	Hi, Jenny, can I ask you for a **favor**?	嗨，Jenny，可以請妳幫個忙嗎？
Jenny	Sure. What do you need?	當然。你需要什麼？
Hank	I need your help to write a market research report on **consumer goods** covering the last six months. Do you think you could do that?	我需要妳幫忙寫一份針對過去六個月民生消費品的市場調查報告。妳認為妳可以辦到嗎？
Jenny	Yes, I can do that. But when do you need it? I need to finish the meeting **minutes** and submit them to the manager first.	可以，但這份報告你何時要？我必須先完成會議記錄並上呈給經理。
Hank	When can you start?	妳何時可以開始？
Jenny	The day after tomorrow. Is that OK?	後天。可以嗎？

Hank	Perfect! As long as you give it to me by the end of next month, it'll be fine.	太棒了！只要妳能在下個月底前給我都可以。
Jenny	What **sort** of information do I need to gather?	我需要收集什麼類型的資訊？
Hank	A **variety** of information, such as brands, prices, packaging, customer service, etc.	各種類型的訊息，例如品牌、價格、包裝、客戶服務等等。
Jenny	Can you send me an e-mail with more **details**?	你可以把更多的細節部分用e-mail寄給我嗎？
Hank	Of course. Thank you.	當然可以。謝謝妳。
Jenny	Don't mention it.	不用客氣。

★你應該要知道的小小事！

助理多數協助處理的會是文書方面的工作，像是資料匯整、表單製作、打訂單等等，所以文書方面的技能就很重要，要熟悉Office軟體的使用，最常使用的就是Word/Excel/PowerPoint，如果想要讓自己功力提升的話，可以多看看這類的電腦書籍或是上上相關的課程，來增加自己的實務能力，這些能力在你之後的工作職位也是相當有幫助的。

Word Bank

enterprise n. 企業、公司

The enterprise always makes a contribution to the society.
這公司總是對社會做出貢獻。

favor n. 恩惠；善意的行為

May I ask you a favor?
我可以請你幫忙嗎？

consumer goods 消費品

The supermarket sells a variety of consumer goods for options.
這超市販賣多種消費品供選擇。

minute n. 會議紀錄

Please take the minutes and have it finished today.
請製作會議紀錄並於今天完成。

sort n. 類型

What sort of person are you looking for?
你正在找何種類型的人？

variety n. 種類；多樣化

The garden has a variety of flowers.
這花園有各式各樣的花。

detail n. 細節

Please tell me more details about this event.
請告訴我這事情的更多細節。

In Other Words

I need your help to write a market research report on consumer goods covering the last six months.
我需要妳幫忙寫一份針對過去六個月民生消費品的市場調查報告。

- Could you do me a favor to conduct a market research report regarding consumer goods for the past six months?
  可以請妳幫忙做一份針對過去六個月民生消費品的市場調查報告嗎?
- Please do me a favor to write a market research report on consumer goods during the recent six months.
  請妳幫我寫一份針對過去六個月民生消費品的市場調查報告。

What sort of information do I need to gather?
我需要收集什麼類型的資訊?

- What kind of information should I collect?
  我需要收集什麼類型的資訊?
- What kind of information is required to gather?
  我需要收集什麼類型的資訊?

Can you send me an e-mail with more details?
你可以把更多的細節部分用e-mail寄給我嗎?

- Please kindly email me more details.
  請把更多的細節部分用e-mail寄給我。
- Could you please send me more details via email?
  請把更多的細節部分用e-mail寄給我嗎?

3-4 協助交辦事務

The Boom Season
旺季

It is the boom season. Every staff member in the Wholesale Department is as busy as a bee. The manager, Lee, asks the assistant, Miki, to help pack the goods and seal the boxes, making sure they will be ready to ship.

現在正值旺季。批發部的每一個人都忙得不可開交。批發部經理李要助理Miki幫忙包裝貨物及裝箱，確保貨物都準備好出貨。

Lee - wholesale manager 批發部經理
Miki - wholesale assistant 批發部助理

Dialogue

Lee	Every year around this time, our department is **flooded** with goods.	每年的這個時候，我們部門總會被貨物給淹沒。
Miki	It's the boom season. I'm very excited about it. Our business is good.	現在正值旺季。我為此感到很興奮。我們的生意興隆。
Lee	Good, you are **energetic**. By the way, how many **tasks** do you have to do this afternoon?	很好，妳很有精神。對了，妳今天下午工作會很多嗎？
Miki	Not many, actually, besides finishing the **inventory checklist**.	事實上不多，除了要完成庫存清單。
Lee	Forget about the checklist; you can finish it tomorrow. I need you to help pack the goods and seal the boxes.	先別管清單了，妳可以明天再做。我需要妳幫忙打包貨品和封箱。

Miki	Yes. I'll start packing the goods right after the lunch break.	好的。午休過後我會立刻開始包裝貨物。
Lee	I almost forgot. There is one more thing. <u>You will have to work fast because all the goods have to be ready for shipment at 5 P.M.</u>	我差點忘了，還有一件事。妳動作可能要快一點，因為所有的貨物必須在下午五點準時送出。
Miki	I will try my best.	我會盡力的。

★你應該要知道的小小事！

公司遇到旺季的時候，出貨量大增，這時各單位都會忙翻天，為了讓各筆訂單都能順利出貨，將貨品準時送達顧客手中，各家貨運公司收送的時間就要特別留意，一定要請公司內各部門配合在時間之內將要寄貨運的物品包好，並填好貨運單，貼在包裝外。

假設有一間公司，有透過郵局、貨運公司、便利帶收送貨物的習慣，如果公司規模大、人數多的話，其實可以在各樓層或是各部門規劃出一個集貨區，擺上三個箱子，在箱子上貼上郵局、貨運公司、便利帶，代表三種送貨的方式，並將收貨時間用紅筆註明，這樣同仁也比較不會忘記，對於公司的新人來說也會比較方便，只要跟他們說集貨區的位置，時間看箱子就不會忘記了。

另外貨運單的填寫也很重要，通常一份會有好幾張，每一個欄位都要確實填寫，尤其是公司如果單位很多，自己的單位和自己的名字一定要寫清楚，不然到時貨物有問題，很難查詢相關訊息，還有在寄出貨物前，一定要再次確認收件者的名字和電話是否正確無誤，避免造成其他同事或是貨運公司處理上的困擾哦！大家如果在每一個環節都多一份細心，那貨物運送就會更順利哦！

wholesale n. 批發

All the goods are bought at wholesale.
所有貨品都是以批發買入。

seal v. 密封

The bottle has to be sealed tightly.
這瓶子需要緊緊密封。

flood v. 淹沒；充斥

All the farms are flooded by heavy rain.
所有農田都被大雨淹沒。

energetic adj. 精神飽滿的

All the sales persons are energetic to start working in the morning.
早上所有銷售人員都精神飽滿的開始工作。

task n. 工作；任務

It is amazing that the boy completed the task all by himself.
這男孩很神奇地獨力完成此份工作。

inventory n. 庫存

An inventory checklist is updated by the system automatically.
系統會自動更新庫存清單。

checklist n. 清單

It is necessary to have the checklist ready before making a purchase.
在購買前須準備好清單。

In Other Words

Every year around this time, our department is flooded with goods.
每年的這個時候，我們部門總會被貨物給淹沒。

- Our department is always filled with goods around this time every year.
  每年的這個時候，我們部門總會塞滿了一大堆的貨物。
- At this time of the year, our office is stuffed with goods.
  每年到了這個時候，我們的辦公室總是塞滿了一大堆的貨物。

It's the boom season.
現在正值旺季。

- It's the high season.
  現在正值旺季。
- It's the peak season.
  現在正值旺季。

You will have to work fast because all the goods have to be ready for shipment at 5 P.M.
妳動作可能要快一點，因為所有的貨物必須在下午五點準時送出。

- You must hurry to have all the goods ready for shipment at 5 P.M.
  妳動作要快一點，讓所有的貨物準備好在下午五點準時送出。
- Because all the goods must be shipped at 5 P.M., perhaps you'd make haste.
  因為所有的貨物必須要在下午五點準時送出，也許妳動作要快一點。

什麼是市場調查？

簡單而言，市場調查就是透過各種調查和分析方式，協助企業了解市場和顧客。針對企劃這一塊，市場調查必須涵蓋以下項目：

★市場訊息

各種商品的價格，包括供應和需求的狀況。

★市場區隔

依照個人喜好以劃分市場中的消費者；類似喜好、行為及動機的族群歸類在同一圈子裡。

★市場趨勢

市場趨勢有高有低，同一件商品或一項服務於不同時期推出，得到的迴響可能會是全然不同。

★競爭者

除了以上三點，想要有效地達到理想的市佔率，則必須了解你的競爭者，正所謂知己知彼。

★行銷效能

下列技巧能協助你衡量行銷效能：

✧ 客戶分析　✧ 競爭者分析　✧ 產品研究
✧ 廣告研究　✧ 行銷組合模式

助理和秘書有何不同！

也許很多人會問，助理到底和秘書有何差異？一樣都是處理行政工作，包括處理公司上下大小瑣事，甚至是主管或老闆的私事，既然性質相同，為何有兩種職務別呢？！

其實助理和秘書還是有差別的，就大多公司行號而言，助理和秘書的差別取決為兩點：(1)參與決策的層級，以及(2)工作內容的複雜度。

秘書所負責的工作內容大多為文書處理類型（行政），包括打字、寫信、記錄、歸檔、排行程等等。雖然工作內容單調，但在企業內享有一定的自由度，因為秘書的上司通常都是經理層級以上的高階主管，工作責任相對少了一道道層級的關卡。

相反地，助理則不僅僅負責行政類的工作了。許多助理可以參與決策，也同時負責計劃進行設計和規劃。工作內容較為廣泛，上至專案經理，下至泡咖啡、買早點的跑腿人員，就看公司如何用人。也有許多所謂的私人助理，但別忘了，私人助理其實有如時下的經紀人一般，有許多還是老闆的好友兼夥計。

相互體諒、良好溝通

在職場裡，有正式員工、約聘員工、全職、兼職，大家因為工作內容的關係而有不同的職稱，彼此之間應互相尊重，不應該有那種我是正式員工，所以我對兼職員工就可以用比較不禮貌的態度說話的心態。很多時候在公司裡會發現有的同事會對總機、助理或是工讀生的態度比較不好，請他們幫忙的時候也是用命令的方式，這樣的態度其實不太合適，因為大家都是努力在工作，不應該因為職位的關係而受到不同的對待。同在一個職場工作就是一種緣份，應該要好好把握，小小的助理或總機有一天也有可能會在職場上大放異彩，這種事情誰知道呢？所以應該要互相尊重、以誠相待，營造出快樂的工作氛圍，這樣對大家的工作效率也是會有幫助的哦！

4-1 郵件包裹寄送

Delivery Service and Post Office
快遞和郵局

Joe, the senior wholesale assistant, reminds Miki of matters that need to be paid attention to regarding mail and parcels.

資深批發助理Joe提醒Miki關於郵件和包裹寄送應注意的事項。

Miki – the wholesale assistant 批發助理
Joe – the senior wholesale assistant 資深批發助理

Dialogue

Joe	Miki, did you finish sealing and **labeling** the boxes?	Miki，箱子都封好且貼上標籤了嗎？
Miki	Almost, five more boxes to go.	快好了，只剩下五箱。
Joe	You'd better hurry up; we are **running out** of time.	妳最好快一點，我們快沒時間了。
Miki	Why are you in such a hurry? It is only a **quarter** to one.	為什麼你這麼急？現在才十二點四十五分。
Joe	We have to bring some of the boxes to the post office before 3:00 P.M.	我們必須在下午三點以前將一些箱子送到郵局去。
Miki	Is that so? Doesn't the post office close at 5 P.M.?	是這樣嗎？郵局下午5點才關門嗎？

Joe	That's right, but the mailing service ends at 3 P.M. If we don't make it on time, our goods won't be sent until the next morning, and that may cause a delay.	沒錯啊，但寄件服務只到下午三點鐘。如果我們趕不及的話，貨物就會拖到明天早上才寄出，這麼一來可能會造成延遲。
Miki	I see. So, which ones will go to the post office?	我懂了，那麼要送哪些箱子去郵局呢？
Joe	Those smaller boxes by the door. And the delivery service will come to pick up the rest of the boxes before 5 P.M. By the way, did you place **FRAGILE** stickers on the boxes with **marks**?	靠近門的那些小箱子。而快遞會在下午五點以前，來收其他的箱子。對了，那些作記號的箱子，妳已經貼上「易碎物」的標籤了嗎？
Miki	Yes, I did.	有的。
Joe	Good, you are careful and **swift**. Way to go.	很好，妳很細心且動作迅速。再接再厲。
Miki	Thank you so much. Shall we go to the post office now?	謝謝你。我們該出發去郵局了嗎？

★你應該要知道的小小事！

如果要請貨運公司配送的貨物是易碎品的話，除了會在箱子外加貼"Fragile!"的貼紙之外，在包裝時也會以舊報紙、氣泡布先包起來，並在箱子內塞滿保麗龍，避免運送過程中的碰撞對物品造成損害。

Word Bank

pay attention to　注意

Kindly pay attention to what I am talking to you.
敬請注意我現在跟你講的話。

parcel　n.　包裹

She was surprised to receive a parcel for her birthday.
她很驚訝收到生日包裹。

label　vt.　貼標籤

Every bottle is labeled clearly for the ingredients.
每個瓶子都清楚貼上成分標示。

run out of　用完

I have run out of the battery and have to recharge it.
我已用完電池，需要再次充電。

quarter　n.　一刻鐘（十五分鐘）；四分之一

Could you please wait for me for a quarter of an hour?
可以請你等我十五分鐘嗎？

fragile　adj.　易碎的，脆弱的

Please be extremely careful when washing these fragile glasses.
清洗這些易碎的玻璃杯時請要特別地小心。

mark　n.　記號

I always highlight my book as marks.
我總是以螢光筆來做記號

swift adj. 快速的

The manager made a swift response to the customer's complaint.
經理對客户的抱怨做了一個快速的回應。

In Other Words

Did you finish sealing and labeling the boxes?
箱子都封好且貼上標籤了嗎？

- Have you sealed and labeled the boxes?
  你都封好箱子並貼上標籤了嗎？
- Did you have the boxes being sealed and labeled?
  箱子都封好並貼上標籤了嗎？

It is only a quarter to one.
現在才十二點四十五分。

- It is only twelve forty-five.
  現在才十二點四十五分。
- It is only three quarters pass twelve.
  現在才十二點四十五分。

Did you place FRAGILE stickers on the boxes with marks?
那些作記號的箱子，妳已經貼上「易碎物」的標籤了嗎？

- Did you put FRAGILE stickers on the boxes with marks?
  妳有把「易碎物」的標籤貼上那些作記號的箱子了嗎？
- Did you have the marked boxes all placed FRAGILE stickers?
  妳有將那些作記號的箱子都貼上「易碎物」的標籤了嗎？

4-2 郵件包裹寄送

Bulk Mail
大宗郵件

The sales assistant, Cathy, is at the post office trying to send bulk mail. It is her first time sending bulk mail through the post office.

業務助理Cathy到郵局寄大宗郵件。這是她第一次透過郵局寄送大宗郵件。

Cathy - the sales assistant 業務助理
Mark - the post office clerk 郵局人員

Dialogue

Cathy	Excuse me. I'd like to send bulk mail.	不好意思。我想寄大宗郵件。
Mark	Do you have the mail ready?	郵件準備好了嗎？
Cathy	I've got the mail here. This is my first time sending bulk mail. Could you tell me what else I need to do?	都在我手上。這是我第一次寄大宗郵件。可否告訴我還需要些什麼呢？
Mark	Are there **postage** stamps on the envelopes?	信封上有貼郵票嗎？
Cathy	No.	沒有。
Mark	Here is the **detailed list** and the **barcode** label. **Fill out** the list first, and then place the barcode label on the back of the bulk mail.	這裡是明細單和貼條式條碼。先填寫明細單，然後將條碼貼在郵件的背面。

Cathy	Thank you. What is the mailing **code**?	謝謝。請問什麼是郵件編號？
Mark	It's the same number as on the barcode label.	就是條碼上的編號。
Cathy	Finished. What should I do with the list?	好了，那這張明細單呢？
Mark	You can give it to me. Thank you. There are a total of 175 **domestic** letters. That will be $1,500.	把它給我，謝謝。一共為175封國內郵件，總共是1,500元。
Cathy	OK. Here you go.	好的，錢給您。
Mark	Here is your change and **receipt**. Thank you. Please come again.	這是找您的錢和收據。謝謝您。請再度光臨。
Cathy	Thank you very much.	非常謝謝您。

★你應該要知道的小小事！

大宗郵寄寄掛號時，先跟郵局拿掛號貼紙，然後貼在每件信件的背面，郵局會秤重：20公克以內是25元（掛號），21～50公克以內是30，51~100公克以內是35元，超過100公克上會再另外計價；一般公司不見得會有秤重器，所以其實填寫完直接給郵局人員處理即可。交寄完畢後你會拿到二張收據，這收據很重要，一張是該郵件投遞編號，如果之後對方沒有收到的話，可以在網路上用此收據的號碼去查詢郵件進度；二是該郵件投遞資費證明，名為「購票證明」，為公司報帳用收據。要特別留意的就是信封上的地址要寫清楚，掛號的話，一定是對方地址上有人收寄掛號才不會被通知要領件，若超過2次貼單招領，仍未有人前往招領單上郵局領取，此郵件便會被退回（約15天）。

postage n. （不可數）郵資

What is the postage on this the parcel?
這小包郵資多少？

detailed list n. 明細單

You should have the detailed list enclosed with the parcel.
你需要把明細單附在小包裡面。

barcode n. 條碼

The price will be displayed on the screen if you scan the barcode of this item.
如果你掃描這項產品的條碼，就會顯示價格。

fill out 填寫

The new member filled out the application form for registration.
這新會員填寫註冊申請表。

code n. 代碼、代號

What's the zip code of the city you live in?
你居住的城市的郵遞區號是多少？

domestic adj. 國內的

The domestic market has great potential.
這國內市場非常有潛力。

receipt n. 收據

Remember to take the receipt as a proof of purchase.
記得拿收據當購買證明。

In Other Words

Fill out the list first, and then place the barcode label on the back of the bulk mail.
先填寫明細單，然後將條碼貼在郵件的背面。

- First, have the list filled out. Then, have the barcode labeled on the back of the bulk mail.
  先填寫明細單，然後將條碼貼在郵件的背面。
- The list has to be filled out first, and then the barcode label has to be placed on the back of the bulk mail.
  明細單須先填寫，然後條碼須貼在郵件的背面。

It's the same number as on the barcode label.
就是條碼上的編號。

- It's an identical number to the barcode label.
  就是條碼上的編號。
- The number and the barcode labels' are the same.
  編號和條碼上的一樣。

There are a total of 175 domestic letters.
一共為175封國內郵件。

- Here are 175 domestic letters totally.
  共有175封的國內郵件。
- The total amount of the domestic letters is 175.
  國內郵件的總數是175封。

4-3 郵件包裹寄送

Express Delivery Service
快遞服務

Cathy calls an express delivery service.
業務助理Cathy打電話叫快遞。

Cathy – the sales assistant 業務助理
Kenny – the express delivery customer service 快遞客服

Dialogue

Kenny	Good morning, this is Fast Mailing. How may I help you?	早安，這裡是Fast Mailing。有什麼可以效勞的嗎？
Cathy	Hi, I want to send a **package** from Taipei to New Taipei City.	嗨，我有一件包裹，要從台北市送到新北市。
Kenny	What is the package **size** and **weight**?	包裹的大小和重量是多少？
Cathy	I don't know about the size and weight. It's as big as a shoebox. <u>It **contains** two bottles of hair spray.</u> That may give you an idea of how much it **weighs**.	我不清楚尺寸和重量。它的大小和鞋盒一般，裡面裝有兩瓶髮膠，這樣你大概可以估算出重量。
Kenny	Are those glass bottles?	是玻璃瓶裝嗎？
Cathy	No, they are not. When can you come to pick it up?	不是。你們什麼時候可以過來取件？

Kenny	Our delivery person will be there **sometime** between two and five this afternoon.	我們的送貨人員會在今天下午的兩點至五點之間到達。
Cathy	And when will the package arrive?	那麼包裹何時會送達？
Kenny	By tomorrow afternoon.	明天下午之前。
Cathy	Good. How much will it cost?	太好了。費用是多少？
Kenny	It will be $350. Please pay the delivery person when he arrives. Is there anything else I can do for you?	一共是350元。到時請將錢付給送貨人員。還有可以為您服務的地方嗎？
Cathy	No. Thank you.	沒有了，謝謝。
Kenny	You're welcome. Have a nice day. Good-bye!	不客氣；祝您有美好的一天。再見！
Cathy	Good-bye!	再見！

★你應該要知道的小小事！

各家公司通常都會有長期配合的快遞，一般來説若需要快遞服務時，就是填完單，打到快遞公司，告訴對方公司的客編，請他們來收件即可。如果是要到某一個地方收件送回公司的話，這是取件，這種狀況就不必填單據。快遞有分一般件、專件和夜間專件，價位就是由低到高，送達的時間也會有不同，如果遇到很緊急的狀況的話，當然還是以工作為優先考量。

Word Bank

express delivery 快遞

The manager asked his assistant to send the letter via express delivery.
經理請助理將此信以快遞寄出。

package n. 包裹

The package has dimension and weight limitation.
這包裹有尺寸和重量限制。

size n. 尺寸

The store carries garments of a variety of sizes.
這家店有販售很多尺寸的衣服。

weight n. 重量

She has been told to lose weight.
她被告知要減肥。

contain vt. 容納

Green vegetables contain a lot of vitamins.
綠色蔬菜含有很多維他命。

weigh vi. 有……重量

How much does this package weigh?
這包裹有多重？

sometime adv. 在（過去或將來）某一段時間

I hope to take a vacation sometime next year.
我希望明年可以去度假。

In Other Words

It contains two bottles of hair spray.
裡面裝有兩瓶髮膠。

- There are two bottles of hair spray contained.
  裡面裝有兩瓶髮膠。
- It includes two bottles of hair spray.
  裡面裝有兩瓶髮膠。

And when will the package arrive?
那麼包裹何時會送達？

- And when will the package get to our customer?
  那麼包裹何時會送達我們客戶哪？
- When will the package be delivered?
  那麼包裹什麼時候會送呢？

How much will it cost?
費用是多少？

- How much for the delivery?
  運費是多少？
- How much should I pay for the package delivery?
  那包裹的費用是多少？

4-4 郵件包裹寄送

The Package Fails to Arrive
包裹並未送達

Cathy calls an express delivery service and **complains** that the customer has not yet received the parcel.

Cathy打電話到快遞公司，抱怨客戶尚未收到包裹。

Cathy – the sales assistant 業務助理
Tom – the express delivery customer service 快遞客服

Dialogue

Tom	Fast Mailing. What can I do for you?	這裡是Fast Mailing. 有什麼可以效勞的嗎？
Cathy	I sent a parcel the day before yesterday, and it was supposed to be delivered to our customer in the afternoon yesterday. Our customer just called and said that the parcel didn't arrive.	我有一件包裹應該在昨天下午就送達到顧客那，但顧客來電抱怨說，包裹仍尚未送達。
Clerk	Let me check. Do you have the **tracking number**, please?	讓我查一下。您有追蹤號碼嗎？
Cathy	Yes, it is EP998321.	有的，EP998321。

Clerk	One moment, please. Thank you for your **patience**. What happened was that our delivery person delivered the parcel to the **designated** address, but no one answered the door. He called the contact number you gave us twice when he was on the way with the parcel, but no one **answered the phone**. That's why the parcel **failed** to arrive.	請稍等。謝謝您的等候。事情的經過是這樣的，我們的送貨人員將包裹送到指定的地址時，沒有人出來應門。在路上還撥過兩通電話至您給的聯絡號碼，但都沒有人接。所以包裹仍未送達。
Cathy	I see. Where is the parcel now?	原來如此。包裹現在在哪呢？
Clerk	Our delivery person still has it. He will **attempt** to deliver it again this afternoon.	仍在我們的送貨人員那裏。他今天下午會再送一次。
Cathy	Great. I'll call our customer and make sure she will be home this afternoon. Thank you.	太好了。我會打電話給我們的顧客，並確認她今天下午在家裡。謝謝。
Clerk	You're welcome. Thank you for calling. Bye.	不客氣，謝謝您的來電，再見。
Cathy	Bye.	再見。

Word Bank

complain vt. 抱怨

The clerk does not complain even though she has to work overtime.
這員工即使必須加班也不會抱怨。

tracking number 追蹤號碼

Every registered letter has a tracking number.
每一封掛號信都有追蹤號碼。

patience n. 耐心

He has much patience and is a good listener.
他很有耐心，是個很好的傾聽者。

designate vt. 指定

Richard was designated to be the Chairman of Board of Directors.
Richard 被任命為董事會主席。

answer the phone 接電話

The store owner is too busy to answer the phone.
老闆忙到無法接電話。

fail vi. 失敗

The student failed in the examination.
這學生考試不及格。

attempt vt. 試圖

The firefighter attempted to save the child.
消防隊員試圖要拯救這小孩。

In Other Words

I sent a parcel the day before yesterday, and it was supposed to be delivered to our customer in the afternoon yesterday.
我前天寄一件包裹，應該在昨天下午就送達到顧客那。

- The parcel, which was sent the day before yesterday, was supposed to be delivered to our customer in the afternoon yesterday.
  前天寄的包裹，應該在昨天下午就送達到顧客那。
- I sent a parcel the day before yesterday, and our customer supposed to get that parcel yesterday afternoon.
  我前天寄的包裹，我們的顧客應該在昨天下午就要收到。

That's why the parcel failed to arrive.
所以包裹仍未送達。

- So, the parcel did not arrive.
  所以包裹仍未送達。
- It caused that the parcel failed to be delivered.
  所以導致包裹仍未送達。

He will attempt to deliver it again this afternoon.
他今天下午會再送一次。

- This afternoon he will try to deliver it again.
  今天下午他會再送一次。
- He will deliver it again later today.
  他今天稍晚會再送一次。

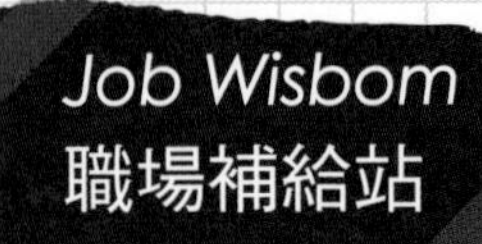

常見的運輸錯誤！

★貼錯標籤/忘了貼標籤

記得在將貨物送上車、準備送往郵局，或是讓快遞公司前來領取之前，一定要再檢查一遍箱子上的標籤是否正確。

★為了省運費而硬將大型物件擠入過小的箱子或包裹裡。

運費的費用不能省，這直接關係到屆時送達顧客手上的貨品是否會有損壞，有可能會導致產生不必要的負面印象。

★錯誤的地址和電話。

聽起來或許有點無厘頭，但此類問題卻層出不窮。越是簡單的事，越容易疏忽。

★忘了提醒貴重或是易碎的物品要特別小心。

儘管專業的快遞公司都會小心地對待物品，但多一次的提醒會更謹慎。

★沒有小心裝箱。

體積較小的包裹常常會在運送的途中「跌個東倒西歪」。這或許和快遞公司沒有直接關聯，自己在裝箱時就得多加注意可以用報紙將空隙填滿，以避免上述狀況發生。

用字篇

! Package 和 Parcel 的差別

若查閱字典，這兩個單字的解釋都是包裹。但是實際上指的是不一樣的物件，而且在動詞的使用上也不相同。

★package

內含非私人物件；尺寸和重量超出特定的規範；動詞的使用→ to mail a package

★parcel

內含私人物件（如信件、證件等）；尺寸和重量並無超出特定的規範；仍能夠投進郵箱中；動詞的使用→ to send a parcel

老鳥巧巧說

郵寄包裹處理要注意些什麼？

通常助理需要幫忙處理公司包裝包裹、郵寄、貨運、快遞等等的事項，但是每天都有這麼多的包裹和郵件需處理，要怎樣才能讓自己有效率地處理這些事，做得又快又好呢？可將公司有配合的收送方式整合在表單中，依每天收件的時間來排序，這樣就不會耽誤到其中一項。至於快遞的部分，算是比較機動性的，所以有快遞需求時，再處理就好，只要留意收件時間，也就是快遞服務加價的時段，這個部分若不清楚，一定要仔細問清楚，才不會成不必要的浪費。還有一種送件方式，叫做「便利帶」，這樣的送件服務，因為價格比較便宜，所以也很受到公司的喜愛。會員需先買袋子，依送的區域、貨品的大小，而有不同的袋子，只要把要送的文件或是物品裝進袋子，填妥單據，打電話請他們來收件即可。這種通常都是下午收件，然後隔天才會到。每種郵寄方式的到貨日都不同，一定要記得問清楚，尤其是很重要又緊急的包裹，才不會造成自己或是他人的困擾。當然，所有的單據都應完整保留，萬一發生什麼樣的狀況，才有個依據。

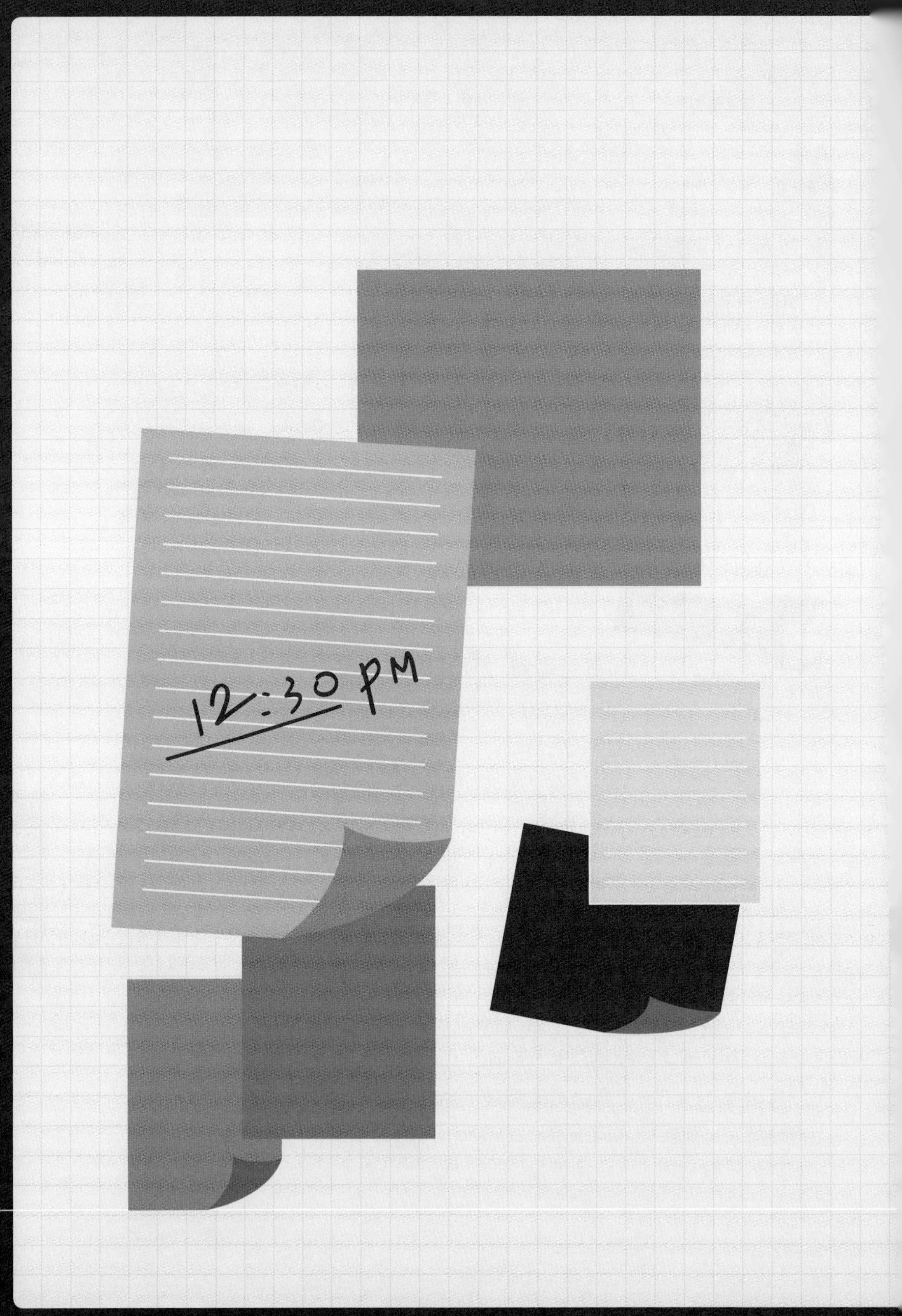
12:30 PM

PART 3

General Affairs / Personnel / Procurement 總務／人資／採購

* Unit 01 公司設備
* Unit 02 人力不足
* Unit 03 比價採買
* Unit 04 內部員訓安排

1-1 公司設備

Office Equipment
辦公設備

Brian calls the general affairs coordinator, Tracy, to say that the printer is not working. Tracy calls the printer company for a solution.

Brian打電話給總務專員Tracy表示印表機無法運作，崔西打電話給印表機公司以解決問題。

Brian - the sales coordinator 業務專員
Tracy - the general affairs coordinator 總務專員

Dialogue

Brian	Hi. Tracy, this is Brian, from the Sales Department.	嗨，Tracy，我是業務部的Brian。
Tracy	Hello, Brian, what's up?	哈囉，Brian，還好嗎？
Brian	The printer is not working.	印表機無法正常運作。
Tracy	Oh, no. Not again. Listen, turn off the printer first. Then **inspect** the **tray** to see if there is paper **stuck** in it.	喔，不，又來了。聽著，先關掉印表機。然後檢查托盤，看看是否有紙張卡住了。
Brian	No, it's not a **paper jam**.	沒有，不是卡紙的問題。
Tracy	It could be out of **toner**. Why don't you restart the printer now and try again?	可能是沒碳粉了。要不要將印表機重開機，然後再試一次。
Brian	It is still not working.	還是不能用。

Tracy	Does it show any error messages?	有顯示任何錯誤訊息嗎？
Brian	No. I'm sorry, but I really need to make some copies of reports and quotations. My supervisor needs them by noon.	沒有。不好意思，但我真的需要影印一些報告和估價單。我的主管中午以前會用到他們。
Tracy	I see. I'll call the printer company and ask them to send someone over to fix it as fast as they can.	了解。我會打電話給印表機公司，並請他們儘快來修理。
Brian	Thank you.	謝謝。

★你應該要知道的小小事！

影印機是一家公司裡非常重要的設備，功能分很多種，有單色影印、彩色影印、掃描、大量文件複印……功能愈多，價格當然也就愈貴！所以公司一般都會依業務上的需求，購買或是租用適合的影印機。影印機最常遇到的問題就是卡紙，有時是跟用的紙有關，像是比較薄的紙張，可能就比較容易遇到這樣的問題；有時是機器內部零件的關係，如果是這樣的狀況，可能就得要換零件或是買新的影印機。為了節省紙張的費用，大家會將單面影印的紙回收再印，但要注意一定要將回收紙上的釘書針或是色膠帶這些東西清除，不然會因此而減短影印機的壽命。

Word Bank

general affairs　總務

You have to ask the General Affairs Department to fix the copy machine.
你需要請總務部的人來修理影印機。

solution　n　解決辦法

The engineer is trying to find out a solution.
這工程師正在想解決辦法。

inspect　vt.　檢查

All the passengers are waiting in line for inspecting.
所有的旅客都在排隊等檢查。

tray　n.　托盤

The waitress brings dishes on a tray.
女服務生用托盤端菜。

stuck　adj.　卡住的

I am stuck on the traffic jam.
我卡在車陣當中。

paper jam　卡紙

The technician is working on the paper jam.
技術員正在解決卡紙問題。

toner n. 碳粉

The printer is required to refill toner.
這印表機需要重加碳粉。

In Other Words

Tracy calls the printer company for a solution.
Tracy打電話給印表機公司以解決問題。

- Tracy makes a phone call to the printer company to figure out the problem.
  Tracy打電話給印表機公司以解決問題。
- Tracy calls the printer company to solve the problem.
  Tracy打電話給印表機公司以解決問題。

Then inspect the tray to see if there is paper stuck in it.
然後檢查托盤，看看是否有紙張卡住了。

- Please check the tray to see if it is a paper jam.
  請檢查托盤，看看是不是卡紙了。
- Next, take a look at the tray to see if any paper stuck in it.
  接下來檢查托盤，看看是否有紙張卡住了。

Does it show any error messages?
有顯示任何錯誤訊息嗎？

- Is there any error messages displayed?
  有顯示任何錯誤訊息嗎？
- Any pop out error message?
  有跳出任何錯誤訊息嗎？

1-2 公司設備

Office Furniture
辦公設備

A new employee will report for duty a week from today. The general affairs manager, Emma, asks Tracy to purchase furniture for the new person.

一位新人將於一個星期後到公司報到，總務經理Emma吩咐Tracy為新員工添購設備。

Tracy – the general affairs coordinator 總務專員
Emma – the general affairs manager 總務經理

Dialogue

Emma	Did you know the Personnel Department just **hired** a new employee to fill a **vacancy**.	你知道人事部剛雇用了一個新人來填補一個空缺嗎？
Tracy	Not really. Who left?	不太知道。誰離職了？
Emma	It's Carrie. The new person will **replace** her **post** as an assistant.	是Carrie。新人將代替她原本助理的職位。
Tracy	Carrie? Didn't she just join the company about two months ago?	Carrie？她不是約兩個月前才進公司的嗎？
Emma	Don't be too surprised. Anyway, the new person will report for duty a week from today, but I just found out that we are short of an office desk and chair.	別太驚訝。總之，新人一個星期後會報到，但我剛剛才發現我們還少一組辦公桌椅。

Tracy	I know there are some desks and chairs in the **storage room**.	我知道儲藏室裡還有一些桌椅。
Emma	Those are damaged. And I just checked with the MIS Department; they don't have any extra keyboards, so we need to purchase a keyboard, too.	那些都壞掉了。還有我才剛和MIS部門的人查詢過，他們沒有多的鍵盤可以給新人用，所以我們也需要再買一副鍵盤。
Tracy	We surely don't take very good care of our furniture.	我們真的很不會照料家具。
Emma	Not me. I've been using the same desk, chair, and computer since the day I came to this company, and that was five years ago.	可不是我。從我第一天來到這間公司到現在，我一直都用同樣的桌子、椅子和電腦，那可是五年前的事了。
Tracy	Okay. I will place an order right away.	好的。我立刻就去下單。
Emma	Don't forget to ask for a discount!	不要忘了要求打折。

★你應該要知道的小小事！

新人報到前，有許多單位就會開始忙著準備，像是人資、總務和資訊部門，新人的座位（seat）安排、桌椅（desk and chair）、電腦（computer）、鍵盤（keyboard）、電腦軟體（computer software）等等，這些都要先準備好，新人報到後才能夠使用。

Word Bank

report for duty　報到

Please come at 8 a.m. tomorrow to report for duty.
請明天早上八點前來報到.

hire　vt.　雇用

Due to the business growth, we need to hire more helpers.
由於業務量增加，我們需要雇用更多幫手.

vacancy　n.　空缺、空位

She is the best person to fill the manager vacancy.
她是補這一個經理空缺的最佳人選。

replace　vt.　取代、替換

Currently, most of the cellular phone devices are replaced by smartphone ones.
目前大部分的手機都被智慧型手機取代。

post　n.　職位

I was offered the post of secretary.
我得到秘書職缺的工作。

storage room　儲藏室

The storage room is located at the basement of the building.
儲藏室位在大樓的地下室.

In Other Words

The new person will replace her post as an assistant.
新人將代替她原本助理的職位。

- The new employee will take over her tasks of an assistant.
  新人將代替她原本助理的職位。
- Her position of an assistant will be replaced by the new person.
  她的助理職位將會有新人補上。

They don't have any extra keyboards, so we need to purchase a keyboard, too.
他們沒有多的鍵盤，所以我們也需要再買一副鍵盤。

- There is no extra keyboard, and buying an additional one is required.
  他們沒有多的鍵盤，所以需要再買一副鍵盤。
- We need to purchase one more keyboard because there's no extra one.
  我們需要再買一副鍵盤，因為沒有多的鍵盤。

Don't forget to ask for a discount!
不要忘了要求打折。

- Remember to request for a discount.
  記得要求打折。
- Keep in mind to ask for a price reduction!
  記得要他們算便宜一點。

1-3 公司設備

Saving Paper and Energy 節約用紙和能源

Emma calls a department meeting to discuss how to save paper and energy in the office.

Emma 召開部門會議討論如何節約用紙和能源。

Tracy – the general affairs coordinator 總務專員
Jim – the general affairs coordinator 總務專員
Gary – the general affairs coordinator 總務專員
Emma – the general affairs manager 總務經理

Dialogue

Emma	Good morning. I called up this meeting to discuss how to save energy and paper.	早安。我召集這個會議，是要討論有關於如何節約能源和用紙。
Gary	Shouldn't we invite the other departments to join us?	難道不該請其他部門一起加入討論嗎？
Emma	They will for sure. The General Manager is not happy about how we have been **consuming** too much energy and wasting too much paper. He wants us to make an energy and paper saving plan. Let's begin with saving paper. And Tracy, please take notes for us.	當然會請他們一起加入討論。總經理對於近來我們浪費了太多能源和紙張感到不悅，他希望我們能夠擬定一個節約能源和節約用紙計畫。先從節約用紙開始。Tracy，請幫我們大家做筆記。
Gary	We should email more often, **instead of** sending letters.	我們應多利用email以代替書信往來。

Tracy	**Recycle** unwanted paper and **shred confidential** documents only. Don't print documents or email unless it is **necessary**.	回收不要用的紙張，用碎紙機切碎的僅限機密文件。除非必要，否則不要列印文件或是email。
Jim	Only use one paper towel after we wash our hands.	洗完手後，只用一張紙巾。
Emma	How about saving energy?	那麼關於節約能源呢？
Tracy	Use "sleep mode" on computers when not in use. Turn off the lights or table lamps during our lunch break.	電腦不用時，讓它處在休眠狀態。午休時間要關燈或是桌燈。
Emma	Good. If you have any thoughts or ideas, tell Tracy and have her write them down.	很好。若你們有任何想法和點子，請告訴Tracy並讓她記下來。

★你應該要知道的小小事！

現在大家都在講『節能減碳』，為了要能創造更大的營收，公司當然會希望員工能儘量地節省不必要的浪費。在以不造成大家工作困擾的前提之下，以下提供幾個方法參考。例如在離開座位或是下班時，順手將電腦螢幕關閉，午休時間也可以將電燈關掉，單面列印的紙，可以在裁切之後，作為memo紙使用，或是利用空白面列印（要記得將釘書針或是色標籤去除），這些都算是還蠻容易做到的小事，長期下來，可為公司省下一筆不小的費用。

Word Bank

energy n. 能源

We are responsible for reducing energy consumption.
我們有責任減少能源消耗。

consume vt. 消耗

The latest technology device consumes less energy.
最新的科技設備消耗較少電力。

instead of 代替

I keep in touch with my friends via emails instead of mails.
我以電子郵件代替郵件和朋友保持聯絡。

recycle vt. 回收

We should acquire a habit to recycle anything recyclable.
我們應該養成習慣回收任何可回收的東西。

shred vt. 用碎紙機切碎

The confidential documents should be shredded.
這些機密文件應該要碎掉。

confidential adj. 機密的

All top confidential documents are only unlocked by passwords.
所有最高機密文件只能用密碼打開。

necessary adj. 必要的

It is necessary to preview the next lesson by next Monday.
下週一前需要預習下一課。

In Other Words

The General Manager is not happy about how we have been consuming too much energy and wasting too much paper.
總經理對於近來我們浪費了太多能源和紙張感到不悅。

- The General Manager is not pleased that too much energy has been consumed and too much paper has been wasted.
  總經理對於近來浪費了太多能源和紙張感到不悅。
- Too much energy has been consumed and too much paper has been wasted makes the General Manager unhappy.
  近來浪費了太多能源和紙張讓總經理感到不悅。

We should email more often, instead of sending letters.
我們應多利用email以代替書信往來。

- We should use emails more, instead of paper letters.
  我們應多多利用email以代替書信往來。
- Use email to share our ideas or documents, instead of print it out.
  利用email來分享我們的構思或是文件，而不要將它印出來。

Recycle unwanted paper and shred confidential documents only.
回收不要用的紙張，用碎紙機切碎的僅限機密文件。

- Have unwanted paper recycled and shred only confidential documents.
  回收不要用的紙張，用碎紙機切碎的僅限機密文件。
- Reuse paper that's already printed on one side, try to use the both side of a sheet of paper. But remember, the unwanted confidential document must be shred.
  回收使用已經印了一面的紙張，試著將紙張的兩面都能利用到。但是要記住，不要的機密文件要以碎紙機切碎。

1-4 公司設備

Office Equipment Maintenance 辦公設備維護

The printer company calls Tracy to confirm the date for routine maintenance and tries to convince her to buy the latest model.

印表機公司打電話給Tracy確認例行保養的日期，並試圖說服她購買最新的機種。

Tracy – the general affairs coordinator 總務專員
Johnny – printer company salesman 印表機公司業務

Dialogue

Johnny	Hello, may I speak to Tracy?	哈囉，請問Tracy在嗎？
Tracy	This is she. Who is speaking?	我就是，請問哪裡找？
Johnny	This is Johnny from ABC Printers. I am calling to confirm your routine maintenance this Friday at 2 P.M.	這裡是ABC Printers的Johnny。我想確認星期五下午兩點鐘的例行保養。
Tracy	Oh, yes. You're just in time. We've been having a lot of problems with the printer lately.	喔，是的。你來的正是時候了，近來我們的印表機老是出問題。
Johnny	What kind of problems?	什麼樣的問題？
Tracy	We've had **various malfunctions**. The paper jams quite often, and sometimes it just quits working for no reason.	各式各樣的問題，最近常卡紙、故障，有時候連原因都找不到。

Johnny	When did you buy the printer?	您是什麼時候購買的印表機呢？
Tracy	I don't know. The same printer has been in the office since I came to this company, and I've been working here for nearly four years.	我不知道。從我來到這間公司到現在，用的都是同一台印表機，我在這裡工作已快四年了。
Johnny	Have you considered buying a new one? Our latest **model** is a good choice.	您有沒有考慮過買一台新的呢？我們最新的機種是個很好的選擇。
Tracy	I haven't really thought about that, but tell me about it.	我倒是沒想過，但你還是跟我講解一下。
Johnny	It's an **all-in-one** printer with **built-in** fax, copier, and scanner. It has a duplexing function, which is very helpful if you are looking to save paper. And it is almost the same price as a single-function printer.	這是一台多功能的印表機，內建傳真機、影印機、掃描機，還有雙面列印的功能，特別是您想要節省紙張的話。而且價格幾乎和單一功能的印表機一樣。
Tracy	That sounds very good, but I can't make the decision now. I will consult with my supervisor and get back to you later.	聽起來很不錯，但我現在無法做決定。我必須和我主管商量，然後晚點再回覆你。
Johnny	Certainly. I can assure you it's a great deal.	當然沒有問題。我能向您保證這絕對是物超所值的。

Word Bank

routine adj. 例行的

I go to the dentist for a routine check on my teeth every three months.
我每三個月去看牙醫做牙齒的例行檢查。

maintenance n. 維護

The small garden requires high maintenance.
這一個小花園需要費心的維護。

various adj. 各式各樣的

There are various books in this library.
在這圖書館裡有著各式各樣的書籍。

malfunction n. 機器故障

There is a malfunction on this equipment.
這設備有點故障。

model n. 機種

The company is promoting its lastest model.
這公司目前正促銷最新機種。

all-in-one adj. 多功能的

I prefer buying an all-in-one cell phone.
我比較喜歡買多功能的手機。

built-in adj. 內建的

The laptop has a built-in speaker.
這筆電有內建喇叭。

In Other Words

We've been having a lot of problems with the printer lately.
近來我們的印表機老是出問題。

- There have been many malfunctions with our printer lately.
  近來我們的印表機老是出問題。
- There is something wrong with the printer recently.
  近來我們的印表機老是出問題。

We've had various malfunctions. The paper jams quite often, and sometimes it just quits working for no reason.
各式各樣的問題，最近常卡紙、故障，有時候連原因都找不到。

- There have been many kinds of malfunctions. It gets stuck by paper quite often or just does not work with no reason.
  各式各樣的問題，最近常卡紙或是連原因都找不到就是不動。
- There's a lot of problems, such as paper jam happens all the time, and sometimes just doesn't print, and no reason be found.
  有一大堆的毛病，例如像是常常會卡紙，有時則是不能印但又找不出原因。

I will consult with my supervisor and get back to you later.
我必須和我主管商量，然後晚點再回覆你。

- I will discuss with my supervisor and reply to you later.
  我必須和我主管商量，然後晚點再回覆你。
- I will have to get my supervisor's approval first, and then give you our answer.
  我必須要先徵求我主管的同意，然後才能告知你我們的答案。

辦公室節約用紙！

★若可以的話，儘量透過e-mail或電話來聯繫，而非書信。

★如不需要，不要列印e-mail或是文件。

★若非正式文件，多加利用回收紙張。

★將行事曆儲存在電腦上，少使用便利貼。

★多加使用再生紙產品。

辦公室節約能源！

★不使用的時候，請關燈。

★使用節能的電燈泡或LED燈

★沒有在使用電腦時，將它設定在休眠狀態。

★建立交通工具共乘制度。

★辦公設備沒在使用時，關掉電源。

★多爬樓梯、少搭電梯。

用字篇

! 節約能源相關詞彙

- air pollution 空氣污染
- carbon cycle 碳循環
- carbon reduction 減碳
- climate change 氣候變化

- air pollution 空氣污染
- carbon cycle 碳循環
- carbon reduction 減碳
- climate change 氣候變化
- efficient energy use 有效使用能源
- energy conservation 節約能源
- energy consumption 能源消耗
- energy crisis 能源危機
- energy recovery 能源回收
- energy shortage 能源短缺
- food waste recycling 廚餘回收
- general waste 一般廢棄物
- global warming 地球暖化
- green building 綠色建築
- green consumption 綠色消費
- greenhouse effect 溫室效應
- low energy building 低能耗建築
- low energy vehicle 低能源汽車
- resource recycling 資源回收
- zero energy building零能耗建築

總務工作好繁瑣

公司內的總務要管的東西五花八門，從公司大小設備（像電梯、空調、桌椅、文具用品、衛生紙等等……）到環境整潔（茶水間、洗手間、公共區域），通通都要管。要管理一家公司從上到下，從裡到外真的不是件容易的事，所以當總務的一定要夠細心、有條理，才能將這個工作做好，如果怕遺漏任何一項工作，建議可以將總務的工作分成幾大類，再細分成幾小類去做工作管理，像有些機器有固定維修日期，就可以先將該日期標出，時時可以提醒自己。

2-1 人力不足

Recruitment
招聘新人

Ben, the procurement coordinator, tells his supervisor, Carol, the procurement manager, that there is too much work and the need for **recruitment** is urgent.

採購專員Ben向他的主管—採購經理Carol表示工作量過重，需要趕緊招聘新員工。

Ben - the procurement coordinator 採購專員
Carol - the procurement manager 採購經理

Dialogue

Ben	Carol, could I have a word with you?	Carol，方便說話嗎？
Carol	Sure, come in. What's wrong? Is everything all right? You look awfully tired.	好的，請進。發生了什麼事？一切都還好嗎？你看起來累壞了。
Ben	As you know, I've been working overtime for months. I've missed a lot of dinners and time with my family.	您也知道，好幾個月以來我都一直在加班。我錯過了許多晚餐以及和家人相處的時間。
Carol	I understand, and I am responsible for that. Since Nicole left, I haven't had time to recruit a suitable **replacement**. Sorry, **blame** it on me.	我了解，而我也應該要負起責任。自從Nicole離職之後，我一直沒有時間招聘適合的人選。不好意思，該歸咎於我。

Ben	Don't get me wrong; it's not your fault. I wonder if we could recruit a new assistant.	別誤會我的意思。這不是你的錯。我在想我們或許可以招聘一名新助理。
Carol	I think that's just what we need.	我想這正是我們所需要的。
Ben	That's wonderful to hear.	太棒了。
Carol	You are **indispensable**; you are hardworking and a great communicator. I **regret neglecting** your heavy workload. I will talk to the director about it. As soon as he **approves** it, I'll get right on it.	你是不可或缺的人才，你工作認真，又擅長溝通，很抱歉沒注意到你的工作量大增。我會跟協理談一談。一旦他批准，我就馬上著手去辦。
Ben	Thank you so much. That's a relief.	非常謝謝你。真是讓我鬆了一口氣。
Carol	Don't mention it. I should have done this a while ago.	別提了。我應該更早進行這件事的。

★你應該要知道的小小事！

通常部門內的人力不足可以分成幾個因素：同仁家中突然有急事需請假、同仁休產假、同仁離職、工作量徒然增加等等；前面兩個原因造成短期的人力不足，主管可透過工作上的調度來解決這個問題，儘量將影響減到最低，但若是後面的原因，可能就要好好想想配套措施，像是確認同仁要離職後，儘快找到新人來接替工作，如果遇到業務量徒然增加，在針對部門內人力評估之後，看看是否要提出新增人力的需求。很多公司在景氣不好的時候，會欲缺不補，這時部門主管除了要讓同仁了解狀況之外，也應盡力為部門同仁爭取相關福利，不然很有可能會造成部門向心力不夠、流動率高的結果產生。

Word Bank

recruitment n. 招聘新人

There will be a large recruitment fair held at the city hall next week.
下週在市政府會舉行一個大型就業博覽會。

replacement n. 替代

Soy milk is a good replacement of milk.
豆漿是很好的牛奶取代品。

blame vt. 把……歸咎於

Do not blame yourself. You have made your effort.
不要自責，你已經盡力了。

indispensable adj. 必不可少的

A dictionary is indispensable for learning a language.
字典是學習語言的不可缺工具。

regret vt. 後悔

I have never regretted leaving that company.
我從沒後悔離開那間公司。

neglect vt. 忽略、忽視

The children should not be neglected.
這些小孩不應該被忽視。

approve vt. 批准，同意

My business plan has been approved by the General Manager.
總經理已核准我的營業企劃案。

In Other Words

Carol, could I have a word with you?
Carol，方便說話嗎？

- Could I talk to you for a moment, Carol?
  Carol，方便說一下話嗎？
- Carol, are you available to have a talk with me?
  Carol，方便說一下話嗎？

You look awfully tired.
你看起來累壞了。

- To be honest, you look terrible.
  老實說，你看起來糟透了。
- You look exhausted.
  你看起來累壞了。

Sorry, blame it on me.
不好意思，該歸咎於我。

- Sorry, it is all my fault.
  不好意思，是我的錯。
- I apologize for that, it is my neglect.
  我為此感到抱歉，這是我的疏忽。

2-2 人力不足

Recruitment Requirements 招聘需求

The personnel manager, Lynn, confirms the content of the recruitment request form with the procurement director, Ian.

人事部經理Lynn向採購部協理Ian確認有關招聘需求的內容。

Lynn – the personnel manager 人事經理
Ian – the procurement director 採購協理

Dialogue

Lynn	Hello, Ian, this is Lynn. I just received a recruitment **request form** from you. I'd like to go over a couple things with you.	哈囉，Ian，我是Lynn。我剛收到你的招聘需求。有幾件事情想跟你確認一下。
Ian	Sure. Go ahead.	當然。說吧。
Lynn	Some of the **required fields** are left **blank**.	有一些必填項目是留白的。
Ian	Really? I'm sorry; I must have missed them. I'll make corrections.	真的嗎？我很抱歉，我一定是漏掉了。我會再做修正。
Lynn	It's all right. I can fill in the **blanks** for you. What is the **minimum** education requirement?	沒關係。我可以幫你填空白處。最低學歷要求是什麼？
Ian	A **bachelor's** degree.	學士學位。

Lynn	How about the age limit?	年齡限制呢？
Ian	20 – 35 years old.	20到35歲。
Lynn	How about the salary **range**?	那麼薪資範圍呢？
Ian	$25,000 to $27,000. I think that is a reasonable range.	兩萬五至兩萬七。我想這是合理的範圍。
Lynn	I think so, too. Business has been bad these years. OK, that's all.	同感。這幾年的景氣不是很好。好了，就這樣。
Ian	Wait! Could you add one thing for me?	等一下！可以請妳幫我增加一個項目嗎？
Lynn	No problem. What is it?	沒問題。什麼項目？
Ian	A short **autobiography** is required. Thank you very much.	必須附上簡短的自傳。非常謝謝妳。

★你應該要知道的小小事！

一般來說，主管在提出招聘需求時，都需將一些徵人的基本條件告訴人資，方便人資在人力網站上刊登職缺，建議在列出徵才條件時，可仔細想想工作實務面的內容，將一些擔任這個職位需要的一些個人特質或是特殊專長一起列上去，這樣比較容易找到適合的人才，才不會浪費刊登廣告的錢和公司內部的人力和時間成本。

request form　需求單

A request form is required to fill in when applying for office supplies.
要申請辦公室用品需填寫需求單。

required field　必填項目

Please fill in all required fields to register an account.
要註冊新帳號需填寫所有必填項目。

blank　adj.　留白的，空白的

It is not acceptable to have the columns blank before logging in an account.
欄位空白是無法在登入帳號的。

minimum　adj.　最低的

What's the minimum quantity of an order?
最低下單量是多少？

bachelor　n.　學士

He eventually earned a bachelor degree after studying hard for many years.
在努力讀書許多年後，他終於拿到學士學位了。

range　n.　範圍

What's the age range of the students in this school?
這學校學生的年齡範圍是多大？

autobiography n. 自傳

The autobiographies of celebrities are well-sold.
名人的自傳銷售得很好.

In Other Words

I'd like to go over a couple things with you.
有幾件事情想跟你確認一下。

- I want to confirm several things with you.
  有幾件事情想跟你確認一下。
- There are a lot of things which I desire to confirm with you.
  有幾件事情想跟你確認一下。

I'll make corrections.
我會再做修正。

- I'll make amendments.
  我會再做修正。
- Some adjustments will be made by me.
  我會再做一些修正。

Business has been bad these years.
這幾年的景氣不是很好。

- There has been a bad business over the past years.
  過去這幾年來的景氣不是很好。
- Business has been depressed in recent years.
  這幾年的景氣都很蕭條。

2-3 人力不足

Job Search Website
求職網站

The personnel coordinator, Penny, calls the customer service line of a job search website to clear up some confusion.

人事專員Penny打電話給一家求職網站的客服，以釐清她的困惑。

Penny – the personnel coordinator 人事專員
Ted – the customer service staff 客服人員

Dialogue

Penny	Hello, I am calling from Green Day. A few days ago, we posted a job opening on your site. Since then, we have received 25 replies. I called some of the applicants, but two people said that they had not responded to our post. I'd like to know what went wrong.	哈囉，我這裡是Green Day。幾天前，我們在你們的網站上貼了一個徵才啟事，在那之後，我們便收到了25個回覆。我打電話給其中一些申請者，但有兩個人說他們並沒有回應我們的啟事。我想知道這當中到底出了什麼差錯。
Ted	In that case, I think it was probably because those applicants did not turn off **automatic** match and active **status**.	若是這樣的話，我想是因為那些申請者並沒有將自動配對和開啟求職身份給關掉。
Penny	What is automatic match?	什麼是自動配對？

Ted	The system automatically selects suitable **candidates** for you, according to your requirements.	系統會根據您的要求，自動為您篩選合適的應徵者。
Penny	What is the active status?	什麼是開啟求職身份？
Ted	It means that that person is still looking for a job. If it shows inactive status, it means that he or she is not looking for a job now.	開啟求職身份則代表該人仍在尋找工作機會。若顯示不開啟求職身份，則代表該人目前沒有在尋找工作機會。
Penny	I see now. Those people should switch their status to inactive, so I don't have to waste time trying to reach them.	我了解了。那些人應該轉為不開啟求職身分才對，那麼一來，我就不用浪費時間連絡他們了。
Ted	Some people are forgetful. It happens **from time to time**.	有些人很健忘。這樣的情況常常發生。
Penny	Thank you.	謝謝。
Ted	You're welcome. Please call us at any time if you have any more questions.	不客氣。若有任何問題，請隨時來電。

★你應該要知道的小小事！

透過人力網站找工作快速又方便，企業徵才時可以多比較，找尋最適合自己公司的方案，有些時候人力網站都會有優惠活動，多比多問就有機會省下一筆開銷哦！如果說職缺開啟之後，人力網站配對的人力重覆性太高或是不符合公司期待，這些問題都可即時反應給人力網站的窗口，請他們協助解決。

Word Bank

clear up　釐清

Could you please explain to clear up what you requested?
可以請你解釋以釐清你所要求的嗎？

confusion　n.　混淆，困惑

I have some confusion about telling from the twins.
我無法分辨這雙胞胎。

automatic　adj.　自動的

The automatic washing machines cost more than conventional ones.
全自動洗衣機售價較傳統的高。

status　n.　身份、狀態

What's your marital status?
你目前的婚姻身分是什麼？

candidate　n.　求職者；候選人

Only one candidate will be chosen for the position.
這個職位只有一位候選人會被選上。

from time to time　不時地

The security walks around the building from time to time to ensure the safety.
保全不時地巡視整棟大樓以確保安全。

In Other Words

The personnel coordinator, Penny, calls the customer service line of a job search website to clear up some confusion.
人事專員Penny打電話給一家求職網站的客服，以釐清她的困惑。

- The personnel coordinator, Penny, calls the customer service line of a job search website to clarify some questions.
  人事專員Penny打電話給一家求職網站的客服，以釐清她的問題。
- Penny, the personnel coordinator, calls the customer service line of a job bank. She wants to know why some applicants claim that they didn't respond to the post.
  人事專員Penny打電話給一家人力銀行的客服。她想要知道為什麼有些應徵者說他們並沒有應徵這一份工作。

The system automatically selects suitable candidates for you, according to your requirements.
系統會根據您的要求，自動為您篩選合適的應徵者。

- The right candidates will be automatically selected by the system to meet your requirements.
  合適的應徵者會被系統自動篩選以符合您的要求。
- According to your requirements, the system will select the suitable applicants and send their resumes to you.
  根據您的要求，系統會自動為您選出合適的應徵者，並將他們的履歷寄給您。

It happens from time to time.
這樣的情況常常發生。

- It happens quite often.
  這樣的情況常常發生。
- That's quite common, and occurs now and then.
  這樣的情況常常發生。

2-4 人力不足

Interviewing a Candidate
面試應徵者

A candidate, Bobby, comes for an interview. Penny asks him to fill out some forms, and Lynn comes in to do the initial interview.

Bobby前來面試，Penny請他填寫表格，然後Lynn進行初次的面試。

Penny – the personnel coordinator 人事專員
Lynn – the personnel manager 人事經理
Bobby – the job candidate 求職應徵者

Dialogue

Penny	Could you fill out the recruitment form and complete the short answers on the second page? I will come back to collect them in fifteen minutes.	可否請你填寫求職表格和完成第二頁的簡答題。十五分鐘後我會過來收。
Bobby	Of course. Thank you.	好的。謝謝。
Penny	Thank you. Please wait a moment. Lynn, the Personnel Manager, will be with you shortly.	謝謝。請稍等。人事經理Lynn馬上就會過來。
Lynn	Hello, I'm Lynn. Here is my card.	哈囉，我是Lynn。這是我的名片。
Bobby	Hello, nice to meet you.	哈囉，幸會。
Lynn	Are you currently **employed**?	你目前仍在就業中嗎？
Bobby	No, I am **unemployed** at the moment.	沒有，我目前待業中。

Lynn	So, how long have you been out of work?	所以，你失業多久了？
Bobby	About three months. I was **laid off** by my former **employer** because of budget cuts.	大約三個月。因為預算削減的原因，我被前任雇主裁員了。
Lynn	Could you tell me a little bit about your **previous** work experience?	可以說說你之前的工作經驗嗎？
Bobby	Yes, after graduating from college I worked at Hello Market as a procurement assistant for two years. That was my first job.	好的，大學畢業後，我在Hello Market工作了兩年。那是我第一份工作。
Lynn	You did not put down an **expected salary**.	你沒有寫希望待遇。
Bobby	I expect to be paid according to the company's salary scale.	依照公司的薪資規定。
Lynn	OK. We will let you know the result as soon as possible, but there may be a second interview.	OK。我們會儘快讓你知道結果，但可能還會有第二次面試。
Bobby	Thank you very much.	非常謝謝您。

Word Bank

initial adj. 最初的

The man becomes very successful and beyond his family's initial expectation.
這男人變得非常成功超乎他家人最初的期待。

employed adj. 就業中

He has been employed for three months.
他已經去工作三個月了。

unemployed adj. 待業中

The workshop is planned for unemployed people.
這研討會是針對失業人士設計的。

laid off 解雇

Many people have been laid off in the past few years.
過去幾年有許多人被解雇。

employer n. 雇主

It is required to build a good relationship between employers and employees.
勞資雙方必須建立好關係。

previous adj. 之前的

Please ignore my previous message and replace with this one.
請勿理會我之前的訊息，並以這次的取代。

expected salary 希望待遇

What's your expected salary for this position?
你對此職位的希望待遇是多少？

In Other Words

Could you fill out the recruitment form and complete the short answers on the second page?
可否請你填寫求職表格和完成第二頁的簡答題。

- Please have the recruitment form filled out and the short answers on the second page completed.
  可否請你填寫求職表格和完成第二頁的簡答題。
- Could you fill in the recruitment form and answer the short answers on the second page?
  可否請你填寫求職表格和回答第二頁的簡答題。

No, I am unemployed at the moment.
沒有，我目前待業中。

- No, I am between jobs currently.
  沒有，我目前待業中。
- No, I am not hired now.
  沒有，我目前待業中。

I was laid off by my former employer because of budget cuts.
因為預算削減的原因，我被前任雇主裁員了。

- My former employer choose to downsize the business, so I got laid off.
  因為前任雇主選擇縮編，所以我被裁員了。
- Due to the budget reduction by my former employer, I've been downsized.
  因為前任雇主預算削減的原因，我被裁員了。

如何聘用到最佳員工？

★僱用比你聰明的人

能夠做到這一點的人，必須要對自己很有自信才行。其實，下屬的表現出色，間接地也代表你是個出色的主管。不要害怕僱用比自己更出色的人，這其實並不困難。

★光是聰明不夠，還要熱情。

僱用個性爽朗且積極的人。

★觀察應徵者的舉止。

先不要開口交談。想知道他/她是個活潑、親切，或是親和力十足的人嗎？先測試一下對方，看他/她是否會主動交談，然後再觀察其口吻、態度、用字遣詞等。

★將心比心的態度。

所謂「己所不欲勿施於人」。你想別人如何對待你，那麼你就要用相同的態度對待別人。

主動出擊尋找人才！

有些公司行號不僅篩選主動應徵的求職者，也會主動去尋找有志之士，特別是主管階層的職位。如何迅速又有效的找到理想人才，下列是幾種方式。

★透過親友、有生意往來的人，或是以前同事的介紹

★請公司員工推薦

★推薦新員工獎勵制度，有些企業為鼓勵員工介紹親朋好友來公司上班，擬定了獎勵方法，如果經員工介紹進來的求職者，在經過公司評估後成為正式職員，員工可以領取獎金，當作鼓勵。

★聯繫以往印象深刻卻未僱用到的求職者，看看他們是否有意願。

★請人脈很廣的合作廠商或是供應商介紹

★被大公司裁員的員工。有些被裁員的員工並非因為自身的錯而被開除，而是原本服務的公司面臨不得不裁員的危機。或許你可以從中找到千里馬。

★建教合作，和高中或大專院校合作，提供實習的機會。

用字篇

! applicant和candidate的差別！

- Applicant（申請者）

  任何看到徵才啟事便主動給予回覆的職務申請者。公司尚未做出篩選或甚至沒注意到的求職申請者。申請的意願取決為自己。

- Candidate（候選人）

  經過公司這一方的最初篩選，但尚未做出最後決定的求職應徵者。取決於公司方。

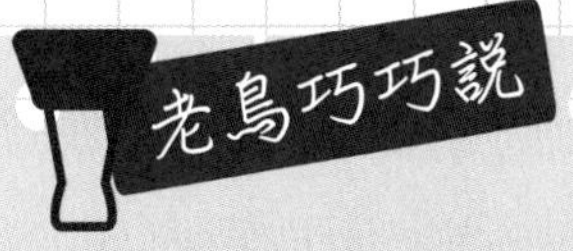

善用人力網站資源

你是不是只有在找工作時才會上人力網站去更新履歷和自傳呢？其實現在人力網站提供了許多實用、即時的資訊報到，三不五時可以上去逛逛增加新知喔！

假設你有換工作的打算，在確認這個想法時，可以先去人力網站上看看相關職缺，他們的條件有哪些？有沒有哪些是你所欠缺的，可以趕緊學習加強，以增加你自己的競爭力。或是你想轉換跑道，你也可以先去看看你需要加強哪方面的專業知識與技能，讓你的轉換能夠更順利。時間就是金錢，除非有計畫要休長假或是進修，能減短工作轉換時間的空窗期，這應該是大家心中共同的想法，多利用網路上這些免費的資源為自己加分吧！

3-1 比價採買

A Copy of a Book for All Employees
人人一本書

Ian asks Carol to purchase a copy of a book for every employee in the company because the president has found the book very useful and helpful.

Ian要Carol為每一位員工添購一本書，因為董事長認為這本書既實用且有幫助。

Carol - the procurement manager 採購經理
Ian - the procurement director 採購協理

Dialogue

Carol	Ian, were you looking for me?	Ian，你剛剛在找我嗎？
Ian	I need you to look for a book and purchase a copy for every employee in the company.	我需要你去找一本書，然後為每一位員工都買一本。
Carol	A book? Why?	一本書？為什麼？
Ian	The president found the book very **worth** reading. <u>He said it could be very useful, helpful, and **inspiring** for us.</u>	董事長發現此書很值得一讀。他說這本書對我們很實用、有幫助且具啟發性。
Carol	What is the title?	書名是什麼？
Ian	It is called The **Key** to **Sustainable** Development, a **translated** book.	書名叫做永續經營的秘訣，是一本翻譯的著作。
Carol	How lovely!	太迷人了！

Ian	Don't **joke**. The president is very serious about it, and we'd better have the books ready by the end of the month.	不要開玩笑。董事長是很認真的，而且我們最好在月底以前將書準備好。
Carol	That's too soon! Ordering and shipping take time, and I'll need to look for the book first.	太趕了吧！訂購和運輸都需要時間，更何況我還得先找書。
Ian	It's the best-selling book this month. You can find it from every bookstore and online shops. The president wishes to **discuss** the book during the next monthly meeting, and he expects us to finish reading it by that time. So, the earlier the books arrive, the more time we have.	這是這個月的最暢銷的書籍。你可以在各家書局或網路商店找到。董事長希望能在下個月的會議中討論此書，他期許我們能在那之前都閱讀完畢。所以，越快買到書，我們就有越充分的時間。
Carol	Alright, I will try my best.	好的，我會盡力。

★你應該要知道的小小事！

一般公司的採購人員的工作內容包括：

1. 根據原物料的庫存量，進行訂購作業。
2. 供應商的開發、拜訪與評核。
3. 供應商資料的建立與更新，以及選擇最佳供應商。
4. 驗收作業，確認貨品的品質與規格。
5. 請款作業及整理相關表單，像是請款單、驗收單、訂購單等。

通常每家公司對其採購程序都會有標準的SOP，新進人員要特別留意的是，在處理金錢的時候，要格外小心謹慎，秉持著公正公平的心態，才能避免不必要的紛爭產生。

Word Bank

worth adj. 值得的

It is worth spending time with your children.
花時間跟你的小孩相處是很值得的。

inspiring adj. 具啟發性的

The movie is very inspiring and encouraging.
這部電影非常有啟發性且激勵人心。

key n. 秘訣

One of the keys to success is working hard.
成功的祕訣之一就是認真工作。

sustainable adj. 能維持的

We expect the sustainable growth in sales can last from now on.
我們希望從現在開始銷售可以持續成長。

translate v. 翻譯

The Bible has been translated in many languages.
聖經已被翻譯成很多語言。

joke vi. 開玩笑

He's only joking.
他只是在開玩笑。

discuss vt. 討論

We need to discuss our future.
我們需要討論一下我們的未來。

In Other Words

He said it could be very useful, helpful, and inspiring for us.
他說這本書對我們很實用、有幫助且具啟發性。

- He said we could be helped and inspired by this useful book.
  他說我們可能會從這本實用書得到幫助和啟發性。
- He mentioned we could be given an advantage of being helped and inspired by this useful book.
  他提到這一本書相當的實用，對我們會有幫助，也具有啟發性。

Don't joke.
不要開玩笑。

- Please take it serious.
  請認真地對待這件事。
- Don't be kidding.
  不要開玩笑。

Ordering and shipping take time, and I'll need to look for the book first.
訂購和運輸都需要時間，更何況我還得先找書。

- It takes time to order and ship, and not to mention that I have to look for the book first.
  訂購和運輸都需要時間，更何況我還得先找書。
- I'll have to find out the book first, and it will take some time to order and deliver.
  我需要先找書，更何況訂購和運輸都需要時間。

3-2 比價採買

Ordering Books in Bulk
大量購書

Carol calls a bookstore and wishes to make a bulk order of a book.

Carol 打電話到書店，想大量訂購一本書。

Carol – procurement manager 採購經理
bookstore clerk – 書局店員

Dialogue

Clerk	Hello, Taipei City Bookstore, how may I help you?	哈囉，Taipei City Bookstore 您好，有什麼可以為您服務的嗎？
Carol	I'd like to make a bulk order of a book.	我想要大量訂購一本書。
Clerk	Could you tell me the title of the book?	可以告訴我書名嗎？
Carol	It's called The Key to Sustainable Development, written by Tim Smith.	書名是《永續經營的秘訣》。作者是Tim Smith。
Clerk	Do you know the **publisher**'s name?	您知道出版社的名字嗎？
Carol	I am not sure, but I think it is **published** by Lantern Books.	我不太確定，但我想它是Lantern Books出版的。
Clerk	One moment, please… Here it is. How many copies would you like to order?	請等一下……找到了。您想要訂購多少數量？

Carol	150 copies. How much discount would you offer me?	150本。你能給我多少的折扣？
Clerk	Would that be the **paperback** or **hardcover version**?	平裝還是精裝版本？
Carol	Paperback.	平裝。
Clerk	Where would you like it shipped? Will it be outside Taipei?	您希望送到哪裡呢？是台北以外的地區嗎？
Carol	No, within Taipei.	不，在台北市內。
Clerk	150 copies in paperback…We can offer you a 40% discount. How does that sound?	150本平裝書…我們可以提供六折的優惠。您意下如何呢？
Carol	Good. I'll place an order. Do you have a fax number? I will fax you our contact information, including the **uniform invoice number**.	很好。我要下單。你有傳真號碼嗎？我會傳真我們的聯絡資料給你，包括統一編號。
Clerk	It's 721-0906. Thank you.	傳真號碼是721-0906。謝謝您。

Word Bank

publisher　n.　出版社

The respected publisher has released thousands of good books in the past years.
這信譽好的出版社近年來已發行上千本好的書籍。

publish　vt.　出版

The English book is published and printed in U.S.A.
這本英文書是在美國出版印製。

paperback　n.　平裝本　adj.　平裝的

The novel is only available in paperback.
這本小說只提供平裝本。

The paperback novel is cheaper.
這本平裝本小說較便宜。

hardcover　n.　精裝書　adj.　精裝本

The novel is only available in hardcover.
這本小說只提供精裝本。

The hardcover novel is more expensive.
這本精裝本小說較昂貴。

version　n.　版本

An updated version of this software is available.
這軟體的更新版本已經出來了。

uniform invoice number n. 統一編號

Do you need a receipt, including the uniform invoice number?
你的收據需要開立統一編號嗎？

In Other Words

I'd like to make a bulk order of a book.
我想要大量訂購一本書。

- I want to place a huge order on a book.
  我想要大量訂購一本書。
- I'd like to order a large quantity on one book.
  我想要大量訂購一本書。

How many copies would you like to order?
您想要訂購多少數量？

- What's the quantity would you like to place an order?
  您想要訂購多少數量？
- How many volumes would you like to order?
  您想要訂購多少本？

We can offer you a 40% discount.
我們可以提供六折的優惠。

- The 40% discount can be offered.
  我們可以提供六折的優惠。
- 40% off is the best discount that I can provide you.
  六折的優惠是我所能提供給您最好的折扣了。

3-3 比價採買

Bulk Quotations
大量訂購估價單

Ian calls a computer store to make a price inquiry on flat panel monitors.

Ian打電話給一間電腦公司，詢問有關平面電腦螢幕的價格。

Ian – procurement director 採購協理
Store Clerk – 店員

Dialogue

Ian	Good morning. This is Ian, the procurement director at Green Day. I'd like to know the price of a Samsung 23-**inch** flat panel monitor.	早安，我是XXX的採購協理Ian。我想知道你們的三星23吋平面電腦螢幕的價格。
Clerk	$5,800. <u>That's the tax-exclusive **rate**.</u>	$5,800，這是不含稅的價格。
Ian	What is the lowest price you can offer if I buy in bulk?	若我大量購買，你們的最低價是多少？
Clerk	How many units would you like to buy?	您想買幾台？
Ian	I'd like 65 monitors.	六十五台。
Clerk	I can give you 25% off. That's the best we offer to any customer.	我可以給您七五折的優惠。這是我們給顧客的最優惠價格了。

Ian	Can't you make an exception for me?	不能為我破個例嗎？
Clerk	Sorry, that's the company policy.	很抱歉，這是公司規定。
Ian	Could you fax me details of prices and **terms of payment**, including **delivery charges**? My fax number is 349-9871.	那可以請你將價格、付費方式，還有運費的細節傳真給我嗎？我的傳真號碼是349-9871。
Clerk	Certainly. Is the delivery address in Taipei?	當然可以。運送地點是在台北嗎？
Ian	Yes. Can I deliver my order to **multiple** addresses?	是的。貨物可以送達至超過一個地點以上嗎？
Clerk	Sorry, we cannot deliver to multiple addresses from the same order. If you wish to deliver monitors to more than one **recipient**, you must fill out a **separate** order for each address.	抱歉，同一份訂單無法送達到多個地點。若您希望將螢幕送達至超過一個以上的接收者，就必須每一個地址填寫一份訂單。
Ian	I see. Forget about that. Please fax me the details as soon as possible.	了解，那就不用了。請儘快將明細傳真給我。
Clerk	I will. Thank you so much.	我會的。感謝您。

★你應該要知道的小小事！

在詢價的過程中，當對方依據你所想要購買的數量，提供估價單給你時，要記得確認該價格是否含稅，假設一個品項單價為600元（稅外），總數量是20，這樣的話，總價應該是600×20×1.05＝12,600。這個部份在你製作成本表要提供給主管檢視時，要特別留意。

Word Bank

inch n. 吋

Apple's iPhone 6 Plus, which has a 5.5-inch display, will be soon on the U.S. market.
蘋果公司具有 5.5 吋螢幕的 iPhone 6 Plus 很快就會在美國上市。

rate n. 價格

What's the room rate per night at this motel range?
這汽車旅館的每晚房價為多少？

terms of payment 付款條件

The terms of payment are required to be listed on the quotations.
報價單上需列出付款條件。

delivery charge 運費

It usually costs more delivery charge for an international package.
國際包裹通常會運費較高。

multiple adj. 多個的

There are multiple-option questions on the test sheet.
這考試卷上有複選題。

recipient n. 接收者

A recipient's signature is required for a registered mail.
掛號信需要收信人簽名。

separate adj. 分開的

Please pack these in separate bags.
請分開包裝。

In Other Words

That's the tax-exclusive rate.
這是不含稅的價格。

- That price excludes tax.
  這價格是不含稅的。
- That price does not include tax.
  這價格是不含稅的。

Can't you make an exception for me?
不能為我破個例嗎？

- Can't I have a special discount?
  不能給我一個特別的折扣嗎？
- I'll appreciate, if you can make an exception for me.
  如果能為我破個例，我會很感激的。

Can I deliver my order to multiple addresses?
貨物可以送達至超過一個地點以上嗎？

- Is that possible to deliver my order to different places?
  可以將我訂的商品送到不一樣的地方嗎？
- Can I have my order be shipped to more than one address?
  貨物可以送達至超過一個地點以上嗎？

3-4 比價採買

Ordering Books in Bulk
大量購書

Ian shows price quotes for the book The Key to Sustainable Development and the flat panel monitors to the president, Mr. Lo. The president is not satisfied with the price of the monitors, so he wants Ian to go back and **bargain** with the supplier.

Ian給董事長羅先生看《永續經營的秘密》這一本書和平面電腦螢幕的報價單。董事長對於螢幕的報價不太滿意，所以他希望伊恩回去向供應商議價。

Ian – procurement director 採購協理
Mr. Lo – President 董事長

Dialogue

Ian	Mr. Lo, what do you think of the book and the flat panel monitor prices?	羅先生，你認為書和螢幕的報價還可以嗎？
Mr. Lo	I am fine with the price of the book, but not that of the flat panel monitors. Did you visit the online stores?	我可以接受書的價格，但無法接受平面電腦螢幕的價格。你有到網路商店查詢價格嗎？
Ian	Yes. I have made inquiries at two **physical stores** and two online stores. This offer was provided from an online store, and its price is the **fairest**.	有的。我分別向兩間實體商店和兩間網路商店詢價。這份報價是由一間網路商店所提供，它的報價是最合理的。
Mr. Lo	The price they suggested is still above our limit. How much discount did they offer us?	他們所建議的價格還是高於我們的底限。他們給我們多少折扣呢？

Ian	30% discount. They said it was the best price they could offer and couldn't possibly go any lower. Prices of larger computer monitors haven't dropped much in the market.	七折。他們說這是最優惠的價格了，不可能更低。在市場上，尺寸較大的電腦螢幕，價格的跌幅都不是很多。
Mr. Lo	But **competition** is **intense**. It's just a matter of time. **Eventually**, the price will drop.	但是市場競爭相當激烈。這只是時間問題，到頭來，價格還是會跌的。
Ian	How about second-hand ones?	那二手貨呢？
Mr. Lo	DO NOT buy used 3C products. The used items will **end up** costing us more money.	不要買用過的3C產品。這些二手產品會讓我們花更多的錢。
Ian	I see. Should I do more shopping?	了解。我是否應該再多看看幾家店？
Mr. Lo	No. Just go back and make a better deal with the online store.	不用了。再回去和那家網路商店議價看看。
Ian	Yes, I will.	是的。

★你應該要知道的小小事！

通常在詢價過後要製作表單，供決策單位做出決定時，可以把握以下幾個原則：

1. 儘量將比價結果數據化、文字簡單化：
   讓決策單位能在最短時間掌握相關資訊。
2. 清楚地將各項比價結果之間的差額列出：
   可利用圖表來呈現差異性。
3. 簡化並整合相關資訊：
   像是後續訂貨的交貨期、配合特殊事項等等。

比價過程中一定會跟對方談到折扣等問題，建議一定要對該品項有明確的了解，像是內容、品質、市場價格，才不容易被騙上當。

Word Bank

bargain vi. 討價還價

The woman is bargaining with the store owner over the price.
這女人正在和老闆討價還價。

physical store 實體商店

Many people still like to visit physical stores.
許多人仍然喜歡逛實體商店。

fairest adj. 公正的，合理的

I expect your fairest comments.
我期待你的公正評論。

competition n. 競爭

Competition in the automobile industry is intense.
汽車市場競爭相當激烈。

intense adj. 激烈的

People today are under intense pressure to survive.
現代人面臨巨大生存壓力。

eventually adv. 到頭來

Eventually, the store manager apologized for the fault.
最後店經理為了這個過失道歉。

end up 最終成為、變成

Due to a persistent effort, she ends up being a famous singer.
由於持續不懈的努力，她最終成為一個有名的歌手。

In Other Words

This offer was provided from an online store, and its price is the fairest.
這份報價是由一間網路商店所提供，它的報價是最合理的。

- The price, which was provided from an online store, is the lowest.
  這份由一間網路商店所提供的報價是最低的。
- The most reasonable price was offered by an online store.
  這份最合理的報價是由一間網路商店所提供的。

The price they suggested is still above our limit.
他們所建議的價格還是高於我們的底限。

- The price they offered is over our budget.
  他們所提供的價格超過我們的預算。
- The offer they provided is above our bottom line.
  他們所提供的價格超過我們的底線。

But competition is intense.
但是市場競爭相當激烈。

- Anyway, the market is in an intense competition.
  但是市場競爭相當激烈。
- However, the market is in an extreme competition.
  但是市場競爭相當激烈。

大量訂購的撇步！

大量訂購對於公司行號來說，是一個省錢的管道。不過呢，大量訂購和單件訂購的原則是相同的，還是必須貨比三家。

★貨比三家

無論是大型的販賣場或是中小型的商店，都要親自前往調查。如果從中找到合適的長期供應商，也是收穫一樁。

★檢查商品的有效期限

市場中難免會有不守規矩或是粗心大意的店家。不要嫌麻煩，每一件物品都要仔細檢查、再三確認。

★計算單件的價格

將店家提供的價格除以所購買的數量，這麼一來才能清楚知道對方給的折扣究竟是多少。有些店家會提供你一個相當漂亮的數字，但當你以單件計算來看，才發現其實根本沒有便宜多少。

★詢問運費

這個部分在詢價時一定要確認清楚，因為運費對廠商來說其實是必要成本，通常超過一定金額以上會免運費。但也是有特例，這也是在議價過程中可以討論的空間。比方說，你可以用妥協的方式，以按照店家所說的折扣，要求店家自行吸收運費的部分。最重要的是運費的部分必須要在議價時就提出並確定，以免事後增加一筆不必的費用開支。

用字篇

! President、Chairman，以及CEO的差異！

- 英漢字典中，有很多單字的解釋常會讓人搞不清楚，而chairman就是其中之一；因為chairman的解釋有很多，除了主席、委員長之外，還包括董事長。而president則較單純，可稱為所謂的董事長（亦可稱之為總裁），也可以是總統了。

- 那麼在企業界中，president、chairman，以及CEO哪一個的權力地位較大呢？一間企業的chairman就是董事會的主席，管理企業的大小事務（董事會中），但不會親自上陣管理企業的實際運作。另外，主席通常是由董事會的成員選拔出來的。

而president（董事長或總裁）呢？就是真正的老大了；是的，權力地位比董事會主席大。不過呢，在目前許多中大型的企業中，很多董事長基本上是不管事的，只掛了個榮譽的頭銜。

那麼CEO（執行長）又是什麼呢？執行長是企業內部的最高階主管，掌管各部門的所有運作。不過呢，CEO不參加董事會，而是直接對主席和董事長負責。

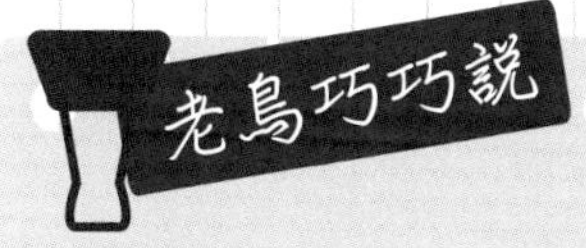

採購工作說分明

想扮演好採購這個角色，首要的就是要對公司的產品有詳細的了解。同一個品項，可能有很多種不統的等級，品質有差，價格當然也會有差別，如何在當中挑出品質和價格都符合公司期待的品項就很重要囉！當採購成本降低，不管是單位成本降0.5元或是1元，對公司來說就是好消息，因為成本降低，表示公司的獲利就會增加，學習如何降低成本，就是採購面臨到最大的課題，建議可以多看一些相關書籍，了解談判技巧，或是多看一些報章雜誌來掌握市場動向。在交涉的過程中，必須一直跟對方溝通，有良好的溝通能力和高EQ對交涉是很有幫助的。最後一個就是具有強烈的道德感，很多廠商為了要爭取訂單，可能會給採購人員回扣，但羊毛還是出在羊身上，這些成本會轉嫁到產品上，如果說萬一東西品質不好、或是報價變高，採購對公司其實都不好交代，所以一定要憑著良心做事，才不會為自己帶來不必要的麻煩。

4-1 內部員工訓練安排

Employee Training Courses 員工訓練課程

Staff members from Personnel are in a meeting to discuss and determine next year's training courses for all employees.

人事部同仁在會議中討論並決定明年員工訓練的課程。

Lynn – personnel manager 人事經理
Wendy – personnel coordinator 人事專員
Sam – personnel coordinator 人事專員

Dialogue

Lynn	Have you collected all the **questionnaires**?	你們回收所有的問卷了嗎？
Wendy	Yes, we have.	是的，我們都收齊了。
Lynn	What are the top four choices with the most votes?	獲得最高票的四個選項是什麼？
Wendy	You might be a little surprised. The top four choices for next year's employee training courses are **Stress Management**, Yoga, English Language, and Aerobic Dance.	你可能會感到一點驚訝。明年員工訓練課程的前四高票是壓力管理、瑜珈、英文，以及有氧舞蹈。
Lynn	Our colleagues seem to care about workplace wellness very much. But we can't have yoga and aerobics courses at the same time because they **resemble** each other.	我們的同仁好像很關心職場健康。但我們無法同時開瑜珈和有氧舞蹈課程，因為它們性質很類似。

Sam	Yoga improve physical, **mental**, and **spiritual** health.	瑜珈可以改善生理、心理及心靈方面的健康。
Lynn	I agree. I think we need to **cross out** stress management, too. Yoga helps **resolve** stress.	我同意。我想我們應該將壓力管理刪掉才對。瑜珈有助於消除壓力。
Wendy	So, Stress Management and Aerobic Dance are out. Now we need to choose two other courses. What do you suggest?	所以，壓力管理和有氧舞蹈已經被刪去了。現在我們需要選擇兩種其他課程。你有什麼建議嗎？
Lynn	I think each of you should suggest one.	你們何不一人建議一項？
Sam	I want to suggest Communication Skills.	我想建議溝通技巧。
Wendy	For me, Time Management.	至於我，時間管理。
Lynn	Good choices. So, here are the four courses we will have for next year's employee training: Yoga, English Language, Communication Skills, and Time Management.	很好的選擇。所以，現在我們已經有明年度的四種員工訓練課程了–瑜珈、英文、溝通技巧還有時間管理。

★你應該要知道的小小事！

比較有規模的公司為了培養優秀的人力，除了在新人報到時會有新人訓練課程幫助他們早一點適應該職場，針對全公司的員工，也會固定安排一些員工訓練，來幫助員工提升自己的能力，內容可能包括讀書會、演講、外訓課程等等，也會依在公司的職別不同而有不同的訓練課程，建議可以多多把握這樣的機會，充實自己。

questionnaire n. 問卷

I received a questionnaire about the customer service.
我收到有關一份客户服務的問卷。

stress management 壓力管理

Stress management is one key to success.
壓力管理是成功的一個關鍵。

resemble vt. 類似

She so resembles her mother.
她長得很像她的母親。

mental adj. 心理的

Doing exercises can bring mental health.
做運動可使心理健康。

spiritual adj. 心靈的

The topic of speech is regarding spiritual issues.
這演講是有關心靈議題。

cross out 去除

I cross out the item from the shopping list after I put it in the shopping cart.
當我把東西放到購物車後，我就從購物清單刪除該項目。

resolve vt. 消除

His answer resolved our confusion.
他的回答消除了我們的困惑。

In Other Words

Our colleagues seem to care about workplace wellness very much.
我們的同仁好像很關心職場健康。

- It seems that our colleagues are concerned about workplace wellness very much.
  這樣看起來，我們的同仁似乎都很關心職場健康。
- It looks that our coworkers are interested in workplace wellness very much.
  這樣看來，我們的同仁對職場健康很感興趣。

But we can't have yoga and aerobics courses at the same time because they resemble each other.
但我們無法同時開瑜珈和有氧舞蹈課程，因為它們性質很類似。

- We don't think that we should have yoga and aerobics courses at the same time, because they are quite the same.
  我們不認為我們應該同時開瑜珈和有氧舞蹈課程，因為它們性質非常相近。
- Due to the similarity, we can't have yoga and aerobics courses at the same time.
  我們無法同時開瑜珈和有氧舞蹈課程，因為它們性質很類似。

Yoga helps resolve stress.
瑜珈有助於消除壓力。

- Yoga helps to de-stress.
  瑜珈有助於舒壓。
- By doing Yoga, it helps to relieve stress.
  做瑜珈有助於消除壓力。

4-2 內部員工訓練安排

Looking for an English Teacher
找英文教師

Wendy calls an English teacher agency to look for a suitable English teacher.
Wendy打電話給英文教師仲介公司，尋找一位合適的英文教師。

Wendy – personnel coordinator 人事專員
Paul – receptionist 總機接待

Dialogue

Paul	Hello, Taipei English Teacher **Agency**. How may I help you?	您好，這裡是Taipei English Teacher Agency。有什麼我能效勞的嗎？
Wendy	This is Wendy, calling from Green Day. I am looking for a **native** English speaking teacher to teach business English in our company.	您好，我是Wendy。我想找一位以母語為英語的英文教師，來我們公司教授商業英語。
Paul	Could you please describe your needs and requirements **specifically**?	可否請您明確地敘述您的需求和條件？
Wendy	We'd like the teacher to teach a group of 40 people three times a week from 7–9 P.M. Classes will be held in our meeting room.	我們希望有一個老師，一週三次，一次40個學生，從晚間七點到九點，上課地點在我們的辦公室。
Paul	Do you need us to design a **curriculum** for you?	需要我們為您們設計課程嗎？

Wendy	Yes, of course.	當然需要。
Paul	Allow me to explain. Each company has its own language goals for their staff, and we will need to discuss your **goals in order to** design a suitable curriculum.	請容我解釋一下。每一間公司都有自己對旗下員工的語言目標，我們必須和你們先討論過後，才能設計合適的課程。
Wendy	So, what are we supposed to do now?	那我們現在應該怎麼做？
Paul	We will send someone to your office to discuss the job requirements with you first, and then we will find an experienced and **qualified** teacher for you.	我們會先派人去公司和你們討論，然後我們會為您們找一名有經驗且合格的教師。
Wendy	That sounds good. Let's do that.	聽起來不錯，就這麼辦吧

★你應該要知道的小小事！

由於目前與國外廠商合作的機會增加，英語在商務溝通上變得也相對的重要，為了要掌握先機，很多企業會對內部的員工進行英語訓練，有的公司還會希望同仁能夠考取相關的英語證照，來提升公司員工內部的素質。在安排這類課程的時候，可以找一些比較有公信力的英語補習班，詢問他們外派師資授課的相關細節與費用，並讓對方了解公司的屬性以及同仁在實務面上比較常遇到的狀況，當作授課的主題，這樣不但比較容易引起同仁學習的興趣，學習效果也會比較好。

Word Bank

agency n. 仲介

The travel agencies are very busy in the summer season.
旅行社在夏天非忙碌。

native adj. 本國的

Mark is excellent in English because he is a native speaker.
Mark 英文很強，因為英文是他的母語。

specifically adv. 明確地

The marketing manager proposed his strategy specifically.
行銷部經理很明確地提出他的策略。

curriculum n. 課程

English is the essential part of the school curriculum.
英文是學校課程的主要項目。

goal n. 目標

I am a goal-oriented person.
我是一個以目標為導向的人。

in order to 為了

My sister saves a lot of money in order to study overseas.
我姐姐存很多錢為了要出國念書。

qualified adj. 合格的

The Human Resource Department is looking for some qualified candidates for interviews.
人力資源部正尋找許多合格的候選人來面談。

In Other Words

I am looking for a native English speaking teacher to teach business English in our company.
我想找一位以母語為英語的英文教師，來我們公司教授商業英語。

- I am seeking an English teacher, who is a native English speaker, to teach business English in our company.
  我想找一位以母語為英語的英文教師，來我們公司教授商業英語。
- Our company needs a native speaker of English to teach business English.
  我們公司需要一位英語的母語人是來教商業英文。

Could you please describe your needs and requirements specifically?
可否請您明確地敘述您的需求和條件？

- Could you please clarify your needs and requirements?
  可否請您明確地敘述您的需求和條件？
- Would you please specify your needs and requirements in more detail?
  您是否可以明確地敘述您的需求和條件？

So, what are we supposed to do now?
那我們現在應該怎麼做？

- What should we do then?
  那我們現在應該怎麼做？
- So, what do we have to do next?
  那我們接下來應該怎麼做？

4-3 內部員工訓練安排

Booking the Whole Club
包下整間俱樂部

Sam wishes to book the whole country club for the yoga course.
為了瑜珈課程，山姆想包下整間鄉村俱樂部。

Sam – personnel coordinator 人事專員
Cindy – receptionist 總機接待

Dialogue

Cindy	Rainbow **Country Club**, how may I help you?	Rainbow Country Club，有什麼我可以效勞的地方？
Sam	Yes, we want to book the whole club for our company's employee training. Do you normally do that?	是的，我們想包下整間俱樂部進行公司員工訓練。請問你們平常會這麼做嗎？
Cindy	Yes, we accept whole-facility booking. I must inform you that a **minimum fee** per night applies to the whole-facility booking, but the use of **central** hall and kitchen is included.	是的，我們接受包場的預約。我必須先跟您説明，每晚包場的預約有最低收費的限制，但中央大廳和廚房的使用包括在裡面。
Sam	That is fine.	好的。
Cindy	We provide full **catering**, but self-catering is also welcoming in our kitchen facilities.	我們提供完善的飲食和服務，若想自行準備，也歡迎您們使用我們的廚房設備。

Sam	That is good to know. With no doubts, I am sure we will be having your catering service.	謝謝您的說明。無庸置疑地，我確定我們會需要你們的餐飲服務。
Cindy	Certainly. Our maximum **capacity** is about for 200 people. May I know that how many people will you have?	好的。我們最多一次能容納約200人左右。我可以知道您們的人數有多少呢？
Sam	150 or more.	150人以上。
Cindy	How long would you like to stay with us?	您們要住多久？
Sam	Two days.	兩天一夜。
Cindy	And when will that be?	什麼時候呢？
Sam	May first and second next year.	明年的五月一日至二日。
Cindy	Oh, no. The **entire** month of May next year is available except the 1.	喔，不。明年五月一整個月都是可以的，除了一號之外。
Sam	In that case, I will have to get to back to you later.	那樣的話，我必須等會兒再回覆你。
Cindy	Certainly. <u>I **look forward to** hearing from you.</u>	當然。期待您的回覆。

★你應該要知道的小小事！

公司外部的場地租借，通常要考量的就是預算和交通問題，像會話當中提到的體育活動，如果需要這類型的場地，可以先詢問學校或是公家的運動中心，費用通常比較低，預算有高一點的話，也可以考慮到俱樂部或是渡假村舉辦，設備和服務也會比較好一點。還有像那種兩天一夜的會議研習，可以詢問商務飯店，通常它們會有那種會議專案（含會議室的使用和住宿），在會議中也會提供餐點服務，如果預算是OK，這種配套專案還滿方便的。

country club　鄉村俱樂部

I really enjoy having a vacation at a country club.
我很喜歡在鄉村俱樂部度假。

minimum fee　最低收費

There is a minimum fee per customer in this restaurant.
這餐廳有個人最低消費。

central adj.　中央的

The city hall is located in the central part of the city.
市政府位在市中心。

catering　n.　提供飲食及服務

The catering service is very convenient to people today.
承辦酒席的服務對現代人非常方便。

capacity　n.　人數

The conference room has a seating capacity for about 100.
這會議室可容納超過 100 人的座位。

entire　adj.　整個的、全部的

It took me an entire year to finish this project.
我花了一整年完成此計畫案。

look forward to　期待

I look forward to seeing you soon
我期待很快和你見面。

In Other Words

We want to book the whole club for our company's employee training.
我們想包下整間俱樂部進行公司員工訓練。

- We would like to reserve the whole club for our company's employee training.
  我們想預定整間俱樂部進行公司員工訓練。
- For the company's employee training, we would like to make a reservation of the entire club.
  我們想預定整間俱樂部進行公司員工訓練。

May I know that how many people will you have?
我可以知道您們的人數有多少呢？

- Is that possible for you to give me a certain number of the participants?
  是否有可能可以 我　加　的确切人 呢？
- Could you please tell me that how many people for the training?
  能否告知貴公司員工訓練的人數有多少人呢？

I look forward to hearing from you.
期待您的回覆。

- I expect your response soon.
  期待您的回覆。
- I look forward to your reply soon.
  期待您的回覆。

4-4 內部員工訓練安排

The Class is Overbooked
課堂爆滿

Lynn instructs Wendy and Sam to make an announcement concerning the English class.

Lynn交代Wendy和Sam公布英文課的相關資訊。

Lynn – personnel manager 人事經理
Wendy – personnel coordinator 人事專員
Sam – personnel coordinator 人事專員

Dialogue

Lynn	<u>Is the schedule for the English class **finalized**?</u>	英文課的行程定案了嗎？
Sam	Yes. Every Tuesday, Wednesday, and Thursday, from 7–9 P.M.	是的。每星期二、三、四，從晚上7點到9點。
Wendy	Three **consecutive** days?	連續三天？
Sam	Nobody wants to have a class on Monday or Friday nights.	沒有人會想要在星期一或星期五晚上上課。
Lynn	It doesn't matter. There will be different students for each day, anyway. **Speaking of which**, has everyone decided on the day they want?	無所謂。反正每一天的學生都不同。說到這裡，每個人都決定好日子了嗎？

Sam	There is a problem. Tuesday night is **overbooked,** while only twenty people have **signed up** for Wednesday night.	有一個問題。星期二晚上太多人預約了，而星期三卻只有20個人報名。
Wendy	Why is that? Having a class on Wednesday is not so bad!	怎麼會這樣？星期三晚上上課也不錯啊！
Sam	I guess not everyone prefers to have a class on Wednesday night. It's a **weekend Wednesday**.	我想不是每個人都喜歡在星期三晚上上課吧！這可是小週末呢。
Wendy	But each class is limited to 50 people. What are we going to go with that?	但是每堂課不能超過50個人，我們該怎麼辦呢？
Sam	We've got to **persuade** people to sign up for Wednesday and Thursday nights.	我們得說服大家報名星期三和星期四的課。
Lynn	Well, I will talk to each department's manager to see whether they can talk people out of booking the same class, and then you can make an announcement.	嗯，我會和各部門經理談一談，看他們是否能說服大家不要都報名同一堂課，然後你們就能發公告了。

★你應該要知道的小小事！

在安排內部員訓的時候，留意以下細節，會讓整個員訓更順利哦！

時間：時間點的安排盡量避開旺季，避免同仁太過勞累。

地點：先確認參與人數，以方便安排適當的會議室來進行員訓。

配套措施：如果安排在下班時間，可以準備小點心或簡單的晚餐，不要讓同仁餓肚子。

意見回函：請同仁協助填寫意見回函，檢視此次活動的成效，也可做為之後的參考。

Word Bank

finalize　vt.　完成；定案

Eventually, the business plan is finalized.
這企劃案終於定案了。

consecutive　adj.　連續不斷的

We have training courses for three consecutive weeks.
我們連續三週都有受訓課程。

speaking of which　說到這裡

Speaking of which, do you need my help?
說到這裡，你需要我幫忙嗎？

overbooked　adj.　預訂超過席位的，爆滿的

The flight seats are always overbooked during summer seasons.
夏季時機位總是爆滿。

sign up　報名

You have to sign up as a new member to log in the website.
你需要先註冊為新會員才能登入網站。

weekend Wednesday　小週末

I feel more relaxed on weekend Wednesday.
我在小週末時會覺得較輕鬆。

persuade　vt.　說服

The sales person persuades the customers into buying the newest products.
這銷售員說服客人購買最新產品。

In Other Words

Is the schedule for the English class finalized?
英文課的行程定案了嗎？

- Is the schedule for the English class set?
  英文課的行程定案了嗎？
- How about the schedule for the English class, is it arranged?
  英文課的行程安排好了嗎？

Tuesday night is overbooked, while only twenty people have signed up for Wednesday night.
星期二晚上太多人預約了，而星期三卻只有20個人報名。

- The reservation for Tuesday night exceeds the limit, while the registration number for Wednesday night is only twenty.
  星期二晚上的預約超過限額了，而星期三報名人數卻只有20個人。
- There are too many people booked for Tuesday night; however, there are only twenty people signed up for Wednesday night.
  星期二晚上的預約人數超過限額了，而星期三卻只有20個人報名。

But each class is limited to 50 people.
但是每堂課不能超過50個人。

- But the maximum class size is 50 people.
  但是每堂課最多只能有50個人。
- However, there is a limitation of 50 people for each class.
  然而每堂課不能超過50個人。

員工訓練小撇步！

訓練有素的員工是促進公司發展、進步的關鍵之一。有研究指出，生產力高的員工往往都是那些好學的員工。員工訓練的目的不只是增強員工的技能和擴展其知識領域，也是企業主向員工證明其愛惜人才的一片心意。

★強調訓練如同投資

訓練需要花錢，但就長遠的眼光來看，它能創造的利益會遠遠地超越所支出的費用。買新的設備很快，但是培養人力則需要時間的累積，當公司的人力優於其他企業時，公司的競爭力自然就高。

★決定需求

要將經費、時間發揮到最大的效益，必須先釐清最重要的需求是什麼。

★培養辦公室學習文化

當公司將學習成長、永續經營變成企業精神，很自然地就能在企業內營造出一種學習的氛圍，企業內的員工就會相互影響，激勵彼此學習，企業才能一直充滿活力。

★主管階層必須以身作則

主管的態度和接受度會直接影響旗下同仁。

★結果評量

訓練完後，一定要徹底且清楚地衡量員工（業績和表現）究竟成長了多少，不然訓練課程會失去其意義。

★獎勵制度

針對同仁工作所需的考試或是證照，像GEPT/NEW TOEIC考試有通過某一個程度的資格檢定或是考取工作所需的專業證照，可以發給獎金予以獎勵，以帶動同仁對自我專業技能的提升。

★補助申請

除了公司所舉辦的員訓之外，同仁如果想利用假日進修，參與一些專業訓練課程或是演講，公司可以提供部分的補助，以實際的行動支持同仁，也鼓勵大家多多參與。

員工健康的重要性！

員工是一家企業最為重要的資產，健康的員工才能充分將其能力表現出來。

★健康的員工不常生病。
★健康的員工擁有活力。
★健康的員工散發自信、抗壓性較高。
★健康的員工激發、鼓舞他人。
★健康的員工具有領導的潛力、較能激發團隊精神。
★健康的員工擁有良好的態度、注意力較集中。

五花八門的員工訓練

公司的員訓很多元化，可以分成以下幾類：

1. 部門讀書會－固定活動，鼓勵各部門挑選適合部門工作面的書籍進行閱讀及討論，以增進各部門的實力。
2. 講座－每年會規劃幾場的座談會，內容除了安排與該產業工作相關的演講之外，也有心靈講座，希望透過這類的內容，可以幫助員工排解工作壓力，讓員工的工作效率提高。
3. 外訓課程－這類活動通常參與的是主管階級的人，外面有一些比較具有公信力的機構不定期會舉辦類似的課程，因為課程主題的關係，會安排公司主管參加，也能夠與同業甚至是不同領域的專業人士做交流。
4. 內部考試－固定時間舉辦內部考試，做為晉升的標準，也是一種鼓勵同仁提升自我能力的方法。

12:30 PM

PART 4

Secretary 秘書

*Unit 01　客户拜訪

*Unit 02　會議行程安排

*Unit 03　老闆出差

*Unit 04　老闆交辦的事務處理

1-1 客戶拜訪

Greeting an Office Visitor
招待來訪的訪客

A visitor comes to see the general manager, but he is not in. The general manager's secretary, Stacy, greets the visitor.

訪客來拜訪經理，但經理不在。經理的秘書Stacy招待訪客。

Stacy – secretary 秘書
Mr. Chen – visitor 訪客

Dialogue

Stacy	Sir, how may I help you?	先生，有什麼可以效勞的地方嗎？
Visitor	I am Jackie Chen from Lily's Club. I have an **appointment** with Mr. Tsai at 1:30.	我　是Lily's Club的Jackie陳。我一點半和蔡總有約。
Stacy	Oh, yes. Please have a seat, Mr. Chen.	是的。陳先生，請坐。
Visitor	Thank you.	謝謝。
Stacy	I'm very sorry to tell you that our manager, Mr. Tsai, is not in the office right now.	很抱歉，蔡總目前人不在辦公室。
Visitor	But we just talked on the phone this morning. He knew I was coming to see him.	但我們今早才通過電話，他知道我要來拜訪他。

Stacy	Yes, he did. He had an **emergency**; his car got **towed away** while he was having lunch.	是的，他知道。但事發突然，他中午外出用餐時，車子被拖走了。
Visitor	How **unfortunate**! Where did he **park** his car?	真倒霉！他車子停在哪？
Stacy	He parked it on a **red line**.	他把車停在紅線上。
Visitor	Well, he shouldn't do that. When will he be back?	天啊，他不應該那樣做的。他什麼時候會回來？
Stacy	He just called five minutes before you arrived. He wanted to **apologize** to you and said that he would be back in fifteen minutes, and could you wait for him?	他五分鐘前才打過電話。他想跟您道歉，他在十五分鐘之內就會回來，您可以等他嗎？
Visitor	Sure.	當然。
Stacy	Could I get you some coffee?	要來點咖啡嗎？
Visitor	No, just water please.	不，水就可以了。

★你應該要知道的小小事！

身為老闆的好幫手，秘書要隨時隨地懂得變通：

如果老闆因上一個行程delay，影響到接下來的行程，秘書要趕緊通知接下來的訪客，如果來不及的話，要記得在訪客抵達公司時，要先婉轉地跟訪客說明原因，老闆可能會晚一點進來，請對方耐心等候。

如果老闆“不小心”忘記某個約會，人根本不在公司，也因為行程的關係趕不回來，這時身為秘書的你千萬要沉著面對，編一個好一點的理由跟訪客說明，讓對方能夠諒解。如果對方只是單純的例行性來訪，可以看看是否有些相關資料由你轉交給老闆，但如果對方有一些工作上的事情必須跟老闆親自洽談，那就要客氣地跟對方約下次的時間，並再次致上歉意。

appointment n. 約會

I have an appointment with my dentist tomorrow.
我明天跟牙醫有預約。

emergency n. 突發事件

It is very important to learn how to deal with an emergency matter.
學習如何處理突發事件是非常重要的。

tow away 被拖走了

Steve called someone to tow away his broken-down car.
Steve 打電話請人來拖走他的故障車。

unfortunate adj. 倒霉的

It was unfortunate that we got stuck in the traffic jam.
我們很倒楣卡在塞車中。

park v. 停車

Your car will be towed away if you park it at a prohibited area.
如果你將車停在禁停區域，你的車會被吊走。

red line 紅線（全日禁止停車的標線）

All the red line zones are not allowed for parking cars.
所有區域都不可以停車。

apologize vi. 道歉

I would like to apologize for my fault.
我要為我的錯誤道歉。

In Other Words

The general manager's secretary, Stacy, greets the visitor.
經理的秘書 Stacy 招待訪客。

- The general manager's secretary, Stacy, welcomes the visitor.
  經理的秘書 Stacy 歡迎訪客。
- Stacy, the general manager's secretary, receives the visitor.
  經理的秘書 Stacy 接待訪客。

He wanted to apologize to you and said that he would be back in fifteen minutes, and could you wait for him?
他想跟您道歉，他在十五分鐘之內就會回來，您可以等他嗎？

- He would like to make an apology to you first and asked if you could wait for him and he promised that he would be back in fifteen minutes.
  他想先跟您致歉，他問您是否能等他一下，他保證會在十五分鐘之內回來。
- He would like to say sorry to you and said that he would be back within fifteen minutes, and could you please wait for him?
  他想跟您道歉，他在十五分鐘之內就會回來，您可以等他嗎？

Could I get you some coffee?
要來點咖啡嗎？

- Would you like some coffee?
  要來點咖啡嗎？
- Would you like to have something to drink?
  您要喝點什麼嗎？

1-2 客戶拜訪

Making an Appointment on the Phone
電話上預約會面

The secretary, Stacy, receives a call from someone wanting to make an appointment to see the general manager.

秘書史黛西接到一通某人想和總經理預約會面的電話。

Stacy - secretary 秘書
Mr. Lin - caller 來電者

Dialogue

Stacy	General Manager's Office. How may I help you?	總經理室，請問有可以效勞的地方嗎？
Mr. Lin	Hello. This is Timmy Lin from DTC, and **ISO certified** company. We make fragrance oils. We would like to make an appointment with Mr. Tsai.	您好，我是DTC的提米・林，是一家通過ISO認證的公司代表。我們生產相經由。我們想跟貴公司合作。所以我想約個時間跟蔡先生見面。
Stacy	Please wait for a minute. Let me check Mr. Tsai's **schedule**. Well, Mr. Lin, how about next Tuesday at 11 A.M.?	請稍等一下，讓我確認一下蔡先生的行程表。嗯，林先生，那下週二早上11點可以嗎？
Mr. Lin	Can we do it sometime this week? I only need twenty minutes.	我們可以約這個星期嗎？我只需要20分鐘。
Stacy	Sorry about that, but Mr. Tsai's schedule is already full this week.	真的很抱歉，但是蔡先生這週的行程都已經排滿了。

Mr. Lin	All right. Next Tuesday at 11 A.M. will fine.	好的。下星期二早上11點我可以。
Stacy	Could you please give me your name and phone number?	可以請您給我您的大名和電話嗎？
Mr. Lin	Of course. My name is Timmy Lin, T-i-m-m-y L-i-n. My phone number is 2596-4856, and my **extension** is 201.	沒問題。我的名字是Timmy林，T-i-m-m-y L-i-n。我的電話是2596-4856，分機號碼是201。
Stacy	OK. I've written them down. Mr. Lin, could you please send me a **catalog** and the **profile** of your company before next Tuesday? So, Mr. Tsai can get a snapshot of your company before the appointment.	好的，我已經寫下來了。林先生，可以請您在下週二前將型錄及您公司的簡介寄給我嗎？這樣的話，蔡先生在碰面之前能先對您的公司有大概的了解。
Mr. Lin	Sure. Could you give me your e-mail address, please?	當然。您可以給我您的e-mail地址嗎？
Stacy	My e-mail address is stacy.chang@greenday.com.tw.	我的e-mail地址是stacy.chang@greenday.com.tw。
Mr. Lin	OK. I will e-mail the related information to you right away. Thank you for your help.	好的，我將馬上把相關的資訊寄給您。謝謝您的幫忙。
Stacy	You're welcome. See you next Tuesday.	不客氣。那下週二見。

Word Bank

ISO (International Organization for Standardization)　國際標準組織

All our products meet the ISO certification.
我們所有產品符合 ISO 認證。

certified　adj.　被證明的

The financial statements are audited by a certified public accountant.
這財務報告是由一個認證會計師所審核的。

schedule　n.　行程表

I have a tight schedule next Monday.
我下週行程很滿。

extension　n.　分機

This is my direct line, and I have no extension number.
這是我的專線，沒有分機號碼。

catalog　n.　型錄

The paper catalogs are replaced by e-catalog gradually.
紙本目錄漸漸被電子目錄取代。

profile　n.　簡介

I post a job profile on the job bank.
我在人力銀行放上我的工作簡介。

In Other Words

Let me check Mr. Tsai's schedule.
讓我確認一下蔡先生的行程表。

- Let me have a look at Mr. Tsai's planned time.
  讓我確認一下蔡先生的行程表。
- I'll check the schedule of Mr. Tsai for you.
  我將為您查看一下蔡先生的行程表。

Sorry about that, but Mr. Tsai's schedule is already full this week.
真的很抱歉，但是蔡先生這週的行程都已經排滿了。

- Sorry about that, but Mr. Tsai's schedule is very tight this week.
  真的很抱歉，但是蔡先生這週的行程很緊湊。
- I'm apologized that Mr. Tsai has a very tight schedule this week.
  我很抱歉蔡先生這週的行程十分地緊湊。

So, Mr. Tsai can get a snapshot of your company before the appointment.
這樣的話，蔡先生在碰面之前能先對您的公司有大概的了解。

- So, Mr. Tsai can preview roughly about your company profile before the appointment.
  這樣的話，蔡先生在碰面前能先預覽您的公司資料。
- And, Mr. Tsai can get a general understanding of your company before the appointment.
  這樣的話，蔡先生在碰面之前能先對您的公司有大概的了解。

1-3 客戶拜訪

Changing an Appointment On the Phone
電話上更改會面時間

The secretary, Stacy, receives a call requesting to change an appointment.
秘書 Stacy 接到一通想更改會面時間的電話。

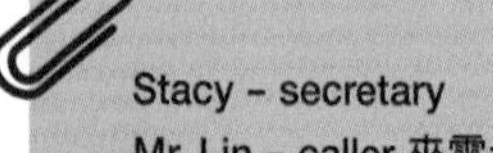

Stacy - secretary
Mr. Lin - caller 來電者

Dialogue

Stacy	General Manager's office, what can I do for you?	總經理辦公室，請問有可以為您效勞的地方嗎？
Mr. Lin	Hello, this is Timmy Lin calling from DTC. I've scheduled an appointment to see Mr. Tsai next Tuesday at 11 A.M., but I couldn't get a **high speed rail** ticket because there were some faults in the **electronic ticketing system**. So I won't be able to make it.	哈囉，我是DTC的提米・林。我之前預約了下星期二早上11點與蔡先生見面，但我買不到高鐵車票，因為電子售票系統有問題。所以我無法赴約。
Stacy	Would you like to cancel or **reschedule** your appointment?	您想取消或是重新安排會面呢？
Mr. Lin	I'd like to reschedule for another time. May I come to visit Mr. Tsai next Thursday?	我想當然是重新安排另一個時間。我可以下星期四拜訪蔡先生嗎？

Stacy	Let me see. Erm, yes, Mr. Tsai is available next Thursday. What time would be **convenient** for you?	我看一下。嗯，沒問題，蔡先生下星期四有空。您何時方便呢？
Mr. Lin	Any time in the afternoon is fine for me.	下午的任何時間都可以。
Stacy	How about 2 P.M.?	兩點鐘可以嗎？
Mr. Lin	Yes, 2 P.M. is fine. Thank you very much. And I'm very sorry for the **inconvenience**.	兩點鐘可以。非常謝謝你。為你帶來不便真是不好意思。
Stacy	That's okay, and I'll see you next Thursday. Thank you for calling.	不用客氣。那下星期四見了。謝謝您的來電。

★你應該要知道的小小事！

如果遇到跟廠商／客戶約好要碰面，但有事得取消，一定要記得盡早告知對方，避免擔誤對方處理公事的時間。另外，雖然智慧型手機愈來愈普遍，APP和Line也都是大家會使用的軟體，又快又方便，在公事上的連絡，尤其是要約開會、取消開會的這種事情，還是親自打電話跟對方連絡比較好，感覺比較正式。秘書在接到更改會議的通知之後，要記得馬上在行事曆上註明，這樣才有辦法能提供老闆最新的資訊，千萬不要想說等等再記，如果不小心忘了的話，有可能會讓一連串的行程都受到影響。

★你應該要知道的小小事！

reschedule = re + schedule

字首"re"：再一次

schedule：當名詞的時候，可以當計劃表、行程表、清單、報表，當做動詞的時候，就是將…列入清單、將…列入計畫或是時間表。Schedule management就是進度管理，這個也是工作上會用到的詞。

Word Bank

high speed rail 高鐵

I plan to visit my friend by high speed rail next month.
我計畫下個月搭高鐵去找我朋友。

electronic adj. 電子的

Personal electronic devices have been very popular in the past few years.
最近幾年個人電子設備非常受歡迎。

ticketing n. 售票系統

Most travel agencies are using electronic ticketing now.
現在大部分的旅行社都使用電子售票系統。

cancel vt. 取消

The outdoor concert was cancelled due to the heavy rain.
户外音樂會因為大雨取消了。

reschedule v. 重新安排

The meeting is rescheduled to next Monday.
這會議改期到下星期一。

convenient adj. 方便的

There are a lot of convenient stores located in the central of the city.
位在市中心有很多便利商店。

inconvenience n. 不方便

I am sorry for any inconvenience caused.
很抱歉造成不便

In Other Words

I've scheduled an appointment to see Mr. Tsai next Tuesday at 11 A.M.
我之前預約了下星期二早上11點與蔡先生見面。

- I have made an appointment with Mr. Tsai next Tuesday at 11 A.M.
  我之前預約了下星期二早上11點與蔡先生見面。
- I have an appointment with Mr. Tsai next Tuesday at 11 A.M.
  我下星期二早上11點預定要與蔡先生見面。

Would you like to cancel or reschedule your appointment?
您想取消或是重新安排會面呢？

- Would you like your appointment cancelled or rescheduled?
  您預定的會面時間是要取消或是重新安排呢？
- Would you like your appointment called off or rearranged?
  您想要取消預定的會面時間或是另做安排呢？

What time would be convenient for you?
您何時方便呢？

- What is your convenient time?
  您何時方便呢？
- What is the best time for you?
  您何時方便呢？

1-4 客戶拜訪

Meeting Reminder
會議提醒

Mr. Tsai asks his secretary to remind him of an important meeting.
蔡先生指示秘書提醒他一個重要的會議。

Stacy - secretary 秘書
Mr. Tsai - general manager 總經理

Dialogue

Mr. Tsai	Mr. Su is coming to see me on at 10 A.M. this Friday. Remember to **remind** me **prior** to the appointment.	蘇先生這個星期五早上10點會來找我，記得在會面之前要提醒我。
Stacy	But you have to host a conference on Friday morning. Mr. Lo will be present in the conference.	可是您星期五早上要主持一個會議。羅先生會出席該會議的。
Mr. Tsai	Oh, my! I totally forgot about it. How could I ever forget about the meeting with our boss?	天啊！我完全忘了。我怎麼能忘了和老闆開會的事呢？
Stacy	Well, you've been **occupied** with other things. So, what should I do about Mr. Su's appointment?	您太忙了。所以，與蘇先生的會面我該如何處理？
Mr. Tsai	Why don't you call Mr. Su and see if he could see me at a different time? Ask him to come on Thursday, if possible.	你不妨打給蘇先生，看看他是否可以在其他時間來見我。若可以的話，請他星期四過來。

Stacy	I'll do that, but let me remind you that you have an appointment on Thursday in the afternoon with Mr. Lin.	我會的，但讓我提醒您星期四的下午，您和林先生有預約。
Mr. Tsai	Who is Mr. Lin?	林先生是哪位？
Stacy	Mr. Lin is from DTC, a company that **manufactures** fragrance oils. They want to know if there is a chance to cooperate with us.	陳先生是DTC的人，一間製造香精油的公司，他們想知道是否有和我們合作的機會。
Mr. Tsai	Any more **details**?	有更多的細節嗎？
Stacy	I have put the profile of DTC, the **up-to-date** catalog and Mr. Lin's **proposal** on your desk.	我已經將DTC的簡介、及最新的型錄和林先生的企劃書放在您的桌上了。
Mr. Tsai	Very good, thank you.	很好，謝謝。

★你應該要知道的小小事！

Office 軟體中的Outlook除了可以用來做信件管理，還可以用來提醒自己什麼時候有什麼會議要開、有什麼重要事項要處理，非常方便。拜科技之賜，智慧型手機問世，也為現代人的生活帶來許多的便利性，網路上有很多應用軟體，都可以用來做提醒，可以將重要事項輸入（對象、主題、時間、地點等等），還可以設鬧鈴提醒，看需要在事件發生前多久發出鈴響提醒都沒有問題，避免自己在工作忙碌之餘不小小忽略掉哪一件重要的事，趕緊上網找個你喜歡的手機軟體來幫你管理你的schedule吧！

Word Bank

remind vt. 提醒

The teacher reminds the students of the quiz next week.
老師提醒學生下週有小考。

prior adj. 在……之前

Please ignore my prior email correspondence.
請忽略我之前的電子信件。

occupied adj. 無空閒

All my time is occupied with work.
我所有時間都忙於工作。

manufacture vt. 製造、生產

The electronic device is manufactured in Taiwan.
這電子設備是台灣製造。

detail n. 細節

Could you tell me more details?
你可以再告訴我詳細一點嗎？

up-to-date adj. 最新的

I always access the internet for up-to-date information.
我總是上網得知最新資料。

proposal n. 提案；企劃書

The manager submitted a marketing proposal to the general manager.
經理提出行銷企劃書給總經理。

In Other Words

Remember to remind me prior to the appointment.
記得在會面之前要提醒我。

- Please tell me that again before the appointment.
  在會面之前要再跟我說一次。
- Prior the appointment, remember to give me a cue.
  在會面之前，要記得提醒我。

Well, you've been occupied with other things.
您太忙了。

- Well, you've been taken up by other things.
  您太忙了。
- Well, your schedule is too tight.
  您的行程太緊湊了。

I have put the profile of DTC, the up-to-date catalog and Mr. Lin's proposal on your desk.
我已經將DTC的簡介、及最新的型錄和林先生的企劃書放在您的桌上了。

- The profile of DTC, the latest catalog, and Mr. Lin's proposal are already put on your desk.
  DTC的簡介、及最新的型錄和林先生的企劃書放在您的桌上了。
- You can find the DTC profile, the latest catalog and Mr. Lin's business plan on your desk.
  您可以在您的桌上找到DTC的簡介、及最新的型錄和林先生的企劃書。

如何做一名稱職的秘書？

1. 秘書工作並不如外界所想像的那般制式化。不同的公司行號有不同的規定，而秘書所負責的項目和權責也不盡然相同。例如，一間生技研發公司和一間室內設計公司的秘書，所負責的職務以及所需具備的專業知識全然不同。除此之外，大型企業的秘書和中小型企業的秘書之職務也不一樣，若再加上公司經營型態，例如擁有董事會或是較單一的家族企業等，秘書的職務和專業也會有所區別。
2. 首先，你必須先清楚了解自己所任職或是欲求職的公司是屬於哪一種產業。雖然秘書的工作不外乎是處理文件、安排行程等等，但仍需具備產業和市場的基本專業知識，不然就無法有效處理文書和應付客戶。接下來，則要知道公司的規模是多大，大公司的秘書，其專業和態度馬虎不得，尤其是辦事效率。而在中小企業或是小型企業任職的秘書，儘管規章或許不比大型企業來的嚴謹，但職務不見得輕鬆。大型企業的制度較完善，每一個職位和職務都細分的很清楚，而中小型企業在此上頭則較模糊，意指秘書必須處理的事情可能會很瑣碎且不一致。
3. 不要排斥處理職務之外的事項。有時候，頂頭上司或是老闆會將秘書當作自己的私人特助一般，無論公事還是私事，都會交代秘書辦理。若是您的上司或老闆是個極為會「用人」的人，請不要感到氣餒，將它當成一種學習的機會，藉此增強自己的處理能力並提升自己的EQ，轉換心情，當成免費的就職訓練吧。

接待訪客的撇步！

不同於電話接待，來到公司的訪客不僅需要好語氣，還需具備專業和親切的態度！

★站起身問候對方

看見訪客要立刻（起身）招呼，若手邊有電話或是急事在進行，也需先跟訪客打聲招呼，請對方等候。

★專業及親切的態度

親切表示面帶微笑，專業表示不過度興奮和熱情的舉止。

★語調自然、音量適中

語調不能懶洋洋的，也不能不耐煩或是讓人覺得很冷淡。

★無論對方是否有預約，仍先詳細詢問

一來是為了展現專業的一面，二來是再三確認以免搞錯對象。

★先請對方稍待一下，並送上飲料

不要一進門就將訪客帶進辦公室或是會議室。給對方以及公司內部的職員一點緩和的空間和時間，先為訪客倒茶，然後詢問訪客欲見面的人。

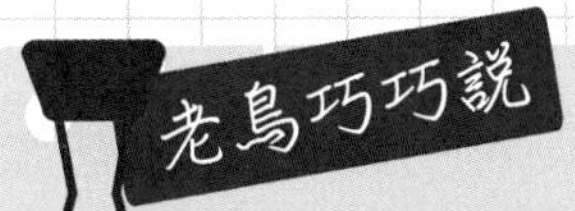

**想要當一名稱職的秘書
該具有哪些條件呢？趕緊確認一下吧～**

Qualities a great secretary requires!

- ☐ 組織性高、反應快、注重小細節。
- ☐ 對於老闆所交代的任務，全力以赴。
- ☐ 就算忙碌，面對訪客或來電者時，切記面帶笑容、語氣溫和不慌張。
- ☐ 不斷地充實自己。
- ☐ 拿捏分寸、適當得宜：開口說話的時機和尺度應分清楚。
- ☐ 不鑽牛角尖、不輕易陷入自己的私人情緒。
- ☐ 用公正的角度評估看待事情。
- ☐ 時時刻刻保持專業的態度和從容的情緒。
- ☐ 學習效率快、理解力強。
- ☐ 書寫技巧的培養。
- ☐ 細心與貼心－不要拿瑣碎的事去煩老闆。

2-1 會議行程安排

Writing an Email Concerning Meeting Time
寫 E-mail 告知開會的時間

Mr. Tsai asks his secretary, Stacy, to write an email to inform every department head of the time of a directors' meeting and of items needing attention.

蔡先生要他的秘書Stacy寫一封E-mail通知各部門主管，關於主管會議的時間以及需注意事項。

Stacy - secretary 秘書
Mr. Tsai - general manager 總經理

Dialogue

Mr. Tsai	Mr. Lo wants to call a **directors' meeting** next Tuesday at 10 A.M. I want you to write an email to inform every department head.	羅先生想在下週二的早上10點召開主管會議。我要妳寫封E-mail通知各部門的主管。
Stacy	So this is not a regular directors' meeting.	所以這不是定期的主管會議囉。
Mr. Tsai	You're right; it's not a regular directors' meeting. A company from Hong Kong wishes to be our **local importer**. Mr. Lo would like to discuss this matter during the meeting.	妳答對了；這並非定期的主管會議。一間香港的公司有意成為我們的當地進口商，羅先生想在會議上討論這件事。
.Stacy	In Hong Kong?! This is good news, isn't it?	在香港？！這真是個好消息，不是嗎？

Mr. Tsai	Correct. It's good news indeed that it will help us to establish a **distribution center** later in Hong Kong.	沒錯，這確實是好消息，這將有助於我們日後在香港設立一間配送中心。
Stacy	What should I include in the e-mail, **in addition to** the time of the meeting?	除了會議的時間之外，我還該在e-mail上寫些什麼？
Mr. Tsai	Mr. Lo would like all of us to visit that company's website first, and try to **gather** as much information as we can about the company. I'll send you the **link** to the website later.	羅先生希望我們先上那間公司的網站了解一下該公司，然後試著蒐集越多關於該公司的資料越好。我等一下就將該公司的網址傳給你。
Stacy	Is that all?	就這樣嗎？
Mr. Tsai	There's one more thing. It will be a long meeting, so don't forget to have the receptionist order lunches for us.	還有一件事。會議時間將會很長，所以別忘了交代總機接待人員替我們訂午餐。
Stacy	Okay, no problem.	好的，沒問題。

★你應該要知道的小小事

以下是使用outlook常用的功能設定：

1. 副本：通常副本的收件者是為了讓對方可以留備份；一般收件人在收到這封信的同時，也能看到發信者cc給誰。
2. 密件附本：不想讓其他人知道你這封信有寄給誰，可將收件人寫在這裡。
3. 要求送達回條：信件有成功送達給收件者，系統會回報讓你知道。
4. 要求讀取回條：信件若被收件者開啟讀取，系統會回報讓你知道。
5. 使用投票按鈕：如果有選項供收信者選擇並回覆時可使用。

Word Bank

directors' meeting　主管會議

The regular directors' meeting is scheduled on every Monday morning.
例行主管會議在每週一早上開會。

regular　adj.　定期的

I always have a regular check-up for my teeth every three months.
我每三個月定期檢查牙齒。

local　adj.　當地的

The local supermarkets in U.S.A. are very competitive.
美國當地的超市非常競爭。

importer　n.　進口商

Costco is one of large importers in the world.
Costco 是全世界大型進口商之一。

distribution center　配送中心

Our company would like to establish a distribution center in U.S.A. to expand globally.
我們公司要在美國設立配送中心以拓展全球市場。

in addition to　除……之外

In addition to the activation fee, a service fee will be charged.
除了啟用費用外，還會收取服務費。

In Other Words

Mr. Lo wants to call a directors' meeting next Tuesday at 10 A.M.
羅先生想在下週二的早上10點召開主管會議。

- Next Tuesday at 10 A.M., Mr. Lo would like to schedule a directors' meeting .
  下週二的早上10點，羅先生要召開主管會議。
- Mr. Lo requested to hold a directors' meeting at 10 A.M. next Tuesday.
  羅先生要求要在下週二的早上10點召開主管會議。

I want you to write an email to inform every department head.
我要妳寫封E-mail通知各部門的主管。

- Please inform every department head via email.
  請寫E-mail通知各部門的主管。
- Please notify every department head by email.
  請寫E-mail通知各部門的主管。

So this is not a regular directors' meeting.
所以這不是定期的主管會議囉。

- So this is not a routine directors' meeting.
  所以這不是定期的主管會議囉。
- And this is an unscheduled directors' meeting.
  那這是臨時召開的主管會議囉。

2-2 會議行程安排

Prior to the Directors' Meeting
主管會議之前

Stacy reports back to her boss, the general manager, about how things have been going prior to the directors' meeting.

Stacy向總經理報告有關主管會議的事前準備事項。

Stacy - secretary 秘書
Mr. Tsai - general manager 總經理

Dialogue

Mr. Tsai	Have you sent the **notice** of the meeting to every department head?	是否已經將會議通知寄給各部門的主管了？
Stacy	Yes, I have. But there's a **minor** problem.	都寄了，但是有一個小問題。
Mr. Tsai	What's the problem?	什麼問題？
Stacy	Jacqueline, the director of the Personnel Department, is on vacation with her family in **Cairo** now, and I'm not sure **whether** she has received the e-mail.	人事部的協理Jacqueline目前人在開羅和家人度假中，我不確定她是否有收到email。
Mr. Tsai	Oh, goodness! I remember that now… And she won't be back until the day before the meeting.	天啊！我想起來了…她要到開會的前一天才會回來。
Stacy	When will she come in?	她何時會進公司？

Mr. Tsai	She'll come in on Tuesday, the day we will have the directors' meeting.	她星期二會進公司；剛好是主管會議的那一天。
Stacy	Should I call her?	需要我打電話給她嗎？
Mr. Tsai	You might be unable to **get in touch with** her. There would be no **reception** if they were out of the city.	你可能聯絡不上她，如果他們不在市區內的話，電話可能無法接收訊號。
Stacy	What do you suggest me to do?	那您建議我怎麼做呢？
Mr. Tsai	Call her next Monday evening and ask her to be **prepared**.	下星期一傍晚再打給她，並請她做好準備。
Stacy	Yes, I'll do that.	好的，我會去做。

★你應該要知道的小小事！

秘書在主管要開會之前，記得要將相關資料先整理完畢，標出重點，連同開會議題一起交給主管，讓主管在開會之前能夠快速消化所有訊息，並針對開會議題進行思緒的整理。秘書也有可能會需要協助製作簡報檔（PPT）、會議記錄等等，所以相關軟體的應用，對秘書實務工作上也是很重要的。

Word Bank

notice n. 通知

The notice of salary raise rate has been posted on the billboard.
加薪比例的通知已貼在公告欄上。

minor adj. 較小的

Most of the troubles except minor ones have been solved.
除了一些較小問題，大部分的問題已被解決了。

Cairo n. 開羅（埃及首都）

Cairo is the capital of Egypt.
開羅是埃及首都。

whether conj. 是否

I am not sure whether she can go to the movies with us.
我不確定她是否可以和我們去電影。

get in touch with 與……取得聯繫

Let's get in touch with each other forever.
我們要永遠保持聯絡喔！

reception n. 接收

The reception of communication is not good in the basement.
地下室的接收通訊不好。

prepare vt. 使……有準備

My older brother is preparing for a camping trip.
我哥哥正在準備要露營的東西。

In Other Words

And she won't be back until the day before the meeting.
她要到開會的前一天才會回來。

- And she will come back till the day before the meeting.
  她要到開會的前一天才會回來。
- She probably won't be in town until the day before the meeting.
  她可能到開會的前一天才會回來。

You might be unable to get in touch with her.
你可能聯絡不上她。

- You probably can't reach her.
  你可能聯絡不上她。
- She probably couldn't be contacted with at this moment.
  這個時候有可能聯絡不上她。

There would be no reception if they were out of the city.
如果他們不在市區內的話，電話可能無法接收訊號。

- If they are not in the city, there would be no signals.
  如果他們不在市區內的話，電話可能會沒有訊號。
- There would be no connection if they are outside of the city.
  如果他們不在市區內的話，電話可能無法接收訊號。

2-3 會議行程安排

Dinner Reservation
預約晚餐

Stacy makes a dinner reservation for her boss.

史黛西幫老闆預訂餐廳

Stacy - secretary 秘書
Cindy - hostess 領台人員

Dialogue

Cindy	Sushi Garden, this is Cindy speaking, how may I help you?	Sushi Garden, 我是Cindy，有可以為您效勞的地方嗎？
Stacy	I'd like to make a **reservation.**	我想訂位。
Cindy	For which day and for what time?	哪一天和什麼時間？
Stacy	For Friday night, the 11th, at 7:30.	11號，星期五晚上七點半。
Cindy	I'm sorry. We are fully booked at 7:30 on Friday night. How about eight o'clock?	對不起，星期五晚上七點半的預約都滿了。八點可以嗎？
Stacy	No, it's a little bit late. How about seven o'clock?	不，這樣有點晚。那麼七點鐘呢？
Cindy	I am afraid that we don't have any openings at seven o'clock, either. But I have one table available at 6:45.	我恐怕在七點鐘也沒有任何的空位。但是在六點四十五分是可以的。

Stacy	All right, I'll take that.	好的，就我就訂六點四十五分。
Cindy	How many will be in the party?	一共幾個人呢？
Stacy	There will be six **adults** and two children. Can you give me a table near the window and away from the kitchen?	六個大人和兩個小孩。可以給我一張靠窗且遠離廚房的位置嗎？
Cindy	I cannot guarantee you the table, but I will make **notes** about your request. And the name on the reservation?	我不能保證給您那樣的位置，但我會註明您的需求。那麼訂位人的大名是？
Stacy	Mr. Tsai.	蔡先生。
Cindy	Can you give me a number where we could reach you?	可以給我一個聯絡得到您的電話嗎？
Stacy	0952-876-340. My name is Stacy. Do you provide the **valet parking service**?	0952-876-340。我是Stacy。你們有提供代客泊車的服務嗎？
Cindy	We don't have the valet parking service, but there is a **pay parking lot** just **around the corner** from the restaurant.	我們沒有代客泊車，但餐廳附近就有一個收費停車場。
Stacy	Oh I see. Thank you so much.	好的，我了解了。非常謝謝。

Word Bank

reservation　n.　預約

You had better make a reservation for dinner this coming Saturday.
你最好為這週六的晚餐向餐廳預約。

adult　n.　成人

After a teenager turns into an adult, he or she should be responsible for everything.
當青少年轉變為成人後，他或她應該要為每件事負責。

note　n.　註明

Please read the notes of the manual carefully.
請詳細閱讀手冊的註解。

valet parking service　代客泊車服務

The expensive five-star hotel provides the valet parking service.
這昂貴的五星級飯店提供代客泊車服務。

pay parking lot　收費停車場

There are some pay parking lots located in the downtown.
在市中心有許多收費停車場。

around the corner　附近

There is a big shopping mall around the corner.
附近有一間大型購物中心。

In Other Words

We are fully booked at 7:30 on Friday night.
星期五晚上七點半的預約都滿了。

- All our tables are fully booked at 7:30 on Friday night.
  星期五晚上七點半的預約都滿了。
- We can't take any reservation at 7:30 on Friday night, 'cause all tables are booked.
  我們沒有辦法接受星期五晚上七點半的預約了，因為預約已滿。

I cannot guarantee you the table, but I will make notes about your request.
我不能保證給您那樣的位置，但我會註明您的需求。

- I cannot guarantee to seat you at the table that you requested for, but I will make notes per your request.
  我不能保證給您那樣的位置，但我會註明您的需求。
- I will write down your request, but I cannot promise we will be able to seat you there.
  我會將您的需求寫下來，但我不能保證我們一定能給您所要求的位置。

Can you give me a number where we could reach you?
可以給我一個聯絡得到您的電話嗎？

- May I have a number where I can get in touch with you?
  可以給我一個聯絡得到您的電話嗎？
- May I have your contact number, please?
  可以給我您的聯絡號碼嗎？

2-4 會議行程安排

Prepare Documents
準備文件

Mr. Tsai asks his secretary, Stacy, whether she has prepared all the documents needed for his meeting tomorrow.

蔡先生詢問秘書Stacy是否已將明天開會所需的文件準備齊全。

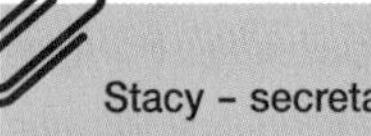

Stacy – secretary 秘書
Mr. Tsai – general manager 總經理

Dialogue

Stacy	Here are the **documents** and reports for tomorrow's meeting with Mr. Cho.	這是您明天和周先生開會所需要的文件和報告。
Mr. Tsai	Did you include the **financial statements**?	你有沒有加入財務報表？
Stacy	No, I didn't know you would need them.	沒有，我不知道您需要報表。
Mr. Tsai	Just go ask the Accounting Department to give you copies of the financial statements from the last six months.	去跟會計部拿過去六個月的財務報表備份。
Stacy	Yes. Is there anything else?	好的，還需要其他的嗎？

Mr. Tsai	Yes, ask Steve from the Sales Department for a list of **vendors** we have worked with over the last two years.	有，去跟業務部的Steve拿一份過去兩年內和我們合作的廠商名單。
Stacy	OK, I'll do that.	好的，我會。
Mr. Tsai	One last thing: Could you **arrange** for a taxi to take me to the office tomorrow?	最後一件事。可以幫我叫一輛計程車明天接我來公司嗎？
Stacy	Certainly. I see you aren't not going to drive by yourself tomorrow.	當然可以。所以您明天不打算自己開車。
Mr. Tsai	My car is **in the shop** for the annual **maintenance** check, and it's easier to take a taxi than take a bus.	我的車子進廠做年度保養了，搭計程車會比搭公車方便多了。

Word Bank

document n. 文件

All the customers' profiles are confidential documents.
所以客户資料都是機密文件。

financial statements 財務報表

The secretary has to collect the financial statements for the general manager.
這秘書必須匯集財務報表給總經理。

vendor n. 廠商

The vendor is reputable and offers guarantees for all the products.
這廠商聲譽佳並提供所有產品保固。

arrange vt. 安排

The parents arrange the top one school for their child.
這父母親替他們的小孩安排最好的學校。

in the shop 車子進廠維修、保養

His car is in the shop for repair.
他的車子進廠修理。

maintenance n. 保養維修

The website is out of service for routine maintenance.
這網站關閉進行定期保養。

In Other Words

Did you include the financial statements?
你有沒有加入財務報表？

- Is the financial statement included?
財務報表 有包括在內嗎？
- I probably will also need the financial statement, did you have it included?
你有沒有加入財務報表？

Yes, ask Steve from the sales department for a list of vendors we have worked with over the last two years.
有，去跟業務部的Steve拿一份過去兩年內和我們合作的廠商名單。

- Yes, I'll also need a list of suppliers we have cooperated with during the past two years, you can get that from Steve of the Sales Department..
有，我還要一份過去兩年內和我們合作的廠商名單，這個可以跟業務部的Steve拿。
- Yes, please call Steve from the Sales Department, ask him for a list of manufactures we have worked with over the last two years.
有，請打電話給業務部的Steve，請他給妳一份過去兩年內和我們合作的製造商名單

Could you arrange for a taxi to take me to the office tomorrow?
可以幫我叫一輛計程車明天接我來公司嗎？

- I'll need a taxi pickup tomorrow, please arrange it for me.
可以幫我叫一輛計程車明天來公司接我嗎？
- Book me a taxi to pick me up to the office tomorrow?
可以幫我預約一輛計程車明天來公司接我嗎？

會議前該注意的事項

如何有效安排一場成功的會議，最能充分展現一個祕書的功力和效率。需注意的事項如下：

★了解會議的主題及目的

有助於會前準備工作，像是行程安排和議題設定。

★清楚參加會議的成員和主持人

★再三同主管確認細項

★確認每位與會人員都有收到會議通知以及注意事項

最簡單的方式即透過email回函；在email上註明參閱者需回覆已讀取的回函。

★會前提醒與會人員開會時間和地點

★準備講義

★檢查會議場所的軟硬體設備

在開會之前務必要再三地確認，避免會議開始進行卻因設備問題而中斷，耽誤到大家的時間。

★訂購茶點或餐點

若會議進行時間較長或是會卡到用餐時間，可主動詢問主管是否要另外準備餐點。

★準備簽到簿

會議中該注意的事項

★簡單清楚、無誤的會議記錄

這絕非一項簡單的任務，可透過多種方式：速記法、錄音（開會員之後再仔細修改和比對）等，重要的是會議中討論過的主題及決策都必須清楚地記錄下來。

會議後該注意的事項

★整理完整的會議記錄

★除了主管之外，同步將會議記錄寄給每一位與會人員，並確認是否有遺漏或需修改的地方。

該怎麼好好安排一場會議？

身為一位稱職的秘書，在主管交代會議安排之後，應該快速地與主管確認開會大項：時間／地點／目的／參加會議者名單，因為主管通常很忙碌的關係，有可能不會注意到每個細節，所以秘書應該全方面思考，在最短的時間之內蒐集好所有的資訊，接著進行後續細項的安排，視情況與主管確認。以下是一個checklist：

Checklist

- □ 時間
- □ 地點
- □ 目的
- □ 參加會議人士
- □ 預約會議場地
- □ 準備相關設備
- □ 發會議通知
- □ 準備茶點
- □ 是否預約用餐
- □ 影印會議資料
- □ 會議前再次提醒

3-1 老闆出差

Planning a Business Trip–Time and Location
規劃出差行程 – 時間和地點

Stacy makes business trip arrangements for her boss, the general manager.

Stacy替總經理安排出差事宜。

Stacy - secretary 秘書
Mr. Tsai - general manager 總經理

Dialogue

Mr. Tsai	I am going to London on a **business trip** next month. I need you to make some arrangements.	我下個月要去倫敦出差,需要妳幫忙安排一些事宜。
Stacy	When will you leave, and how long will you stay there?	您何時離開，且會在倫敦停留多久？
Mr. Tsai	I plan to leave on Saturday, the 20th, and I will stay there for a week.	我計畫20號星期六出發，然後我會在那停留一個星期的時間。
Stacy	I'll book a **flight** right away. Are you going to fly **first class**?	我馬上去訂機票。是頭等艙的位子嗎？
Mr. Tsai	No. Just book me the **business class**; it's much cheaper. Please try to get me an **aisle** seat if possible.	不用。幫我訂商務艙就可以了；商務艙便宜多了。如果可以的話，請幫我劃靠走道的位子。
Stacy	Noted. Should I arrange for a taxi to pick you up at your house?	了解。需要幫您安排計程車到您家裡去接您嗎？

Mr. Tsai	No, my wife will take me to the airport.	不用了，我太太會開車載我去機場。
Stacy	Will you need an **airport pick-up service** when you arrive in London?	您抵達倫敦的時候需要幫您安排接機服務嗎？
Mr. Tsai	I don't think I'll need the pick-up service. I think the company I'm visiting will arrange **transportation** for me. Can you confirm the related details with them for me?	我不認為我需要接機服務。我想我要去拜訪的公司應該會替我安排交通事宜。可以幫我跟他們確認相關細節嗎？
Stacy	Sure. I'll go ahead and book a flight first.	好的。我現在先去訂機票。
Mr. Tsai	Thank you.	謝謝。

Word Bank

business trip　商務旅行、出差

My boss will have a business trip to Japan next month.
我老闆下週要出差到日本。

flight　n.　航班

The flight from Taipei to Tokyo is delayed.
從台北到東京的航班已延遲。

first class　頭等艙

I was lucky to win a first class flight ticket at this game.
我很幸運在這次比賽贏得頭等艙機票。

business class　商務艙

The fare of a business class seat is more expensive than an economic one.
商務艙的機位比經濟艙貴。

aisle　n.　走道

I prefer a seat by aisle.
我比較喜歡坐在靠走道位置。

airport pick-up service　機場接送服務

The credit card company provides VIP customers with free airport pick-up service.
這信用卡公司提供免費機場接送服務給 VIP 客户。

transportation n. 交通

The transportation is very convenient in downtown.
市中心的交通很方便。

In Other Words

I am going to London on a business trip next month.
我下個月要去倫敦出差。

- I will have a business trip to London next month.
  我下個月要去倫敦出差。
- I am going to London on business next month.
  我下個月要去倫敦出差。

Are you going to fly first class?
是頭等艙的位子嗎？

- Should I book a first class seat for you?
  我要幫您訂頭等艙的位子嗎？
- Would you like to take a first class seat?
  你要搭頭等艙的位子嗎？

Please try to get me an aisle seat if possible.
如果可以的話，請幫我劃靠走道的位子。

- If possible, please try to book a seat by aisle.
  如果可以的話，請幫我訂靠走道的位子。
- If possible, please try to reserve a seat by aisle for me.
  如果可以的話，請幫我訂靠走道的位子。

3-2 老闆出差

Planning a Business Trip–Hotel Reservation
規劃出差行程－飯店訂房

Stacy makes a hotel reservation for her boss.

Stacy幫老闆訂飯店房間。

Stacy – secretary/ 秘書
Teddy – hotel reservation agent 飯店訂房人員

Dialogue

Teddy	Good morning, Reservations. Teddy speaking. How may I help you?	早安，訂房組。我是Teddy。有什麼能為您效勞的嗎？
Stacy	Hi, I would like to book a room.	嗨，我想要訂房。
Teddy	Certainly, when would you like to stay with us?	好的，什麼時候呢？
Stacy	September 20.	9月20日。
Teddy	How long will you be staying?	要住多久呢？
Stacy	For Six nights.	六個晚上。
Teddy	How many people will be staying?	請問一共有幾位呢？
Stacy	Just one. I would like to book a **single room** with a **view** over the city?	只有一位。我要一間可以看到市景的單人房。

Teddy	Wait a moment, please. Let me check our reservation… Yes, we do have a room on the twenty-first floor with a **magnificent** view.	請稍後，讓我查一下我們的預約……有的，我們有一間位於21樓的房間，景色壯觀。
Stacy	What is the rate for that room?	那間房間的價格是多少？
Teddy	Would you like it with breakfast?	要附早餐嗎？
Stacy	Yes, please.	好的。
Teddy	It's £115 **pounds** per night. Would you like to make a reservation now?	一個晚上115英鎊。您要現在預訂嗎？
Stacy	Sure.	好的。
Teddy	May I have your name, please?	請問您的大名是？
Stacy	Please make it under Mr. Tsai, that's T-S-A-I.	請登記蔡先生，T-S-A-I.
Teddy	Here is your **confirmation** number #9806541. Thank you for choosing **Palace Inn**. Is there's anything else I can do for you?	這是您的確認號碼#9806541。感謝您選擇Palace Inn。請問還有什麼需要幫忙的嗎？
Stacy	No, thank you and good-bye.	沒有了，謝謝，再見。

single room n. 單人房

I would like to book a single room.
我要訂一間單人房。

view n. 景色

The luxury hotel has a fantastic view at the ocean.
這豪華飯店有很棒的海景。

magnificent adj. 壯觀的；華麗的

The sunrise in Ali Mountain is very magnificent.
阿里山的日出景觀非常壯觀。

pound n. 英鎊

The room rate of the hotel is calculated by pound.
這飯店的房價是以英鎊計算。

confirmation n. 確認

Please get a confirmation number after booking a flight.
在訂完機位後記得拿確認號碼。

palace n. 皇宮

The girl's room is as huge as a palace.
這女孩的房間像皇宮一樣大。

inn n. 小飯店

We enjoyed staying at an inn in Kenting and had a good time.
我們很享受住在墾丁的小飯店，也玩得很愉快。

Yes, we do have a room on the twenty-first floor with a magnificent view.
有的，我們有一間位於21樓的房間，景色壯觀。

Yes, we do have a room on the twenty-first floor with a marvelous view.
有的，我們有一間位於21樓的房間，景色壯觀。

Yes, one of our twenty-first floor rooms is with a magnificient view.
有的，我們21樓的房間中的其中一間，有著壯觀的景色。

What is the rate for that room?
那間房間的價格是多少？

What's the room rate?
那間房間的價格是多少？

How much does it cost for one night?
那間房間的一個晚上的價格是多少？

It's £115 pounds per night.
一個晚上115英鎊。

It costs £115 pounds per night.
一個晚上115英鎊。

£115 pounds for one night.
一個晚上115英鎊。

3-3 老闆出差

Planning a Business Trip–Business Trip Agenda
規劃出差行程－行程確認

Stacy confirms the itinerary of her boss's business activities with the staff of another company, BCC.

Stacy與BCC公司確認老闆的出差行程。

Stacy – secretary 秘書
Perry – BCC representative BCC 代表

Dialogue

Stacy	Hi, this is Stacy, Mr. Tsai's secretary. I'm calling to confirm the activities during his business trip, as noted on the **itinerary**.	嗨，我是蔡先生的秘書Stacy。我想確認一下蔡先生的出差行程。
Perry	Hello, this is Perry.	哈囉，我是Perry。
Stacy	Will you have someone to pick Mr. Tsai up when he arrives in London on 20th?	蔡先生20號抵達倫敦時，您們會派人去接他嗎？
Perry	Yes. Transportation has already been arranged.	當然，相關的交通接送都已安排妥當。
Stacy	Mr. Tsai will have a meeting with your CEO, Mr. Patterson on 22nd at 11 A.M., is that correct?	蔡先生會在22日的早上11點和貴公司執行長Patterson先生開會，這樣正確嗎？

Perry	That's correct, and he will be visiting our **branches** and factories during the next three days.	沒錯，然後接下來的三天，他會參觀我們的分公司和工廠。
Stacy	And how about after that?	在那之後呢？
Perry	After that, we will take him to the **London Eye** which is a giant **Ferris wheel** and the Elizabeth **Tower** where the bell Big Ben is housed within. Those are the most popular tourist attractions in London.	在那之後，我們會帶他去倫敦眼這一座大型的摩天輪還有大笨鐘所在的伊莉莎白塔。這些是倫敦最著名的觀光景點。
Stacy	Great! And you will have someone take him to the airport on September 27th, won't you?	太棒了！那麼9月27號您也會派人送他去機場嗎？
Perry	Of course, unless he decides to stay for few more days.	當然囉，除非他選擇多待幾天。
Stacy	I see. Thank you very much.	了解：非常謝謝您。

★你應該要知道的小小事！

老闆到國外出差，客戶應該會安排當地的接待，包括交通、食宿等等，所以秘書在老闆出差時，其實可以幫忙準備一些伴手禮，讓老闆出差時可以帶去給客戶，選擇伴手禮時要留意不要挑那種很笨重、又不好攜帶的禮物，因為老闆還要帶筆電、會議資料、隨身行李等，東西太多真的不好拿，伴手禮的選擇像阿里山的茶、鳳梨酥、太陽餅等都很有名，也很具有地方特色，很適合拿來當伴手禮哦！

Word Bank

itinerary　n.　議程

The general manager asks for his itinerary for previewing.
總經理要先看一下他的行程表。

branch　n.　分公司

The large corporation has many branches all over the world.
這大公司在全世界有很多分公司。

the London Eye　倫敦眼

The London Eye is a famous landmark in London.
倫敦眼是倫敦的有名地標。

Ferris wheel　摩天輪

Ferris wheel is a popular entertainment site.
摩天輪是一個受歡迎的娛樂景點。

tower　n.　塔

I have been to the Observation Tower at 101 Building in Taipei.
我去過台北 101 大樓的瞭望台。

popular　adj.　著名的

She wants to be a popular singer, but the stage fright crippled her.
她想成為有名的歌手，但卻因怯場而心生畏懼。

attraction　n.　景點

Disneyland is a huge attraction with millions of tourists visiting it every year..
迪士尼樂園是有名的景點，每年吸引了幾百萬的遊客造訪。

In Other Words

I'm calling to confirm the activities during his business trip, as noted on the itinerary.
我想確認一下蔡先生的出差行程。

- I'm calling to assure his business trip schedule is the same as his itinerary.
  我想確認一下蔡先生的出差行程。
- The purpose I call is to check how his business trip itinerary is scheduled.
  我想確認一下蔡先生的出差行程。

Will you have someone to pick Mr. Tsai up when he arrives in London on 20th?
蔡先生20號抵達倫敦時，您們會派人去接他嗎？

- Will you send someone to pick up Mr. Tsai when he gets to London on 20th?
  蔡先生20號抵達倫敦時，您們會派人去接他嗎？
- Will Mr. Tsai be picked up when he arrives in London on 20th?
  蔡先生20號抵達倫敦時，您們會派人去接他嗎？

And you will have someone take him to the airport on September 27th, won't you?
那麼9月27號您也會派人送他去機場嗎？

- And I suppose that someone will accompany him to the airport on September 27th, right?
  那麼9月27號也會派人送他去機場，對吧？
- And will you assign someone to take him to the airport on September 27th, won't you?
  那麼9月27號您也會派人送他去機場嗎？

3-4 老闆出差

Planning a Business Trip–Business Trip Postponed
規劃出差行程－出差延期

Mr. Tsai's business trip has been postponed. Stacy, his secretary, needs to inform Perry, the representative of BCC.

蔡先生的出差延期了，他的秘書史黛西必須通知BCC公司的代表派瑞。

Stacy - secretary 秘書
Perry - BCC representative

Dialogue

Stacy	Hello, Perry. This is Stacy, Mr. Tsai's secretary.	哈囉，Perry。我是蔡先生的秘書Stacy。
Perry	Hi, Stacy, what's up?	嗨，Stacy，還好嗎？
Stacy	I'm very sorry to inform you that Mr. Tsai's business trip has to be **postponed**.	很抱歉，我要通知您蔡先生的出差必須延期了。
Perry	How come? We've already arranged everything.	為什麼呢？我們一切都已經安排好了。
Stacy	Something **unexpected** came up, and Mr. Tsai must **remain** here to **solve** the problem. He has asked me to apologize for him. None of us expects it to happen.	突然有狀況發生，蔡先生必須留在公司協助解決問題。他要我代他向你們道歉。沒有人希望此事件的發生。

Perry	What a **pity**! When does he plan to visit us?	真令人遺憾！他打算何時來拜訪我們呢？
Stacy	He will arrive in London on October 7th, and stay for seven days.	他將於10月7日抵達倫敦，會待七天。
Perry	So, the schedule remains the same.	所以，行程照舊。
Stacy	That's right. Nothing changes except the dates.	沒錯。什麼都沒變，除了日期不同之外。
Perry	Got it. We look forward to his visit.	了解。我們期待他的來訪。
Stacy	Thank you so much. We **deeply** apologize for any inconvenience this may **cause** you.	非常感謝您。若造成你們的困擾，請多多包涵。

★你應該要知道的小小事！

Stacy最後那句話 "We deeply apologize for any convenience this may cause you." 是一句還滿常用的話，建議大家可以背起來哦！

句型：We deeply apologize for + N/V-ing… 我們對…深感抱歉

for的後面可加名詞或是動名詞片語，就是感到抱歉的內容，像是有時接待人員的態度惹怒客戶、出貨delay等等都可以套用這個句型。

* We deeply apologize for his/her attitudes/behavior.

我們對他／她的態度／行為深感抱歉。

Word Bank

postpone vt. 使……延期

The outdoor concert is postponed due to the typhoon.
室外音樂會因為颱風延期了。

unexpected adj. 突如其來的

I am very surprised at this unexpected birthday gift.
我對這個突如其來的生日禮物很驚喜。

remain v. 留待

Please remain at the reception desk if you get lost.
如果迷路了，請留在服務台。

solve v. 解決

I have to solve the problem before I am off tomorrow.
在我明天休假前，我必須要把此問題解決。

pity n. 遺憾

It is a pity that you cannot join us.
很可惜你不能加入我們。

deeply adj. 深深地

I felt deeply touched when I read this novel.
我看這本小說時深深覺得感動。

cause vt. 導致

The traffic jam caused many cars got stuck on the road.
塞車導致許多車子卡在路上

In Other Words

What's up?
還好嗎？

- What's wrong?
  有什麼不對勁嗎？
- What happened?
  發生什麼事？

I'm very sorry to inform you that Mr. Tsai's business trip has to be postponed.
很抱歉，我要通知您蔡先生的出差必須延期了。

- Unfortunately, I want to advise you that Mr. Tsai's business trip has to be delayed.
  不幸地是，我要通知您蔡先生的出差必須延期了。
- I feel so sorry to have you noticed that Mr. Tsai's business trip has to be put off.
  很抱歉，我要通知您蔡先生的出差必須延期了。

Something unexpected came up, and Mr. Tsai must remain here to solve the problem.
突然有狀況發生，蔡先生必須留在公司協助解決問題。

- Mr. Tsai is forced to stay here to figure out the problem due to some incidents.
  突然有狀況發生，蔡先生必須留在公司協助解決問題。
- Something was incurred unexpectedly, and Mr. Tsai has to stay here to solve the problem.
  突然有狀況發生，蔡先生必須留在公司協助解決問題。

Job Wisbom
職場補給站

替主管規劃出差事宜

★確認目的地、出發時間及停留的天數

確切知道此次出差要前往的地點、出發的時間和停留的天數，以便安排老闆的食宿及預訂機票。

★詢問出差預算

出差的費用包括機票、食宿、交通安排、公關費用（拜訪的禮物採買）等，所以在做各項安排前最好先知道預算上限。

★留意住房需求、特殊飲食習慣

像是飯店住宿時是否需要非吸煙樓層、不吃牛肉、素食等等細節。

★飛機艙等、位置安排

主管偏愛搭頭等艙或是商務艙？如果出差的目的地比較遠，飛行時間比較長，可詢問是否要升艙等，或是請航空公司安排位置比較大的位置。

★機場接送

主管出差當天前往機場與返抵國門時接送由誰來負責，請公司同仁協助，或是安排機場接送。

★目的地的交通安排，是否有接機人員

主管抵達目的地時，會由當地飯店的人員接機，先至飯店放行李稍做休息，或是由預定拜訪的公司派人接送，這些都要先確認好。

★確認出國相關文件是否備齊

出國所需的護照及簽證，或是有些落地簽證國家所需的相關文件。

★零用金的準備

可以根據行程規劃，估計大概需要多少零用金，在兌換外幣前記得要再次確認欲兌換的外幣金額。也別忘了提醒主管要帶公司的商務信用卡或是其私人的信用卡以備不時之需。

★特殊旅行物品提醒

在出發之前，可提醒老闆攜帶類似轉接頭、充電器等的小物品。

補充相關詞彙中的中英對照表

place of departure 出發地	visa 簽證
destination 目的地	type of visa 簽證類別
airline航空公司	visa application 簽證申請
airline ticket 機票	entry visa 入境簽證
hotel reservation 飯店預約	re-entry visa 再次入境簽證
flight reservation 航班預約	work permit 工作許可證
accommodation 住宿	exchange rate 匯率
passport 護照	currency 貨幣
passport renewal 護照更新	rental car service 租車服務
passport number 護照號碼	travel's cheque 旅行支票
passport validity 護照有效期	travel agent 旅行社
date of expiry 有效日期	itinerary 路線、旅程
Taiwan Compatriot Travel Certification 台胞證	
overseas travel insurance 海外旅遊保險	

在為主管安排出差行程的時候，有很多地方要留意，因為通常主管在出發之前會很忙，必須將手邊的公事處理到一個段落，以避免在出國期間會有無人銜接或是無人管理的情況發生，也必須先準備好出差時所需要的文件、簡報、對方公司的資料等等。這時候，善盡職責的好秘書便能為主管“看頭看尾”，以減輕主管在出國之前因公事或是一些瑣事所造成的壓力。除了這些，還可以先詢問是否有那一些是需要協助留意進度、繼續追蹤follow的項目，還有在緊急事務時的職務代理人是誰，由誰來處理相關事項，讓主管在出差期間能專心的處理出差的業務。

4-1 老闆交辦的事務處理

Overseas Clients Come to Visit
海外客戶來訪

A major client from Singapore is coming to visit the company and factory. The president, Mr. Lo, gives instructions to his secretary, Helen.

來自新加坡的重要客戶即將來參觀公司和工廠。董事長羅先生交代他的秘書Helen該做些什麼。

Helen - the secretary to the president 董事長秘書
Mr. Lo - the president 董事長

Dialogue

Mr. Lo	Our **major** client in Singapore, Mr. Do, will come to visit our company and factory with his wife and two assistants next week. I need you to make some arrangements.	我們在新加坡的重要客戶杜先生，將於下個星期和他的太太以及兩名助理來參觀我們公司和工廠。我需要妳幫忙做一些安排。
Helen	Yes. When will they arrive?	是的。他們何時抵達？
Mr. Lo	October 12th, at 10 A.M. Arrange a car to pick them up at the airport. Hold on… **On second thought**, please ask the sales director to have his assistant to pick them up.	10月12日，早上十點鐘。派一輛車去機場接他們。等一下……我仔細想一下，還是叫業務部協理讓他的助理去接他們好了。
Helen	Yes, I'll do that. How long will they stay?	好的，我會處理。他們會待多久？

Mr. Lo	About a week. I need you to make room reservations at Star Hotel.	大約一星期左右。我需要妳幫忙訂Star Hotel的房間。
Helen	What type of rooms?	哪種房間？
Mr. Lo	A suite for Mr. and Mrs. Do and **deluxe** rooms for Mr. Do's assistants. I also need you to make a dinner reservation at the hotel's **buffet** on their arrival day at 7 P.M.	杜先生和杜太太住一間套房，兩位助理住豪華客房。我還需要妳預約他們抵達當天晚上七點的飯店自助餐。
Helen	How many will be in the party?	幾個人用餐呢？
Mr. Lo	There will be six of us, including my wife and me. They will come to visit our company on October 13th, and I want the sales director to give them a **tour**.	總共六個人，包括我和我太太。他們十三號會來參觀公司，我需要業務部協理當他們的嚮導。
Helen	What if the sales director is not available on that day?	如果業務部協理當天不在呢？
Mr. Lo	Ask him to put all other things aside. Mr. Do is a very important client of ours. They will visit our factory on the next day, and I want the production manager and the director to show them around.	請他先將其他的事情擱在一旁，杜先生對我們而言是很重要的客戶。他們會在隔天參觀我們的工廠，我需要生產部經理和協理陪同他們一同參觀。
Helen	Will that be all?	就這樣嗎？
Mr. Lo	That's all for now.	目前先這樣。

Word Bank

overseas adj. 海外的

He saves a lot of money to study overseas in the future.
他存很多錢，未來要到海外讀書。

major adj. 重要的

English is a major language in the world.
英文是世界上重要的語言。

on second thought 再三考慮；回頭一想

I changed my mind to stay at home on second thought.
再三考慮後，我改變心意留在家裡。

assistant n. 助理

Connie has applied for the position of sales assistant.
Connie 已經應徵業務助理的工作。

deluxe adj. 豪華的

Rates are higher for the deluxe accommodations.
豪華客房的房價比較貴。

buffet n. （可數）自助餐

We usually have a buffet in a hotel for a family union.
我們家族聚餐通常都在飯店吃自助餐。

tour n. 遊覽

There are many visitors from China coming to Taiwan for a tour recently.
最近有很多中國觀光客來台灣遊覽。

In Other Words

What type of rooms?
哪種房間？

- What kind of rooms?
  哪種房間？
- What sort of rooms should I book?
  要預定哪種房間呢？

Ask him to put all other things aside.
請他先將其他的事情擱在一旁。

- Ask him to take this matter as the first priority.
  請他把這件事當第一優先。
- Ask him to leave all other things aside.
  請他先將其他的事情擱在一旁。

Mr. Do is a very important client of ours.
杜先生對我們而言是很重要的客户。

- Mr. Do is our VIP client.
  杜先生是我們的VIP客戶。
- Mr. Do is our top priority client.
  杜先生是我們的首要優先客戶。

4-2 老闆交辦的事務處理

Book a Holiday
預訂旅遊團

Helen calls a travel agent to book a holiday.

Helen打電話給旅行社想預訂旅遊團。

Helen - the secretary to the president 董事長秘書
Tim - the travel agent staff 旅行社員工

Dialogue

Tim	Good morning, how may I help you?	早安，有什麼能為您服務的嗎？
Helen	Yes, I'd like to book a holiday in Hualien and Taitung.	是的，我想預訂去花蓮和台東度假的行程。
Tim	How long would you like to go for?	想去玩多久？
Helen	Three to four days.	三到四天。
Tim	In that case, we have a suitable and **cost-effective package** for you. It's a three-day trip, and you'll see both Hualien & Taitung.	那樣的話，我們有一個合適且價格划算的計畫可提供給您，叫做「花東三日遊」。
Helen	That sounds interesting. How about the price?	聽起來滿有趣的。價格如何？
Tim	$7,500 per person.	一個人$7,500。

Helen	Is that the best price you can offer?	這已經是你所能給的最好的價格了嗎？
Tim	It's the lowest price you can find in the **current** market.	這是您在目前市場上所能找到的最低價格了。
Helen	How is the quality?	品質如何？
Tim	It's **worth every penny**. When do you want to go, and how many people will there be?	物超所值。您想何時去，一共有幾個人呢？
Helen	On October 15th, and there will be six people.	10月15日，一共六個人。
Tim	Could I have your name and contact number?	可以給我您的名字和電話嗎？
Helen	My name is Helen, and my number is 388-7008.	我叫海倫，我的電話是388-7008。
Tim	Thank you for choosing us. I'll call you with the details of the trip as soon as possible.	謝謝您的光顧。我會儘快告知你旅遊的細項。
Helen	Can you send or fax me a **brochure** first?	你可以寄或是傳真一份廣告小冊子給我嗎？
Tim	Of course. May I have your **facsimile** number, please?	當然可以。方便給我您的傳真號碼嗎？
Helen	It's 388-7010. Thank you very much.	號碼是388-7010。非常謝謝你。

Word Bank

travel agent　旅行社

I booked a group tour to Yellow Stone Park with a local travel agent.
我向當地旅行社預訂到黃石公園的團體旅遊。

cost-effective　adj.　划算的

I am pleased to buy a cost-effective watch.
我很高興買到一個划算的手錶。

package　n.　組合

There are a variety of vacation packages options on the tour websites.
旅行網站上有各式各樣的假期套裝行程。

current　adj.　最近的；目前的

What's the current exchange rate for New Taiwan Dollar to US Dollar?
目前新台幣和美金的兌換匯率是多少？

worth every penny　值回票價

Although the fare of the opera is quite expensive, it is worth every penny.
雖然這歌劇費用很貴，但值回票價。

brochure　n.　廣告小冊子

The Marketing Department printed brochures for promoting their latest products.
行銷部印製廣告小冊子來推銷最新產品。

facsimile n. 傳真

Do you have a facsimile machine?
你有傳真機嗎？

In that case, we have a suitable and cost-effective package for you.
那樣的話，我們有一個合適且價格划算的計畫可提供給您。

- We do have a proper and suitable package for you.
  我們有一個合適的計畫可提供給您。
- Well then, you might like to consider a tour package which is very inexpensive.
  這樣的話，您也許會想要考慮一下套裝行程。

It's the lowest price you can find in current market.
這是您在目前市場上所能找到的最低價格了。

- It's the best offer you can find in the present market.
  這是您在目前市場上所能找到的最低價格了。
- Currently, you cannot find any better offer than this in the market.
  目前你在市場上找不到更好的價格了。

I'll call you with the details of the trip as soon as possible.
我會儘快告知你旅遊的細項。

- I'll let you know about the details of the trip promptly.
  我會儘快告知你旅遊的細項。
- I'll keep you informed of the details about the trip as quickly as possible.
  我會儘快告知你旅遊的細項。

4-3 老闆交辦的事務處理

Catering Service
外燴服務

The president, Mr. Lo, would like to invite overseas clients and company directors to dine at his home. He asks Helen, his secretary, to help arrange a catering service, and to inform the company directors.

董事長羅先生想在自家宴請海外客戶以及公司主管，他要秘書海倫協助安排外燴服務並通知各主管。

Helen – the secretary to the president 董事長秘書
Mr. Lo – the president 董事長

Dialogue

Mr. Lo	I want to invite our overseas guests and the directors of the company to **dine** at my house on October 18th. I've been thinking about **hiring** a catering service. What do you think?	我想邀請我們的海外客戶及公司主管在18號時來家裡用餐。那天我想請外燴服務，妳認為呢？
Helen	A catering service is a good choice.	外燴服務是很好的選擇。
Mr. Lo	Any **suggestions**?	妳有什麼建議嗎？
Helen	I've never hired a catering service before, but I can gather some information and make a list of restaurants that offer catering services.	我從來沒有請過外燴服務，但我可以蒐集資料並列出有提供外燴服務的餐廳的名單。

Mr. Lo	Great. Why don't you just choose a restaurant for me after you finish the list?	很好。清單列好後，妳就幫我選定一家餐廳吧？
Helen	What kind of food do you prefer?	您喜歡哪種菜色？
Mr. Lo	**Western** food; French **cuisine** will be the best choice. I've learned that Mr. Do enjoys **exquisite** French cuisine and fine wine.	西式料理；最好是選擇法國菜。我知道杜先生喜愛精緻的法國餐及上等紅酒。
Helen	I'll see what I can do. What if I cannot find a French restaurant that offer catering?	我看看是否能找到。如果沒有法國餐廳有在做外燴的呢？
Mr. Lo	In that case, try Italian restaurants. And don't forget to send out **invitation** cards to our guests and the directors, and yourself, too.	那樣的話，就試試義大利餐廳吧。別忘了向我們的客人和主管發出邀請，還有妳自己。
Helen	Thank you, Mr. Lo.	謝謝你，羅先生。

★你應該要知道的小小事！

像會話中提到的聚會，秘書就要製作邀請卡invitation card，邀請卡製作時有哪些東西要注意呢？

1. 清爽、大方、有質感–如果要加上一些花邊點綴時，要特別留意。
2. 放上公司的logo
3. 聚會的時間、地點、交通方式–如果可以的話，可附上簡要的地圖說明。
4. 特殊事項–可不可攜伴參加、需不需要著正式服裝等等。
5. 署名–就是老闆或是主管的名字。

邀請卡寄出之後，記得要再次以電話確認賓客是否有收到，也趁這個時候確認人數，以便安排聚會所用的餐點。

dine v. 用餐

My parents plan to dine at a nice restaurant at their marriage anniversary.
我父母親打算在结婚週年到一間不錯餐廳用餐。

hire vt. 租用；聘用

Due to the fast growing business, the company would like to hire more people.
因為業務快速成長，這公司打算雇用更多人。

suggestion n. 建議

Please provide suggestions, if there are any.
如果有任何建議，請提供。

western adj. 西式的；西方的

Western cultures are more acceptable by young people.
年輕人比較可以接受西方文化。

cuisine n. 菜餚；料理

The chef is very famous for this signature cuisine.
這主廚以這一道招牌料理聞名。

exquisite adj. 精緻的

Many exquisite meals are served at French restaurants.
在法式餐廳供應許多精緻的餐點。

invitation n. 邀請

Every VIP client will receive our invitations for free buffet.
每個 VIP 客人都會收到我們免費自助餐的邀請。

In Other Words

What do you think?
妳認為呢？

- How do you think about that?
  妳覺得呢？
- What's your comments?
  妳認為呢？

A catering service is a good choice.
外燴服務是很好的選擇。

- Hiring a caterer sounds like a good idea.
  請外燴服務聽起來是很好的選擇。
- It seems like a good idea to select a catering service.
  外燴服務是很好的選擇。

Any suggestions?
妳有什麼建議嗎？

- Any recommendations?
  妳有什麼建議嗎？
- Do you have any good suggestions?
  妳有什麼好的建議嗎？

4-4 老闆交辦的事務處理

Choosing a Present
選擇禮物

One of Mr. Lo's close business **associates** is having a birthday soon. Mr. Lo asks his secretary, Helen, for suggestions on what to buy.

羅先生一位商場上的好友生日就要到了，羅先生詢問他的秘書Helen該買什麼當生日禮物。

Helen - the secretary to the president 董事長秘書
Mr. Lo - the president 董事長

Dialogue

Mr. Lo	My good friend's birthday is coming soon. I have no clue on what to buy him.	我朋友的生日快要到了。我不知道該買什麼送他。
Helen	Who is this friend of yours?	是您哪一位朋友呢？
Mr. Lo	You know him, too. It's Mr. Tang from the OPA.	妳也認識他啊，就是OPA的湯先生。
Helen	I remember you gave him a **delicate calligraphic** painting last year.	我記得您去年送他一幅精緻的字畫。
Mr. Lo	Yes, and he liked it very much. But, this year…	是啊，而且他很喜歡。但是今年……
Helen	I've got it. <u>I heard him saying that he was very into **wine** collecting.</u>	我想起來了。我曾聽他說過他很熱衷於收藏葡萄酒呢。

Mr. Lo	That's right. I almost forgot about that.	沒錯，我差點都給忘了。
Helen	Why don't you give him a very fine bottle of wine?	您何不送他一瓶很棒的紅酒呢？
Mr. Lo	Great idea! <u>I need you to do that for me.</u>	好主意！我需要妳幫忙。
Helen	<u>I'd love to, but I am **clueless** about wine.</u>	我很樂意，但我對葡萄酒的了解不多。
Mr. Lo	That's easy. Just go to a **liquor** shop and ask the clerk to introduce you a couple bottles of **world-class** wine. I want to give him two bottles as his birthday presents.	那簡單。直接進入賣酒的店，請店員介紹幾瓶世界級的葡萄酒。我想送他兩瓶酒當做生日禮物。
Helen	Yes, I'll do that.	好的，我會處理。

★你應該要知道的小小事！

上述會話中講到送禮，以下有一些酒的小常識供參考：

1. 紅酒 Red wine：紅酒的顏色主要是來自葡萄皮中的花色素苷。
2. 白酒 White wine：釀酒過程中會將葡萄皮分離，以避免色素滲入葡萄之中。
3. 粉紅葡萄酒 Rose wine：顏色較淡，呈粉紅色澤的葡萄酒。
4. 氣泡酒 Sparkling wine：原料為葡萄，但酒中含有二氧化碳形成的氣泡，而二氧化碳則是來自於釀酒過程中所自然產生的。
5. 香檳 Champagne：特指在法國香檳區出產的氣泡酒。
6. 威士忌 Whiskey/Whisky：美國或愛爾蘭產的，拼做Whiskey，而加拿大及蘇格蘭產的則拼為Whisky。
7. 白蘭地 Brandy：包含常聽到的XO，干邑白蘭地等。

Word Bank

associates n. 夥伴

The boss appreciates all the supports from his business associates.
這老闆非常感謝他所有商業夥伴的幫忙。

delicate adj. 細膩的；精緻的

My friend bought a delicate music box for my birthday gift.
我朋友買一個精緻的音樂盒當為我的生日禮物。

calligraphic adj. 書法的

The calligraphic writing is an art of Chinese culture.
書法是中國文化的藝術。

wine n. 葡萄酒

Little wine is good for our health.
少許酒對我們的健康有利。

clueless adj. 無頭緒的

He is clueless where he lost the wallet.
他不知道在哪裡丟掉錢包。

liquor n. 酒

It is illegal to sell liquor to teenagers under 18 years old.
賣酒給未滿 18 歲的青少年是非法的。

world-class adj. 世界級的

Jeremy Lin is a world-class basketball player.
Jeremy Lin 是世界级的籃球員。

In Other Words

I heard him saying that he was very into wine collecting.
我曾聽他說過他很熱衷於收藏葡萄酒呢。

- I heard that he is very enthusiastic in wine collecting.
  我曾聽他說過他很熱衷於收藏葡萄酒呢。
- It is said that he is very passionate about wine collecting.
  我曾聽他說過他很熱衷於收藏葡萄酒呢。

I need you to do that for me.
我需要妳幫忙。

- I need you to do me a favor to choose a really good wine for his birthday.
  我需要妳幫我選一隻好酒送給他做生日禮物。
- Can you do that for me?
  我需要妳幫忙。

I'd love to, but I am clueless about wine.
我很樂意，但我對葡萄酒的了解不多。

- It is my pleasure, but I do not know much about wine.
  我很樂意，但我對葡萄酒的了解不多。
- Sure, certainly. I would love to, but I don't really know how to choose a good wine.
  當然，沒問題。我很樂意，但我不知道怎麼挑選葡萄酒。

選擇優質外燴服務的撇步！

在自家宴客越來越普遍，也使得外燴服務越來越多。身為秘書的你，可能得幫上司或老闆尋找合適的外燴服務喔。

★親自上門品嚐及討論菜色

口味方面需要親自上門品嚐，也需和負責人員討論菜色，一般外燴菜色跟在餐廳吃的不大相同，專門的負責人員能提供專業的意見。

★早點開始規劃

外燴服務的費用通常比較高，食材等也需要及早安排，除了餐點之外，還有桌椅場地等等也都需要安排。

★依照宴客人數來決定外燴的餐廳

依照人數的多寡來決定外燴餐廳的規模，如果是小型的，則可以詢問一般餐廳而且也不一定非得將眼光鎖定在知名且昂貴的餐廳上，有時別具特色的小館也能展現出讓你意想不到的廚藝喔。但如果人數較多，則需考慮專門的外燴公司，因為在設備器具以及出菜速度上都是要考慮到的細節。

★仔細查閱帳單

通常在詢價階段，可以請負責人員開一張估價單，上面會載明如菜式、價錢、定金收取等的相關細節，需仔細確認。在付款時，也要確認是否已扣除定金部分、及發票、統一編號等的細節。

送禮的技巧

老闆或是主管要接洽的客戶很多，秘書常需要協助送禮等等的相關事宜，以下有幾個撇步可供參考。

★記下客戶的喜好及興趣

因為客戶很多，預先建立這樣的情報資料，在送禮時，就能快速地且投其所好的來餽贈禮品。

★蒐集送禮的相關情報，提供給老闆或是主管做選擇

確認送禮方向之後，可以先初步過濾，將整理完的禮品名單（包含金額）交給上司，讓上司做最後的決定。但如果已經被授權全權處理，在採買前最好也先口頭報告，讓上司知道你的決定。

★禮品資訊建檔，以便於查詢

可以將送禮時間、理由、禮品內容、金額等等建檔，方便日後查詢，也可以避免送到重覆禮物等的尷尬場面發生。

★送禮時機

以下幾項為應該提醒老闆或主管送禮的時機

☑ 客戶生日 ☑ 年節（端午節、中秋節、新年）
☑ 婚喪喜慶 ☑ 升遷
☑ 退休 ☑ 生病住院

秘書寶典

許多的主管秘書身邊都會有一本寶典，寶典內裝有許許多多的名片，除了客戶名片之外，還會有一些如飯店、餐廳、花店、水果行等等的名片。這時候可以有系統地將客戶的訊息建檔，無論主管什麼時候問起客戶的相關資訊，都能以最快的速度回答。另外一些餐廳、店家的名片資訊則方便在主管有應酬或是客戶來訪時，為主管預約餐廳，或是安排送禮等的事項。

除此之外，還可以利用一些電腦上或是手機的應用程式，分門別類地建立相關訊息，對於工作效率的提升有相當的幫助。在各式的送禮時機中，禮品的選擇，平時也需要蒐集資訊，例如送給外國客戶的伴手禮或是紀念品，可以依時節而有不同的選擇。但最重要的是要確認預算，依照客戶別的不同來區分，送禮的預算也會有所不同，通常公司裡會有清楚的規範，將客戶分級。但如果沒有這樣的規範的話，記住要先詢問主管，了解預算之後，一邊尋找適合的禮物，一邊歸納整理，建入自己的資料庫寶典，下一次有相同情形時，就能處理得更加得心應手了！

Leader 009

職場菜鳥的英文升職筆記–那一些老鳥不會說的秘密

Experts' Know-how

作　　者　力得文化編輯群

封面構成　高鍾琪

內頁構成　華漢電腦排版有限公司

發 行 人　周瑞德

企劃編輯　陳欣慧

校　　對　徐瑞璞、陳韋佑、饒美君

印　　製　大亞彩色印刷製版股份有限公司

初　　版　2014 年 12 月

定　　價　新台幣 329 元

出　　版　力得文化

電　　話　(02) 2351-2007

傳　　真　(02) 2351-0887

地　　址　100 台北市中正區福州街 1 號 10 樓之 2

E - m a i l　best.books.service@gmail.com

港澳地區總經銷　泛華發行代理有限公司

地址　香港筲箕灣東旺道 3 號星島新聞集團大廈 3 樓

電話　(852) 2798-2323

傳真　(852) 2796-5471

國家圖書館出版品預行編目(CIP)資料

職場菜鳥的英文升職筆記：那一些老鳥不會說的秘密 / 力得文化編輯群著. -- 初版. -- 臺北市：力得文化, 2014.12

面；　公分. -- (Leader ; 9)

ISBN 978-986-90759-8-5(平裝)

1.英語 2.職場 3.會話

805.188　　103023041